Du

"[A] terrific addition to an
—Miranda Ja
the Cat in the Stacks Mysteries

"What a great read! I can't wait to go back to the first title in this
ibrarian, and
rary director
a dog named
vell, it's quite
brary Journal

very authen-
down."
—CrimeSpree

, and chow-
d
ing author of
n Mysteries

erley and a
ki oks Can Be
D
—Ellery Adams, author of the Books by the Bay Mysteries

"Fast-paced and fun, *Books Can Be Deceiving* is the first in Jenn McKinlay's appealing new mystery series featuring an endearing protagonist, delightful characters, a lovely New England setting, and a fascinating murder."

—Kate Carlisle, *New York Times* bestselling author of the Bibliophile Mysteries

continued . . .

PRAISE FOR

JENN MCKINLAY'S CUPCAKE BAKERY MYSTERIES

Red Velvet Revenge

"With a rodeo, a road trip, and the delectable title, *Red Velvet Revenge*, the Fairy Tale Cupcake bakers are back, lassoed into big trouble this time. You're in for a real treat with Jenn McKinlay's Cupcake Bakery Mystery. I gobbled it right up."

—Julie Hyzy, bestselling author of the Manor House Mysteries and White House Chef Mysteries

"Sure as shootin', *Red Velvet Revenge* pops with fun and great twists. Wrangle up some time to enjoy the atmosphere of a real rodeo as well as family drama. It's better than icing on the tastiest cupcake."

—Avery Aames, author of *Clobbered by Camembert*

Death by the Dozen

"It's the best yet, with great characters, and a terrific, tightly written plot."

—*Lesa's Book Critiques*

"Like a great fairy tale, McKinlay transports readers into the world of cupcakes and all things sweet and frosted, minus the calories. Although . . . there are some pretty yummy recipes at the end."

—*Cozy Corner*

Buttercream Bump Off

"A charmingly entertaining story paired with a luscious assortment of cupcake recipes that, when combined, made for a deliciously thrilling mystery."

—*Fresh Fiction*

"Another tasty entry, complete with cupcake recipes, into what is sure to grow into a perennial favorite series."

—*The Mystery Reader*

"McKinlay's descriptions of the cupcakes in Mel and Angie's shop are guaranteed to make the reader salivate—fortunately the recipes are included in the back of the book. Engaging characters, hilarious situations, old movie quotes and, oh yes, a dead body in a hot tub make this a great read." —*Romantic Times*

Sprinkle with Murder

"A tender cozy full of warm and likable characters and a refreshingly sympathetic murder victim. Readers will look forward to more of McKinlay's tasty concoctions."

—*Publishers Weekly* (starred review)

"*Sprinkle with Murder* is one of the better recent cozy debuts, and a few cupcake recipes in the back are, well, icing on the cake." —*The Mystery Reader*

"McKinlay's debut mystery flows as smoothly as Melanie Cooper's buttercream frosting. Her characters are delicious, and the dash of romance is just the icing on the cake."

—Sheila Connolly, author of *Sour Apples*

"Jenn McKinlay delivers all the ingredients for a winning read. Frost me another!"

—Cleo Coyle, national bestselling author of the Coffeehouse Mysteries

"A delicious new series featuring a spirited heroine, luscious cupcakes, and a clever murder. Jenn McKinlay has baked a sweet read." —Krista Davis, author of the Domestic Diva Mysteries

Berkley Prime Crime titles by Jenn McKinlay

Cupcake Bakery Mysteries

SPRINKLE WITH MURDER
BUTTERCREAM BUMP OFF
DEATH BY THE DOZEN
RED VELVET REVENGE
GOING, GOING, GANACHE

Library Lover's Mysteries

BOOKS CAN BE DECEIVING
DUE OR DIE
BOOK, LINE, AND SINKER
READ IT AND WEEP

Hat Shop Mysteries

CLOCHE AND DAGGER

BOOK, LINE, AND SINKER

Jenn McKinlay

BERKLEY PRIME CRIME, NEW YORK

THE BERKLEY PUBLISHING GROUP
Published by the Penguin Group
Penguin Group (USA) Inc.
375 Hudson Street, New York, New York 10014, USA
Penguin Group (Canada), 90 Eglinton Avenue East, Suite 700, Toronto, Ontario M4P 2Y3, Canada (a division of Pearson Penguin Canada Inc.) • Penguin Books Ltd., 80 Strand, London WC2R 0RL, England • Penguin Group Ireland, 25 St. Stephen's Green, Dublin 2, Ireland (a division of Penguin Books Ltd.) • Penguin Group (Australia), 250 Camberwell Road, Camberwell, Victoria 3124, Australia (a division of Pearson Australia Group Pty. Ltd.) • Penguin Books India Pvt. Ltd., 11 Community Centre, Panchsheel Park, New Delhi—110 017, India • Penguin Group (NZ), 67 Apollo Drive, Rosedale, Auckland 0632, New Zealand (a division of Pearson New Zealand Ltd.) • Penguin Books (South Africa) (Pty.) Ltd., 24 Sturdee Avenue, Rosebank, Johannesburg 2196, South Africa

Penguin Books Ltd., Registered Offices: 80 Strand, London WC2R 0RL, England

BOOK, LINE, AND SINKER

A Berkley Prime Crime Book / published by arrangement with the author

PUBLISHING HISTORY
Berkley Prime Crime mass-market edition / December 2012

Cover illustration by Julia Green.
Cover design by Rita Frangie.
Interior text design by Laura K. Corless.

For information, address: The Berkley Publishing Group,
a division of Penguin Group (USA) Inc.,
375 Hudson Street, New York, New York 10014.

ISBN: 978-0-425-25176-8

BERKLEY® PRIME CRIME
Berkley Prime Crime Books are published by The Berkley Publishing Group,
a division of Penguin Group (USA) Inc.,
375 Hudson Street, New York, New York 10014.
BERKLEY® PRIME CRIME and the PRIME CRIME logo are trademarks of
Penguin Group (USA) Inc.

PRINTED IN THE UNITED STATES OF AMERICA

10 9 8 7 6 5 4 3

For Carole Towles and Sheila Levine,
fabulous librarians and priceless gal pals,
you inspire me every day in every way.
Friends until the end and then some, ladies.
XO

Acknowledgments

As always, big thanks to my editor, Kate Seaver; assistant editor, Katherine Pelz; and to my agent, Jessica Faust. Your support and guidance and brilliant input mean the world to me.

To the pirates of my heart, Chris, Beckett and Wyatt, all I can say is "Arr!" Seriously, if I were shipwrecked, I'd pick you three to be with me because I know it would be a blast.

Love to my families, the McKinlays and the Orfs, and to all of my friends who read my books, come to the signings and listen to me when I talk way too much about writing, which is often.

To all of the librarians out there toiling in the stacks, thanks for all that you do to serve your patrons. You are a remarkable breed and the world is a better place for having you in it.

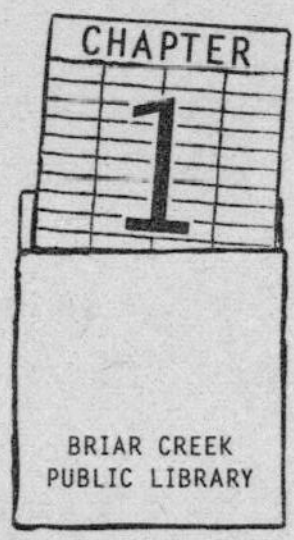

"Daisy Buchanan was an insipid, shallow, soulless woman," Violet La Rue declared. "Jay should have found someone else."

"But he loved her," Nancy Peyton argued.

"Why?" Violet asked. She shuddered. "The woman was a horror."

"She was old money," Lindsey Norris said. "She was everything that the new money, like Jay Gatsby, aspired to be."

It was lunchtime on Thursday at the Briar Creek Public Library, where the crafternoon group met every week to work on a craft, eat yummy food and talk about their latest read. Per usual, Violet and Nancy were the first to arrive. Lindsey was the director of the library, and this group had been one of her ideas to boost the popularity of the library in town.

"Buchanan was a bully. Remember when Daisy has that bruise?" Nancy asked. "What kind of man treats a woman like that?"

"Yeah, I'm pretty sure I've dated him, well, men just like him at any rate," Beth Stanley said as she waddled into the room.

Beth was the children's librarian and today she was dressed as a giant green caterpillar, the puffy underbelly of which seriously impeded her ability to walk. Dangling from one arm, she held a large basket of plastic fruit and foodstuffs.

Lindsey lowered the sampler she was attempting to cross-stitch and studied Beth.

"Don't tell me, let me guess," she said. "Today you read Eric Carle's *The Very Hungry Caterpillar.*"

"What?" Mary Murphy exclaimed as she stepped over the tail end of Beth's costume to enter the room. "I thought we were reading F. Scott Fitzgerald's *The Great Gatsby.*"

"We are," Nancy said. "Beth read the caterpillar book to her story time crowd."

"Oh, phew, you had me worried there," Mary said as she plopped into the chair beside Lindsey.

"Well, you might want to take a gander at some of the picture books," Nancy said. Her look was sly. "You know, if you and Ian ever decide to have some babies."

Mary tossed her long dark curls over her shoulder and sent Nancy a grin. "My husband is all the baby I can handle at the moment, thank you very much. Although things seem to be progressing nicely between Lindsey and Sully, so perhaps you'll have some luck there."

"Ouch!" Lindsey jammed her thumb into her mouth trying to ease the hurt from the round-tipped needle where it had jabbed her skin.

"Interesting," Nancy said, giving Lindsey a piercing look.

"Food's here," Charlene La Rue announced as she stepped into the room, bearing a tray of mini bagel sandwiches paired with cucumber cups stuffed with feta and a carafe of lemonade.

Like her mother, Violet, Charlene was a tall, beautiful black woman with warm brown eyes and a smile that lit up the room. But while Violet had been a stage actress, Charlene was a local news anchor. Lindsey always marveled that she was able to balance her public life, be an exemplary wife and mother and still make time for their crafternoon Thursdays.

Nancy turned her attention away from Lindsey and tucked her cross-stitch needle into the corner of her canvas cloth. She leaned forward to help herself to the food on the tray Charlene was setting out on the table.

"How is Sully?" Violet asked. "I haven't seen him in ages."

Violet and Nancy were not only best friends, but also tag team buddies in the information-seeking game. Where one left off, the other stepped in.

"Did you know that *The Great Gatsby* is considered the greatest American novel?" Lindsey asked.

"There she goes, changing the subject," Beth said.

She shimmied out of her caterpillar costume and hung it up on the coatrack. The static from the costume made her short spiky black hair stand up on end and she ran her fingers through it in a futile attempt to tame it. She grabbed her project bag from where she'd tucked it into her fruit basket and took the last remaining seat in the room.

"I am not," Lindsey said. "I'm just keeping us on task. We're supposed to work on a craft while we discuss our latest book, which is—"

"*The Great Gatsby*," the rest of the ladies said together.

"We know," Charlene said. "It's just that you've been dating Sully for a few months now, so we're curious. Can we assume it's going well?"

Lindsey glanced at Mary for backup, thinking that since she was Sully's sister, surely she wouldn't want to hear about his love life, but no. She nodded at Lindsey encouragingly. Lindsey just shook her head. Her crafternoon buddies were incorrigible.

"Hey, that's not your granny's cross-stitch," Beth declared, looking at the cross-stitch hoop in Lindsey's lap. "I love that."

"Well, we did say we were doing 'subversive' cross-stitch," Lindsey said. She glanced at her sampler, which when she was done would read, "Books are my homeboys," with a border of books on bookshelves going around it. She planned to hang it in her office, if she ever stopped stabbing herself in the thumb, because even with a round-tipped cross-stitch needle, it still hurt when it poked the skin.

"You need a thimble," Violet said. "You're a hazard with that needle."

"I have an extra." Mary reached into her bag and handed one to Lindsey.

"So what do yours say?" Lindsey asked the group.

"Mine says, 'Bake your own damn cookies!' " Nancy said.

Lindsey laughed. Nancy was not just her crafternoon buddy but also her landlady. After sixty-odd years of living in Briar Creek, Nancy had come to be known for her cookie-baking skills, which occasionally annoyed her as she had also become the go-to gal for cookie exchanges and bake sales.

Violet held up her cross-stitch, and in her best stage voice she read, " 'To be or not to be. That is not the question. The question is, what time is lunch?' "

Nancy snorted and gave Violet a high-five.

"I went with an old restaurant standby," Mary said. " 'Kiss my grits.' "

Mary and her husband, Ian, owned the Blue Anchor Café, the only restaurant in town that just happened to serve the best clam chowder in New England.

"Love it," Beth said. "Hang it by the cash register."

"Mine is going in our master bathroom," Charlene said. She held up a pretty cross-stitch with a half-finished border of red swirls. It read, "Cap on. Seat down. Or else."

Mary cracked up and said, "If I pay you, will you make me one just like it?"

Lastly, Beth held up hers. It, too, had a pretty pink border and in the middle, it read, "#@&$!!"

"Oh no, you didn't!" Charlene said with a delighted giggle.

"Yes, I did," Beth said. "I wanted to drop in some really rough language, but I thought this was pithier and more imaginative."

"I think Fitzgerald would approve," Nancy said. "I do love his way with words. Do you remember how Nick describes Gatsby? 'He smiled understandingly—much more than understandingly. It was one of those rare smiles with a quality of eternal reassurance in it, that you may come across four or five times in life.' "

"Lovely," Mary said. "But you can't help but feel that Gatsby will be disappointed."

"Which brings us to the biggest question in the book: Do you think Daisy was guilty of the hit-and-run and Jay took the blame for her or no?" Beth asked.

A knock on the door frame interrupted the conversation. It was Ann Marie, a part-time worker for the library. She was somewhere in her forties, the mother of two rambunctious boys, and favored denim skirts and soft jersey shirts. As she explained it to Lindsey, keeping up with her boys took all of her energy so she did not own any clothing that required ironing. She wore narrow black-framed glasses and was growing out her short brown hair, which had hit the awkward stage of many lengths and was held in place by a handful of hairpins.

"I hate to interrupt," she said. "But there seems to be an altercation happening out front."

Lindsey hopped to her feet. "What sort of altercation?"

"Mostly, it's a yelling match," Ann Marie said. "Between Milton Duffy and Trudi Hargrave."

Milton? The crafternooners exchanged baffled looks. Milton Duffy was a yogi. He didn't yell.

"Excuse me," Lindsey said.

"Holler if you need backup, boss," Beth called.

Lindsey nodded and hurried from the room.

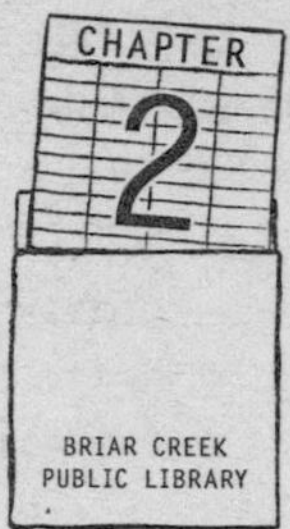

Lindsey could hear the raised voices before she stepped into the library. Standing in the main lobby with the entire library watching them were Milton Duffy and Trudi Hargrave. They were both trying to outshout each other and both were gesturing wildly. Lindsey thought they looked like two wild turkeys trying to intimidate each other with their squawking and ruffled feathers.

"It's a slap in the face of all that the historical society represents," Milton yelled.

"The historical society, you mean the hysterical society," Trudi snapped. "You bring absolutely no revenue into this town."

"It's not all about money!"

"Yes, it is!"

"Trudi! Milton!" Lindsey shouted their names as she stepped between them. "My office—now!"

Trudi opened her mouth to argue, but Lindsey held up her hand.

"Not here," she said.

Milton was in his usual athletic suit. Today's was gray with navy racing stripes up the side. He was bald but sported a neatly trimmed silver goatee that made all of the single ladies over the age of sixty swoon whenever they saw him. Milton was a spry eighty-two. Lindsey figured it was all of the yoga that he did. She had never seen him lose his temper before, but if anyone could do it, she was not surprised that it was Trudi Hargrave.

Trudi was the head of the town's tourism department. Lindsey assumed they were about the same age, but it was hard to tell. Trudi had the whole teeth whitening until they glowed in the dark, hair streaked with every shade from copper to platinum, and she liked to stuff her curvy figure into pencil-thin skirts topped by bust-enhancing jackets. She also wore those silly platform pumps, which added six inches to her short stature but also made her mince her steps, taking away from the whole professional thing she was trying to cultivate.

Lindsey and Milton strode to her office. They waited for Trudi to catch up. Milton was doing deep breathing exercises and Lindsey was relieved to see his face go from tomato red back to a healthy pink.

Trudi came in and shut the door behind her.

"Would either of you care to explain why you are shouting in my library?"

"It's simple," Trudi said. She yanked the lapels of her jacket as if trying to straighten them after a scuffle. "Fossil man here is impeding my ability to build up the town's coffers with an excellent tourism campaign."

"Name calling is for ill-mannered cretins, you tart," Milton snapped.

Trudi screwed up her face like she was about to give as good as she got. Lindsey forestalled her.

"Stop it, both of you," she said, giving Milton a quelling glance. He had the grace to look abashed. "Now it sounds as if your argument has nothing to do with the library, so I want you both to leave—separately. Trudi, you go first. But let me be clear: I don't want to see this sort of behavior from either of you again."

"Fine!" Trudi snapped. She spun on her heel, wobbled for a moment before she caught her balance and quick-stepped out the door, which she slammed behind her.

Lindsey looked at Milton. "Explain."

"She is trying to open Pirate Island up to a treasure-hunting company."

"Meaning?"

"Strangers will be desecrating one of our very own islands," Milton said. He began to turn red again. "Just give me a moment."

He assumed the mountain posture, closed his eyes and started to make soft little "oms" with his mouth.

"Milton, why don't you stay here until you're calmer?" she said. "I need to finish with my crafternoon group, and when I get back, we can talk some more."

Milton gave a very slight nod of his head and Lindsey slipped through her office door, closing it softly behind her.

"What was that all about?" Ms. Cole asked. She was seated at her desk in the workroom, eating her peanut butter and jelly sandwich. For two years now, Lindsey had noticed that Ms. Cole always brought the exact same lunch: peanut butter and jelly on white bread, a bag of baby gherkin pickles and a little carton of milk. She never deviated from the menu, not even getting a wild hair to mix it up by having chocolate milk or dill pickles. Lindsey supposed Ms. Cole appreciated constancy more than epicurean curiosity, or would that be epicuriosity?

Lindsey made a mental note to check the *Oxford English Dictionary* to see if that was a word; if not, it should be.

"It was just a misunderstanding," she said to Ms. Cole, who was watching her over her reading glasses.

"Humph, pretty loud misunderstanding," she said. "Mr. Tupper never had people shouting at each other in the middle of the library."

Lindsey gave her a tight smile. Ms. Cole's unflagging devotion to her predecessor was as constant a presence as her gherkin pickles. She tried to tell herself it was endearing, even when it grated.

"Enjoy your lunch," she said. She glanced at the clock. There were only fifteen minutes left of her own lunch hour. She'd better hurry back before all of Charlene's bagel sandwiches were gone.

She had just gotten back into her seat with her sandwich and a cucumber cup when there was another knock on the door. Hoping it wasn't yet another library situation, she took a quick bite before she turned around.

Standing in the doorway was Charlie Peyton, her downstairs neighbor who was also Nancy's nephew.

"Hello, ladies," he said. "Sorry to interrupt."

"Hi, Charlie," they all greeted him.

"Is everything all right?" Nancy asked.

"Well." He put a hand on the back of his neck. "It's Heathcliff."

"What's wrong?" Lindsey asked as she rose from her seat.

"Oh, he's fine but—" Charlie began but was interrupted when a black fur ball raced through his legs and launched himself on Lindsey.

Lindsey fell back into her chair with an "Oomph" as her dog, Heathcliff, began to lick every part of her face he could reach.

"Hey there, fella." She put her sandwich plate down on the table and scratched his head. He wagged in delight and then jumped off her lap to greet the rest of the crafternooners.

"I'm sorry, Lindsey," Charlie said. "But I got a call for a job interview and I didn't want to leave him alone in the house, you know, with his chewing issues and all."

"No, it's fine," she said. She glanced at her watch. "If I leave now, I have enough time to take him for a walk on the beach before I bring him home."

"I can take him home," Nancy said. "I have no plans for this afternoon. But, Charlie, what job interview do you have? Aren't working for Sully anymore?"

Charlie worked for Mike Sullivan, known to everyone as Sully, who owned a tour boat company that gave tourists rides around the storied Thumb Islands off the shore of Briar Creek. He was the same Sully that Lindsey had been dating for the past several months.

"No, I'll still work for him," Charlie said. "But this is a once-in-a-lifetime opportunity."

"Sort of like that tour your band went on last winter?" Nancy asked. "You know, the one that was supposed to make you famous but ended up breaking up the band?"

"Life on the road is tough," Charlie said. "And no, this is way more solid than that. Besides, the band is back together now."

His flipped back his long stringy hair and Lindsey saw that he had increased the gauges in his earlobes to their next level, giving him even bigger holes. Charlie was very into body art.

"What's the job then?" Violet asked, looking as dubious as Nancy.

"Treasure hunting," Charlie said. "We're going to look for Captain Kidd's treasure."

"Have you lost your mind?" Nancy asked. She looked him up and down as if for signs of the crazy leaking out. Then she frowned. "Sit down and have a sandwich. You look thin."

Charlie rolled his eyes. "You think anyone under two hundred pounds looks thin."

Having greeted everyone in the room, Heathcliff sprawled on the floor and propped his head on Lindsey's feet. This was how he always sat—even with summer fast approaching and temperatures rising, he was still a snuggler.

"Tell us about the job," Lindsey said. She had no doubt that this was the company that Trudi was bringing in to salvage treasure on Pirate Island. She didn't say anything, though, wanting to hear what Charlie had to say first.

Charlie grabbed a sandwich off the table and took a bite. Once he swallowed, he said, "The company's name is Riordan Salvage and they specialize in this sort of thing. They've done loads of shipwrecks off the coast of the Carolinas."

"What do you know about salvage or treasure?" Nancy asked, looking worried. "It sounds dangerous."

"I think they're more interested in using me as a guide," Charlie said. "But I won't know until I interview. Speaking of which, I'd better get going. Sorry about Heathcliff."

"No problem," Lindsey said.

This was a complete lie. If Ms. Cole caught a whiff of a dog in the library, even if he was off in one of the meeting rooms, she would not hesitate to call the town's personnel department to lodge a complaint against Lindsey. She was as reliable as peanut butter and jelly like that.

Charlie headed toward the door, munching his sandwich as he went. He had just opened the door when he spun back around with his eyes wide.

"*She's* coming!" he hissed.

The entire crafternoon group rose as one. Everyone knew there was only one *she* that Charlie could be referring to—Ms. Cole, or as Beth liked to call her, "the lemon" because she always looked puckered about something.

"We have to hide him," Violet said.

"I'll head her off," Charlene said and she slipped around Charlie and through the door.

Lindsey scanned the crafternoon room in a panic. With just two bookshelves for craft books, a fireplace and several squashy chairs, it didn't afford much in the way of nooks or crannies. There was no place to hide a hairy, black, thirty-pound dog.

"I have a plan!" Beth had jumped up from her seat and was scrambling back into her caterpillar costume.

"What plan?" Lindsey asked. "To scare her or threaten to eat her?"

Beth gave a wicked grin. She and Ms. Cole had been at loggerheads since the day Beth had become the children's librarian over ten years before.

"Heathcliff can fit in my tail," Beth said. "It unzips. But hurry."

"Oh, good grief," Lindsey said. "I'll just explain to her that he's passing through. It'll be fine."

"Really?" Beth asked. "How many calls to Human Resources has she made about you? Ten? Twenty?"

"A fair few," Lindsey acknowledged.

"Then start stuffing," Beth said.

Lindsey hefted up Heathcliff. "Okay, buddy, go with Aunt Beth."

Heathcliff raised one of his fuzzy eyebrows as he took in the bright green costume. Lindsey was sure he would balk, but Mary had unzipped the tail and taken out the pillows it was stuffed with. Lindsey placed Heathcliff inside and Mary zipped it up.

"Come on, be my handler," Beth said to Nancy. "We'll go right outside and you can take him from there."

"Are you sure he can breathe?" Lindsey asked, biting her lip.

"It's cotton," Beth said. "For five minutes, he'll be fine."

Just then the door banged open and the lemon strode into the room. Charlie slid along the wall around her and out the door before she noticed him.

Charlene was jumping up and down behind Ms. Cole as if trying to warn them. Lindsey met her gaze and Charlene shrugged, which Lindsey understood. Trying to stop Ms. Cole was like trying to hold back the incoming tide. Impossible.

Beth grabbed up her fruit basket and strode to the door with Nancy at her side. Heathcliff, obviously not liking the abrupt movement, began to growl. Either that, or he could smell Ms. Cole. They had not gotten along during their first and only meeting, most probably because she had been trying to whack him with a broom at the time.

"What's that noise?" Ms. Cole asked, her fat gray sausage curls bouncing as she whipped her head in Beth's direction.

"Me," Beth said. "I am the very hungry caterpillar after all."

With that she hustled from the room, her lumpy tail dragging behind her.

"Finished with your lunch already, Ms. Cole?" Lindsey asked.

Ms. Cole slowly turned back around. Her reading glasses were hanging on a gold chain about her neck. That was the only spot of color on her otherwise drab outfit.

Ms. Cole liked to dress monochromatically, so her outfits were always shades of the same color. Today's color was a mishmash of gray from her orthopedic shoes to her charcoal skirt and pale gray blouse. She looked like her own personal fog bank.

She glanced at Lindsey as if she'd forgotten why she'd come. Then she glowered. "Mr. Duffy left your office and said he couldn't stay but would talk to you later."

With that she turned on her heel and headed back to the main library. Lindsey watched her go and then turned back to the others.

"Is it just me or was that odd?"

Violet shook her head. "Not you, definitely odd."

Mary, Violet, Charlene and Lindsey began to clear away the remnants of their meeting. Violet offered to take both Nancy's and Beth's projects bags out to them, while Charlene and Mary packed up the last of the food.

"I think we should carry forth this week's discussion," Mary said. "Since we didn't get to finish."

"Agreed," Lindsey said. "I'll e-mail everyone and let them know."

It was late afternoon when Charlie came back to the library. He looked even more amped than usual, which was saying something since he lived on a steady diet of energy drinks and candy bars, and he sought Lindsey out immediately.

Lindsey was measuring a section in the adult area for some new shelving she hoped to order. The president of the

Friends of the Library, Carrie Rushton, had been very successful in her fund-raising efforts and wanted a wish list of things the library could use. Lindsey decided some new shelves would really perk the place up, but she wanted to price a few different pieces first.

Charlie popped up behind an old shelf and said, "I got it!"

"Shh!" Ms. Cole hushed him from the circulation desk.

"Sorry," he grimaced.

"It's all right. Come on," Lindsey said. "Help me with the flag."

Together they stepped through the sliding front doors and outside the old stone building that, before it was the library, had once been the residence of a ship builder. One of the things Lindsey loved about Briar Creek was its many historical homes, mostly built and owned by sea captains and ship builders from New England's heyday in the shipping era.

The early June breeze was warm and Lindsey inhaled the intoxicating scent of lilacs mingled with the salty tang of the bay, which lay just across the street. Her gaze went immediately to the pier. At one end sat the Blue Anchor, Mary and Ian Murphy's restaurant, and at the other end was Sully's tour boat company, where he offered boat tours and a water taxi service around the Thumb Islands.

At the moment, the pier was empty of boats, however, and Lindsey knew that meant that Sully was out either giving a tour or picking up or dropping off one of the residents of the hundred plus Thumb Islands, of which only twenty-seven were inhabited and only a few of those year round.

"So tell me about the job," Lindsey said. She led the way to the flagpole, which sat in a small garden in front of the library. Normally, the teen workers took care of flag duty, but Lindsey was restless and this would give her an excuse to be outside and talk to Charlie.

She unwound the rope that held the United States flag and the Connecticut flag and began to hoist them down. Charlie grabbed them before they brushed the ground and draped one over his shoulder while Lindsey tied off the ropes.

"It's just a temporary position," he said. He handed her one end of the flag and they mirrored each other while they folded. "Mr. Riordan wants me to help them locate the most likely spot on the island for Captain Kidd to have buried his treasure."

"How do they know which island it is?" Lindsey asked.

"Well, it's got to be Pirate Island," Charlie said. "I mean, it was named for Captain Kidd and there have been rumors of treasure forever."

"The operative word being *rumors*," Lindsey said as she folded the flag into triangles. She tucked it under her arm and they began to fold the next one.

"I know," he said. He bobbed his head, and his long black hair danced about his face. "But if it is the one, and we find the treasure, Mr. Riordan said I'll get a cut of the profit and I'll finally have enough money to sink into the band and make a real go of it."

Lindsey finished folding the second flag into a large triangle, and she looked at him with concern before tucking that one under her arm as well.

"It sounds dangerous," she said.

"Nah." Charlie waved a hand at her. "I grew up here and I've been working for Sully for five years, I know these islands better than the insides of my own eyelids, which I spend a considerable amount of time studying, as you know."

Lindsey laughed. Charlie's enthusiasm was contagious. She turned to walk back into the building, and he fell into step beside her.

"All right, but how are you going to know where to look on the island?" she asked. "Pirate Island is one of the bigger ones, isn't it?"

"This is the part you'll love," he said. He paused and studied her face.

"Well?" she asked, intrigued.

"Mr. Riordan has a map. An honest-to-goodness, formerly the property of Captain William Kidd, treasure map."

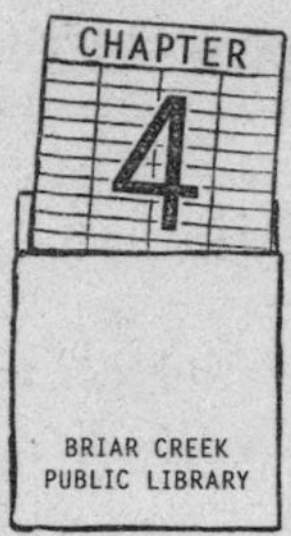

"No!" Lindsey said. She could feel her archivist's soul tingle at the thought of a real treasure map. "For real?"

"That's what he says," Charlie said. He stopped before the sliding doors. "So I was wondering . . ."

"Yes?" Lindsey paused beside him.

"Sully wasn't too keen on my taking this gig," he said.

"And you want me to talk to him on your behalf?" Lindsey guessed.

Charlie gave her his best ingratiating smile. "I'll owe you one."

"I'm only dating the man," Lindsey said. "I don't know that I have that much influence."

"Are you kidding?" Charlie asked. "He's crazy about you. He'll listen to you."

Lindsey ignored the way her heart thumped when he said Sully was crazy about her. She felt her face grow warm and she fought it off with a mock scowl.

"I'll try," she said. She stepped on the rubber mat that triggered the automatic sliding door. "After all, I do have a bathroom that needs painting."

She left Charlie staring at her in mild horror.

Lindsey stowed the flags in the cupboard of the workroom. She still felt restless, and she knew she was probably suffering from an advanced case of spring fever. She glanced around the room, wondering if she should do some cleaning.

Beth came into the room and began riffling through the supply cupboard. She grabbed yellow and orange construction paper, scissors, glue sticks and a box of crayons.

"We don't have any sunflower seeds, do we?" she asked.

"With the office supplies? No, I don't think so. Why?"

"Story time craft for next week," Beth said. "We're making sunflowers, but I really think seeds to glue in the center are critical."

"I'll see if I can spend some petty cash for them at the dollar store," Lindsey said.

"Thanks. Do you and Sully have plans for dinner tonight?" Beth asked.

"He's got an evening boat tour. I was going home to heat up leftovers. Why? Do you have a better offer?"

"Mary told me she's experimenting with the crab salad by putting green olives in it," Beth said. "You know how I love my green olives."

"Count me in," Lindsey said. "White wine and crab salad. Perfect."

"Excellent." Beth left the room, whistling something that sounded like Raffi's "Baby Beluga."

An honest-to-goodness treasure map—the thought wriggled enticingly like a worm on a hook in her brain. Lindsey was intrigued by the idea that such a thing existed.

Back in her office, she did a quick search in the library's catalog for books on Captain Kidd. If treasure hunting was happening in Briar Creek, she wanted to get a display together.

She had already checked out Riordan's website and seen the online videos of his successful excavations in the Carolinas; still Riordan wasn't a cartographer so he could be duped by a map that looked authentic but was, in fact, a fake.

Lindsey got her cell phone out of her desk and flipped through her contacts list. Patti Fulton, her mentor from when she was an archivist at the Beinecke Rare Book and Manuscript Library at Yale University, knew everyone who was anyone in the rare book biz. If there was someone locally who specialized in rare maps, she would know them.

Patti answered on the third ring. "This is Fulton."

Patti wasn't big on small talk.

"Patti, it's Lindsey Norris," she said. "How are you?"

"You're not really calling to find out how I am, are you?" Patti asked.

Lindsey felt her mouth curve up. She'd forgotten how much Patti loathed inanities.

"No, I'm just being polite," Lindsey said. "Although that's not to say I don't care how you're doing."

"Very diplomatic," Patti said approvingly. "I always liked that about you. Although I should hang up on you since the only contact I've had from you was a lousy Christmas card."

"I thought it was a lovely Christmas card, with specialty papers from Japan and vintage typesetting."

Patti was silent and Lindsey suspected she was smiling, well, as much as Patti ever smiled, which would probably appear to be more of a facial tic. She could picture Patti sitting at her desk just as she had when Lindsey worked for her. Her rectangular, black-framed glasses perched on her nose while she fidgeted with a pencil or pen in her right hand. Patti had a lot of nervous energy.

A very attractive woman in her mid-fifties, Patti had a weakness for designer clothes, Italian shoes and red lipstick. And although Patti must have had some gray sprouting in her hair somewhere, Lindsey had never seen it as Patti kept her blunt black bob scrupulously maintained.

"Fine, it was a decent card. So why are you calling me then?" Patti asked.

"I am interested in the possibility that a map, a treasure map, by Captain Kidd might exist."

"Oh, intriguing," Patti said. "Tell me more."

"A salvage company has arrived in Briar Creek, claiming that they have a treasure map which they plan to use to locate a treasure supposedly buried here by Captain Kidd."

Patti was silent for a few seconds. "Have you seen the map?"

"No."

"Then it could be just a rumor," she said.

"Yes," Lindsey said.

"Well, if it's not a rumor, you should talk to Dr. Harris, the maps curator at the Sterling Memorial Library," she said. "He might even be able to authenticate it."

"I was hoping you'd know someone," Lindsey said.

"Here let me give you his number," Patti said. "If he's not in, he has an assistant who is very knowledgeable as well."

Lindsey jotted down the numbers as Patti read them to her.

"And you know his e-mail would be first name dot last name at yale dot edu," Patti said.

"Yes, I remember," Lindsey said. She used to have a Yale e-mail address, before she'd been laid off.

"Was that it?" Patti asked.

"Yes, thanks," Lindsey said.

"Good," Patti said and hung up her phone.

Lindsey smiled again as she hit End on her phone. "Good" was Patti's abbreviated good-bye and she never felt it was necessary to wait for it to be reciprocated.

She returned her attention to her catalog search. The Briar Creek Library did own a few biographies of Captain Kidd, but they were already checked out. She did some online research and found an academic website out of the University of Massachusetts that did mention Kidd's time in New England.

Lindsey preferred URLs that ended in *edu* as they were always a good indicator that the information was verified and not just Joe Shmoe's web page about Captain Kidd.

Like most of the sources she'd checked, however, this one talked about all of the islands Captain Kidd had landed on from New York to Nova Scotia while he was on the run from pirate hunters.

She put a hold on the books and printed out some of the better web pages to read and keep on file for patrons to read as well. If Captain Kidd was going to become the main talk of the town, she wanted to be ready.

At six o'clock, Beth poked her head in Lindsey's office. "Ready?"

"And how," Lindsey said. "I feel like my eyeballs are spinning in different directions from reading all of these different accounts of Kidd's activities in the 1690s."

She shut down her computer and grabbed her purse from her lower desk drawer. Together they made their way through the workroom, which led into the area behind the circulation desk.

Ms. Cole was looming over Ann Marie, one of the library's part-time employees. Ann Marie was one of Lindsey's favorite employees. As the mother of two sons who were fond of bringing frogs, snakes and cockroaches into her home as pets, nothing much fazed her. Suffice it to say, she could handle Ms. Cole without breaking a sweat.

"Have a lovely evening," Ann Marie said with a wave.

"You, too," Lindsey said. "Good night, Ms. Cole."

Ms. Cole frowned, but gave her a small nod. Given that she used to ignore Lindsey completely, Lindsey looked at this as the equivalent of a hug from Ms. Cole.

"Wow," Beth said as they stepped through the sliding doors. "She was positively emotional."

"I must be wearing her down," Lindsey said.

They shared a glance and then broke into chuckles before they crossed the street and entered the small park that overlooked the Briar Creek public beach. They made their way along the path that cut through the park and led to the pier.

The tide had finished coming in while Lindsey had been in her office. The breeze was cool and carried the briny scent of the ocean on it as if it were delivering a message. Several seagulls swooped high and darted low, riding the air currents. Usually Lindsey suspected they were looking for bread or the occasional Cheeto, but today she got the feeling they were just having fun and she wondered if they had the same spring fever she had.

The tables at the Blue Anchor were full, but Mary saw them from across the room and gestured for them to come to her. A busboy was just clearing a table beside her and she motioned for them to take it.

"Check it out," she said, not waiting for them to sit down. "Three stools up at the bar. You can't miss them."

Lindsey peered over the heads of the other diners at the bar, which ran along one wall of the restaurant. Per usual, Mary's husband, Ian, was bartending and Lindsey noticed he was talking to two men, two very big, very blond, very handsome men.

"Oh my," Beth breathed. "Who are they?"

"Steig and Stefan Norrgard, Swedish twin brothers," Mary said. "They work for Riordan Salvage."

"Get out!" Beth said. "I knew I should have gone into salvage."

"As opposed to library school?" Lindsey asked.

"They don't make them like that in library school," Beth said.

"I don't think they make them like that anywhere," Mary said.

"Are you three ogling my customers?" Ian asked as he joined their group.

"If by that do you mean are we undressing them with our eyes?" Mary asked. "No, well, at least I'm not. I'm too busy undressing the bartender."

Ian broke into a grin, looped an arm about his wife and planted a kiss on her, which made Mary blush to the roots of her hair.

Lindsey smiled. Mary, like her brother Sully, was all mahogany curls and big blue eyes, and as if those weren't enough blessings from the gods, she was also quick-witted and kind. Ian, however, was short and bald and wore glasses. He looked more the frog than the prince, but once Ian cracked a joke and smiled at a person, it was impossible not to be smitten with him.

"They are the twin towers of manliness, aren't they?" Ian asked ruefully. "Remind me not to stand next to them. I don't think my ego could take it."

Mary laughed and shook her head. "Your ego is just fine."

"Who is the gray-haired man with them?" Lindsey asked.

She noticed that both of the Swedish men were sipping their beers while leaning down to listen to the man beside them.

"That's the owner of the company, Preston Riordan," Ian said.

Lindsey gave him a quick look. There was a sharp edge to his voice that she'd never heard before. Ian was the sort of person who got on with everybody. He considered strangers to be friends he hadn't met yet, so it was interesting that he sounded less than friendly toward Preston Riordan when the man had been in town for only one day.

"You don't like him?" Mary asked.

Ian shrugged. "Let's just say I don't get the warm fuzzies for him."

Mary's eyebrows rose in surprise, confirming Lindsey's own opinion that it was unusual for Ian not to like Mr. Riordan. As if aware of their scrutiny, the gray-haired man turned around and Lindsey got her first good look at him. He was of medium height and had a powerful build. His skin had the leathered look of a man who'd spent his life aboard a ship. He wore his polo shirt pulled out over his khakis but it didn't hide the beer gut that was hovering over his waistband.

His gaze met Ian's and he waved his empty glass in the air, obviously signaling for a refill.

"Back to my station," Ian said, but before he left to return to the bar, he asked, "Shall I send over the usual?"

"Yes, two chardonnays, thanks," Beth said.

"Okay, ladies, I'll get your order to your waitress. What will it be?" Mary asked.

"Crab salad," Beth said.

"The same," Lindsey said.

"My new recipe with the green olives?" Mary asked.

"Yes," they answered together.

"I do love daring diners," Mary said.

She left them just as their waitress returned with their wine. Lindsey lifted her glass and took a sip. Her eyes strayed over to the Riordan Salvage men and she watched as the door to the Anchor opened and in came Trudi Hargrave.

Trudi wore the same body-hugging suit she'd had on earlier as well as the platform pumps that brought her diminutive height up to about five and a half feet, the half coming mostly from the shoes. She hurried across the room and launched herself at Preston Riordan in a hug that looked as if it strangled.

"Well, this could get interesting," Beth said. She moved her chair so it was next to Lindsey's instead of across and settled back as if expecting a show.

Preston set Trudi back on her feet with a smile that looked forced. Trudi then turned to hug the Swedish brothers but they stood up, which even with her heels made her nose bounce off their sternums as they gave her quick pats on the back as if unsure of what to do with her.

"Awkward," Lindsey said.

"Is it bad that I'm enjoying this?" Beth said. "Trudi and I, we're not what one would call simpatico."

"You, me and Milton," Lindsey said. "It seems none of us belong to the 'I heart Trudi' fan club."

"Cranky of us, isn't it?" Beth asked. "I mean just because she's pushy, rude, loud, selfish and a complete narcissist, that's no reason to dislike the poor girl."

"I think she is the only person I've ever seen Milton lose

his temper with," Lindsey said. "You should have seen them yelling at each other today. He called her a tart."

"No!" Beth chortled and sipped her wine.

"Oh, yes," Lindsey said. "After she called him a fossil."

Beth looked outraged. "That's just mean!"

"And you're surprised because she's known for her niceness," Lindsey said in a tone drier than the wine on her tongue.

Beth glanced back at Trudi, who had just done an over-the-shoulder hair toss with her long, multihued dye job. Then she threw back her head and laughed at something one of the Norrgard brothers said. Her cute little nose wrinkled, and she rested her hand on his arm as if she needed support from laughing so hard.

"Is it me, or is she overselling it?" Lindsey asked.

"The men seem okay with it," Beth said and then sighed.

"Don't fret," Lindsey said. "They'll see through her soon enough. A person can only start so many sentences with 'I' and 'me' before they start boring their listener to death."

"Is that what happened when you met her?"

The waitress appeared with a basket of warm bread and their plates of crab salad. Lindsey waited until she left to answer.

"Pretty much," she said. "I had one of the worst hangovers of my life the day after I met her and I blame her entirely."

"Do tell," Beth said. She buttered her roll and took a bite.

"Well, the mayor was having a party for all of his

department heads and hc had a champagne fountain," Lindsey said. "So whenever I found myself trapped by Trudi and one of her 'I-me' monologues, I would down my glass of bubbly and then excuse myself on the pretext of getting another. Well, I try to stick to the rule of two, but that night I lost count as I tried to get away from her. Luckily, Sully was my date and drove me home. I still blame her."

"Well, since we both rode our bikes to work today, you'd best work out a new strategy," Beth said. "Because here she comes."

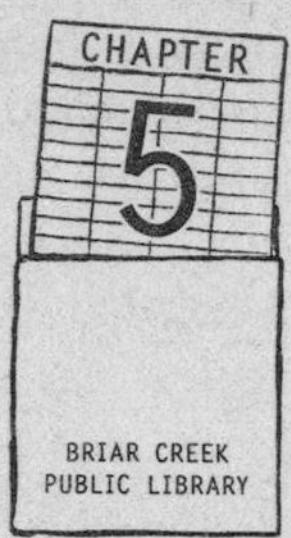

"Oh, good grief," Lindsey muttered and put down her fork. Her crab salad looked so lovely on its leaf of lettuce with cucumber slices surrounding it. It fairly beckoned to be eaten.

"Lindsey!" Trudi called across the room. She was mincing through the café, making for their table and dragging Preston Riordan behind her.

Lindsey rose from her seat and gave Trudi a faint wave. She eyeballed the wine on her table and wondered if she had time for fortification before Trudi landed.

"Preston, I want you to meet our local librarians, this is Lindsey Norris and Beth Stanley," Trudi said. "If you need any research done, these are the two to ask, regular bibliophiles they are."

Beth gave Lindsey a look that said she felt insulted, although she wasn't sure why. Lindsey could have told her it was because nothing Trudi ever said felt like a compliment, but she refrained, knowing that Beth would figure it out for herself soon enough.

Preston Riordan held out his hand to each of them in turn. His hand was rough with calluses and his grip was firm but polite.

"Nice to meet you," Lindsey said. "I believe my neighbor Charlie Peyton is going to be working for you."

"I just signed him on today," Riordan said. His voice was low and gruff. The lines around his eyes were deep, but Lindsey did not get the feeling they were laugh lines; rather, they seemed to be the squint marks of a man who spent his life looking out at the horizon, searching for something he didn't have.

"Charlie is a good kid," Lindsey said.

"He seems like he knows his way about the islands. I really wanted to get that guy who runs the tours, Mike Sullivan, on board, but he turned me down flat."

"Did he?" Beth asked.

"Yeah." Riordan frowned. "Said he was entering his busy season and couldn't afford the time away. I think it was a brush-off, though. I mean, who doesn't want to dig for treasure?"

"Lindsey might be able to help you get Sully on board," Trudi said. "Oh, did you get what I said? 'On board'?"

While Trudi dissolved into laughter, Riordan looked at her and then at Lindsey. Before he could ask her what Trudi was talking about, Lindsey changed the subject.

"Is it true that you have a map?" she asked.

"It is." Riordan's chest puffed out a bit. "Captain Kidd's own map to the Thumb Islands. It was quite a find."

"How did you come by it?" Lindsey asked.

"The Cambridge Auction House in Maine," he said. "They were unloading a whole collection of antique ship furniture, some really amazing stuff."

"The auctioneer didn't realize it was a treasure map?" Lindsey asked.

"No, he didn't even know he had it," Riordan said. "The map was tucked into a secret compartment of an old desk, a desk that supposedly belonged to Captain Kidd."

"Did you know it had a secret compartment?" she asked.

"I suspected," he said. "They were fond of them back in the day."

"I used to be an archivist," Lindsey said. "If you'd care to have the map authenticated . . ."

She let her voice trail off as Riordan turned back and studied her with a sharp brown gaze.

"I know it's genuine," he said. "I don't need to have any academics slicing it up in the name of research."

Lindsey opened her mouth to protest, but Beth cut her off. "When will you start the treasure hunt?"

"As soon as the town gives us the go-ahead," Riordan said. "The mayor has to sign off on some permits and all that."

"Oh, don't bore them with the details," Trudi interrupted. "Librarians don't understand the inner workings of town politics."

"Oh, don't we?" Lindsey asked. "Funny you should say that since I was just going over next year's budget and it looks smaller."

"Well, of course it does," Trudi said. "You're a library. You can't expect a big budget. I mean, it's not like you do anything to increase the town's revenue. What did you earn in overdue fines last year? Seven thousand dollars?"

"Our mission isn't to make money," Lindsey said. "It's to provide residents with access to information in all formats, which costs money. But since it's the residents' choice to have a library, I really don't see why my budget should get diminished while other department budgets get fatter."

Trudi just looked at her and shrugged. "If you want money, you have to make money. Isn't that right, Preston?"

His gaze was on his crew, however. Steig and Stefan were chatting up two lovely young gals, and the drinks were coming fast and furious among their little group.

"Yeah, whatever," he said. He gave them a distracted nod before he went to join his men. Trudi followed in his wake with a little finger wave.

"Just so we're clear, stabbing her with my fork would be bad?" Beth asked.

"Yes," Lindsey confirmed.

"Just checking," Beth said and she jabbed the tines of her fork into her salad instead, leaving Lindsey to suspect she saw Trudi's head in the rounded mound of crab meat.

Lindsey had to admit with the placement of the olives there was a marked resemblance to Trudi and she dug into her salad with gusto.

* * *

Lindsey was sitting on the front porch of the captain's house where she rented the apartment on the third floor. Night had arrived, tucking a blanket of darkness over them, but the porch light illuminated enough of the front lawn for Heathcliff to chase his tennis ball.

Lindsey was throwing to his fetching, while Nancy sat in one chair rocking back and forth as she worked on her cross-stitch and Charlie sat in another, strumming his acoustic guitar.

Lindsey fired the ball across the yard out of the circle of light and Heathcliff ran after it, low to the ground with his paws kicking up dirt as he launched himself across the grass.

Lindsey waited for him to reappear. She stared into the darkness, trying to spot him, but night is the best camouflage for a black dog and there was no sign of him.

"I think he lost it," Nancy said.

Lindsey rose from her seat. She'd been thinking the same. She went down the steps that led to the walkway and crossed the grass toward the fence that ran along the edge of the yard.

"Heathcliff, here, boy," she called. "Where are you, buddy?"

The yellow tennis ball came shooting by her with Heathcliff hot on its tail. Lindsey stared into the darkness and then jumped when a man hopped over the low fence in front of her. Recognizing him, she started to laugh.

"For a second there, I thought Heathcliff had figured out how to throw," she said.

"He is an exceptionally smart dog," Sully said as he reached forward and pulled her into his arms.

Lindsey felt the dizzy, giddy, inexplicably happy feeling bubble up inside her just like it always did when she was near Sully. She wrapped her arms about his neck and planted a proper greeting on him.

"That's what I've been missing all day," he said. He stroked her cheek with one finger as his blue eyes searched her hazel ones. "Good day today?"

"Interesting for sure," she said.

He twined his fingers with hers, and they walked together toward the house.

Lindsey pressed her side against his. She had missed him. He was taller than her with a powerful sailor's build. Dressed in jeans and work boots and a blue T-shirt that molded itself to his brawny build, he looked like he could be the pitch man for an Old Spice commercial.

"Ah, so there's my two-timing employee," he said when he spotted Charlie on the porch. They could hear Charlie plucking out a tune across the yard.

Lindsey glanced at his face, but he was smiling so she knew he wasn't holding any grudge with Charlie.

"I met Preston Riordan," she said. "At the Anchor tonight."

"Mary said you had been in," he said. He let go of her hand to brush a long curly length of blond hair back over her shoulder. Then he circled his hand around her waist and matched his stride to hers. "What was your impression of him?"

"It's hard to say," Lindsey said. "Trudi Hargrave was there, too, and she tends to distort my view of things."

"Ah." Sully nodded in understanding.

"I couldn't really read him," she said.

Again, Sully nodded.

"He told us that he asked you to help find Captain Kidd's treasure," she said. "And that you turned him down."

"True," Sully said. "I couldn't get a feel for him either; besides it's our busy season. As it is, to cover Charlie, I've hired Dale Wilcox to help out."

"Really?" Lindsey asked. "I like Dale. I don't think he's as bad as people say."

Dale Wilcox ran a fishing charter off the same pier as Sully. He had a bad reputation because he was an ex-convict who had served time for assault, but unlike Riordan, when Lindsey had met Dale several months before, she'd gotten his measure immediately. It helped that he was an avid reader, and she liked his taste in authors.

"You only approve of him because he reads Hemingway," Sully teased.

"See? He can't be all bad," Lindsey said. "Besides I heard he's been spending time with Carrie Rushton."

"Another reason I offered him the job," Sully said. "He seems very eager to prove that he has turned over a new leaf and I'd like to help him out with that."

They stepped up onto the porch and Nancy jumped up from her rocking chair to greet Sully with a hug.

"I just made a batch of snicker doodles," she said. "You sit and I'll go get them."

"Oh, don't go to any trouble," Sully said.

"It's no trouble, dear," she said. And she banged through the screened front door with Heathcliff at her side. Lindsey was quite positive that the dog had figured out what "snicker doodle" meant in dogspeak—treat.

"Hi, boss," Charlie said. Sully sat in the empty chair beside him and smiled.

"So is that why you were plucking out 'Working on the Highway' by Springsteen, because your boss showed up?"

"Nice." Charlie bobbed his head and offered up his fist, which Sully banged with his own. "You got it. Yeah, I figured the Boss or my boss. It's all about working for a living."

"You have a new boss now, though," Sully said.

"Yeah, I don't see me playing any songs for that guy," Charlie said. "He's a tad intense."

"Treasure hunters generally are," Sully said. "There have been several people who've tried to find Captain Kidd's treasure on Pirate Island over the years. No one has succeeded yet."

"Really?" Lindsey asked. "I did some research today and it appears there are many islands all along the Northeast that claim to be the spot where Kidd hid his treasure. Do you think it's true—that it could be here?"

The screen door swung open with a screech and out came Nancy and Heathcliff. She had loaded up a tray with four glasses of sweet tea and a plate full of snicker doodles.

Lindsey glanced around her, quickly trying to take it in. A cool evening, people she enjoyed and cookies; it felt as if this was one of those fleeting life moments where everything was right in her world.

"What's true?" Nancy asked as she settled the tray on the glass top wicker coffee table. She and Lindsey took the remaining seats and Charlie put down his guitar so he could tuck into the cookies.

"The stories about Captain Kidd," Charlie said.

"Of course they are," Nancy said. She looked at Sully. "Tell them."

He finished off a cookie and said, "Well, the way I heard it was that in 1699, Captain Kidd was supposed to have buried treasure all along the East Coast from Gardiners Island, New York, all the way up to Oak Island, Nova Scotia, and one of his stopping places is said to be our very own Thumb Islands. Legend has it that he buried the treasure, hoping that the knowledge of its whereabouts would give him bargaining leverage if he got caught since he knew he was a wanted man."

"Did it?"

"No, he was sent back to England to face charges of piracy, and after a speedy trial where he was found guilty, he rotted in Newgate Prison for a year and then was hanged in 1701. So if he did bury treasure here, no one ever found it."

"Was he an evil pirate?" Charlie asked. "Like Blackbeard?"

"Blackbeard?" Sully asked. "You mean Edward Teach?"

Charlie nodded. Lindsey reached for a third snicker

doodle. Not her fault, she told herself. Nancy's cookies and Sully's storytelling were addictive. She chewed while she listened.

"Blackbeard isn't known to have harmed or murdered anyone he held captive," Sully said. "He was only active for three years, from 1716 to 1718."

"I thought he was the scourge of the sea," Nancy said.

"By all accounts, he commanded his ships with the permission of their crews," Sully said.

He bit down on another cookie and Lindsey smiled at him. Heathcliff had propped his head on Sully's feet, ever hopeful for some crumbs.

"I had no idea you knew so much about pirates," she said.

"You can't be a sailor and not know about the ones who went before, and the pirates and privateers make for some interesting reading," he said.

"We should read a pirate book in our crafternoon club," Nancy said. "Something like *Treasure Island*."

"Robert Louis Stevenson was a Scottish author and Captain Kidd was a Scottish sailor, so maybe it'll help you solve the mystery of the buried treasure," Sully said.

Nancy's eyes twinkled with mischief. "You have to admit it is exciting. I don't remember the last time someone tried to find treasure on Pirate Island."

"It's been a few years," Sully said. "I'm surprised with the economy being as bad as it's been, someone hasn't tried it more recently."

"I'm surprised Mayor Henson is letting Riordan and his crew out there," Lindsey said. "Certainly Milton and the historical society are not happy about it, and I can't believe they haven't complained to the mayor."

"I have some information about that," Charlie said through a mouthful of cookie. "Mr. Riordan told me that Pirate Island is owned by the town, and since the town has to send workers out there to trim the brush and clean up the litter from people who sneak out there and go camping, it's really not earning its keep. So Trudi Hargrave proposed to the town council that they make it an island destination for rent."

"I never heard about that," Nancy said.

"Apparently, it was all kept on the down low," Charlie said. "The council was considering it when Mr. Riordan contacted the mayor's office about the island and they referred him to Trudi. She then went to the council with the idea of letting Riordan rent the island as a sort of pilot project and giving him a permit to hunt for the treasure."

"The town gives out treasure hunter permits?" Lindsey asked.

She thought about the special collection of materials she had in the library about the history of Briar Creek and the Thumb Islands and was pretty sure she'd never seen anything like that. She made a mental note to ask Milton if he'd heard of treasure hunter permits before.

"I believe it's a first," Charlie said. "But in any case, Trudi has given the town a win-win situation. If Riordan doesn't find the treasure, the town can go forth and rent out the island and issue treasure-hunting permits, which will make it a tidy profit. If Riordan does find the treasure, then the town promotes the heck out of the find and rents out the island as a destination spot for pirate lovers."

"What happens to the treasure if it's found?" Lindsey asked. "Will the town take it or does it belong to Riordan?"

"I think the town gets a cut, but mostly, they'll be making money off of the tourism dollars that will pour in for having a genuine pirate hideaway."

"Oh." Nancy frowned. "I never thought of that. We get enough summer traffic as it is. I can't imagine what it will be like if a bunch of crazy treasure hunters descend upon us."

"You're awfully quiet." Sully tapped Lindsey's toe with his own. "What are you thinking?"

"That I'd better see what we have in the nonfiction collection about treasure hunting," she said. "Just in case a full-on treasure fever sweeps the town."

"Avast, me hearties," a voice called across the library. It was loud enough that Lindsey heard it in her office and she popped her head up from her computer, where she was writing her weekly report to the library board, to see what the ruckus was about.

Ms. Cole was standing behind the circulation desk, glowering at the person before her. Lindsey hurried from her office to avert any impending disasters.

"Thar be a story time a-brewing in the aft deck in five minutes."

Lindsey squinted. Under the fake beard, eye patch and red bandanna, yes, it was Beth. Lindsey laughed. The kids that had been running amuck in the children's area raced for the story time room in the back.

"Who are you and what have you done with my children's librarian?" she asked.

"Arr, I be Calico Prudentilla Read, and I buttered my toast with that weakling librarian for breakfast," Beth said.

Now Lindsey laughed out loud while Ms. Cole gave her a disapproving look and said, "Mr. Tupper would never have allowed such shenanigans in the library."

"Arr, which is why I ate him, too," Beth said.

Ms. Cole's eyebrows rose to her hairline and then she put on her reading glasses and turned back to her computer screen, obviously hoping that if she ignored them, they would go away.

Beth lifted her plastic sword and said to Lindsey from behind it, "My story time statistics have tripled since he left."

"Can't really argue with that," she agreed. She walked around the desk to join Beth on the other side. "How did you come up with the cool name?"

"The pirate name generator," Beth said. Then she scowled and added, "Arr."

"Explain."

"I found it on the International Talk Like a Pirate Day website," Beth said. She motioned for Lindsey to walk with her as she set out for her story room.

"The who of the what?" Lindsey asked.

"September nineteenth is International Talk Like a Pirate Day, which is not helpful to us in June, but on their website I found the link to www dot pirate quiz dot com. It gives you your pirate's name. How about the last name *Read* on mine—pretty perfect, huh?"

A young girl came up to Beth and studied her, obviously suspicious of this bearded and eye-patched woman.

"Ahoy there, matey," Beth said. "What are ye lookin' at?"

"Your eye patch," the girl said. "Can I have one, too?"

"Arr, course ye can," Beth said. "We'll be craftin' our own at the end of the stories."

The girl clapped and squealed and ran back to the room, looking delighted.

"I think this pirate thing could really work out for me," Beth said and she ducked into her story room with a wave of her sword and one last "Arr!"

Lindsey turned, intending to race back to her office and look up her pirate name. She was hoping for a nice Captain Bloody Mary Flint or something equally terrible, but halfway to her office, she saw a familiar blond head, cut so precisely it seemed as if every hair had been trimmed individually.

She froze. She felt her throat get tight. And then very quickly and quietly, she hurried behind the circulation desk, through the workroom and into her office, which she shut and locked.

"Very mature, Lindsey," she muttered to herself.

Thankful that the solid oak door stood between her and public humiliation, she leaned against it while she caught her breath and willed her heart to stop racing in her chest.

Once she could breathe again, she shook her head. How ridiculous. It probably wasn't even him. She hadn't seen him in over a year. Probably that had just been a summer resident with an unfortunately similar haircut.

She felt like an idiot. In her head, she could hear Ms.

Cole saying, "Mr. Tupper never felt the need to go and hide in his office." Oh, how she loved being compared to her predecessor. Although she suspected in this case Ms. Cole would have been right.

Straightening her shoulders, she heaved herself off the door. Honestly, she needed to get a grip.

She turned and unlocked the door, opening it halfway just as she always did during the workday. And there he was, standing with his fist up as if he had been about to knock. It was John Mayhew, her ex-fiancé.

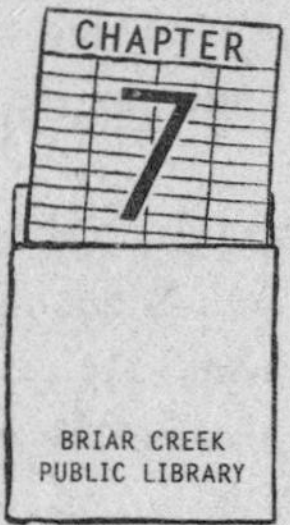

"Hi," she said. Her voice sounded strained and she cleared her throat and tried again. "Hi, John."

"Lindsey," he said. The corner of his mouth turned up and he gave her a wry smile. "I'm sorry, I should have called first."

"No, it's fine," she said.

They were within a haircut of the same height with him only half an inch taller. His pale hair was the same shade as hers and his eyes were the same blue-green hazel. When they'd been dating, it had been a joke among their friends that they looked more like brother and sister than boyfriend and girlfriend. Lindsey wondered if that should have been her first clue that he wasn't the man for her.

"Come on in," she said as she stepped back to allow him to enter.

"Are you sure? I don't want to interrupt your workday," he said.

Lindsey glanced over his shoulder at the library. Now that story time had started, it seemed to have quieted down.

"It's fine," she said. "My staff has it under control."

"Oh, great," he said, looking relieved.

He stepped forward as if to give her a hug, but Lindsey quickly stepped behind her desk. She wasn't angry with him anymore for throwing away their life together, but she wasn't hugging him either.

"So." She picked up a pen and tapped it on her desk. "What brings you to Briar Creek?"

"I've rented a summer place here," he said. "It's that brown-shingled house that overlooks the bay. Well, not the main house, just the guest house. The owner, Paul Gavin, said he'd be away for the summer and wanted someone to keep an eye on the place. He gave me a great rate for the next ten weeks."

He was watching her from beneath his eyelashes. It was an old habit of his that he employed when he was about to say something he thought she wouldn't like.

"Why?" she asked. She tossed the pen down onto the desktop.

"That's what I've always loved about you," he said. "You get right to the point, no hesitation, no talking around a matter, you don't pull any punches."

"Which is funny considering I'd really like to punch you right now," she said.

He tossed back his blond head and laughed. He was trying to charm her. It wasn't working.

"I want the truth, John. Out of all the small shore towns on the Connecticut coast, you picked Briar Creek. Why?"

"Isn't it obvious, Lindsey?" he asked. "I'm here to win you back."

If a tsunami had slammed into the beach across the street, Lindsey could not have been more surprised.

"No," she said, shaking her head. "I'm dating someone. There is no winning me back. I'm done. I've moved on. Good grief, it's been over a year since I left. What happened to the bim . . . excuse me . . . Amy? Aren't you still together?"

A red flush crept into John's cheeks. "No, it didn't work out."

"Sorry," Lindsey said, not meaning it in the slightest. There was an awkward silence, and then just like a scab that she couldn't resist picking at, she asked, "Just out of curiosity, who broke it off?"

John let out a breath from between clenched teeth and said, "She did."

Lindsey studied him. So the pretty, young thing had dumped him. There were so many things she could say that would be like rubbing salt in his wounds and it would feel so good. But that wasn't the person she wanted to be, so she resisted the temptation—barely.

"I'm sorry you were hurt," she said. To her surprise there was a kernel of truth to her words. He had been more than her fiancé; he had also been her friend, and she did feel bad that he'd suffered. Maybe she was more over their breakup than she had realized.

"Don't be," he said. He met and held her gaze. "I deserved to be humiliated after what I did to you. You were the best thing in my life and I ruined what we had. I am so sorry."

Lindsey smiled at him. His words were like a balm on her hurt. She was glad she hadn't given in to the desire to be nasty to him or he might not have apologized, which she realized was all that she had ever wanted from him since their split.

"Apology accepted," she said. An awkward silence fell between them. "I suppose I should get back to work now."

"Of course," he said.

He took the hint and rose from his seat. Lindsey got up, too, and walked him to the door.

"It was good to see you again," she said. She held out her hand, planning to shake his hand and reaffirm that there were no hard feelings.

Instead, John took her hand in his and raised the back of it to his lips.

"I'm glad you think so," he said as he lowered her hand. "I'm not giving up on us, so you can be sure you'll be seeing lots more of me."

Lindsey felt her jaw drop open. No! That certainly wasn't what she'd meant.

"Hey, Lindsey," a voice said from behind John's shoulder.

Lindsey saw Sully looking at her, with one eyebrow

raised, over John's head. She felt a hot flush scald her face and she snatched her hand out of John's.

"Sully," she cried. She reached around John and pulled him forward. Sully wrapped an arm around her shoulders and gave her a quick squeeze before releasing her.

Judging by his expression, Lindsey realized he had no idea who John was. John, meanwhile, frowned up at Sully, looking none too pleased.

"Mike Sullivan, but everyone calls me Sully," he said and extended his hand.

"John Mayhew."

John clasped Sully's hand in his and Lindsey was relieved to see there was no macho hand crushing going on.

"I'm Lindsey's—" John began but Lindsey cut him off.

"Old friend," she said. "From my archivist days at Yale."

"Oh," Sully said. "Are you a librarian, too?"

John looked as if Sully had just kneed him in the crotch, and Lindsey had to press her lips together to keep from laughing.

"No, I'm a law professor," he said. "At Yale."

Sully's gaze snapped to Lindsey's. She knew he was silently asking if John was *that* law professor. She had told him about her breakup with a law professor at Yale but she had never gotten specific enough to share his name, thinking it wasn't important enough to mention. She gave what she hoped was an imperceptible nod.

Either way, he must have understood, because Sully tucked her back under his arm and pulled her up against his side as if he would protect her from any harm. It was nice and Lindsey looped her own arm around the small of his back.

"Well, it was nice meeting you, John," Sully said. "If you don't mind, I need to borrow my girl for just a bit."

John glowered but then said, "Of course. I'll see you around, Lindsey."

"See you," she said.

They waited as he left the building and then Sully turned and led Lindsey back into her office. Closing the door behind them, he glanced up quickly to see that no one was looking and then he cupped her face and planted a swift but thorough kiss on her.

"Are you okay?" he asked.

"I'm fine." She gave him a quick hug. "Never better."

When she stepped back from him, she realized she meant it. There was something so inherently solid about Sully that when he was near, she felt as if everything was exactly as it was supposed to be. In the few short months they'd been dating, he'd become her rock.

"That had to be a bit of a shock," he said.

He sat down in the seat John had just vacated and Lindsey sat down behind her desk.

"A bit," she said. "I had no idea he was going to rent a summer place here."

"He's staying for the summer?" he asked.

"So he says."

"I'm guessing he wants you back."

Lindsey gave him a rueful smile. John had told her as much but she was loath to admit it for fear that it would strain the new relationship she had going with Sully.

"Awkward," she said.

Sully laughed and she felt the tension break.

"Only for him," he said. "I have to feel sorry for the guy."

"Why?" she asked.

"Because he lost you," he said.

Lindsey and Jessica Gallo, a part-time library assistant, spent the afternoon setting up a pirate display by the front door.

Just before closing, Trudi Hargrave arrived, stepping through the sliding doors wearing a pinstriped power suit and a smile that looked like she had been practicing it in front of her mirror for days.

"Lindsey!" she cried. "So good to see you again."

Lindsey handed a stack of books to Jessica and turned to greet Trudi.

"Hi, Trudi," she said. "How are you?"

"Fabulous," Trudi gushed. "Just fabulous. Oh, isn't this darling? Jessica, you are quite the little worker bee, aren't you?"

Trudi was taking in the display of books, movies and maps that they had assembled.

"Er, thank you?" Jessica said in a question. She looked uncertainly at Lindsey as if she wasn't sure what to make of Trudi's effusiveness.

Lindsey smiled to reassure her. "Is there something I can help you with, Trudi?"

"Oh, I'm so glad you asked." Trudi clapped her hands together. "Here's the thing, because *I* am responsible for opening up Pirate Island and for bringing in Riordan Salvage, *I* think *I* should hold a town meeting about the situation for anyone who has questions, and *I'd* like to hold it here at the library, say, tomorrow at six o'clock." Without waiting for a response, she added, "Great. Thanks." Trudi pranced on her stilettos back toward the door. If she was going for the quick getaway, she should have picked different footwear.

"Oh, no you don't," Lindsey said. "Stop right there, Trudi."

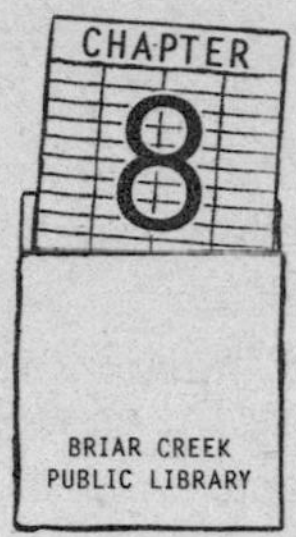

"What? Is something wrong?" Trudi blinked her long false lashes at Lindsey.

"Wouldn't the mayor normally be the one to hold a town meeting?" Lindsey asked.

She hadn't been in Briar Creek long, but she had picked up on a few things about small town life, and one of them was that the mayor was usually the mouthpiece of any big news events within the town.

"Oh, well, this is a different circumstance," Trudi said and her eyes shifted back to the display, which let Lindsey know that she was lying.

"Trudi, Mayor Henson is up for reelection this November," she said. "By any chance are you planning to run against him?"

"Me?" Trudi asked, her eyes wide. "I'm flattered that you think I would be a good candidate, but no, I really couldn't . . ."

"Well, in order to use the library for a meeting, we have to submit a requisition form to the facilities department," Lindsey said. "I have the paperwork in my office, and I'll just need your signature and a deposit."

"Facilities department? Deposit?" Trudi asked. "For me?"

"For anyone who wants to use the room," Lindsey said. "It's procedure."

"Can't we just keep it on the down low?"

"Sorry, it's required," Lindsey said. "Because the library is owned by the town, and the town is run by the mayor, he has mandated that booking any rooms in public buildings has to go through official channels. That way if there were, say, a terrorist group using the library for meetings, there would be a paper trail. At least, that's how it was explained to me."

"Are you calling me a terrorist?" Trudi asked. She looked outraged. "I'll have you know, I am no such thing."

"No, Trudi, I'm not calling you a terrorist, I'm just saying the rules are in place for that sort of reason."

"Well, if you know I'm not a terrorist, then why can't you let me use the room?"

"Because if I make an exception for you, I'd have to make one for everyone," Lindsey said. "Including the terrorists."

She saw Jessica roll her eyes at the ridiculous turn the conversation had taken, and she glanced away so as not to laugh.

"No, you wouldn't have to make an exception," Trudi insisted. "Because no one has to know you waived the deposit and let me use the room."

"Trudi, you've lived in this town your whole life," Lindsey said. "If I give you special treatment, *everyone* will know and probably before supper is on the table tonight."

Trudi narrowed her eyes, looking petulant. "Fine. I see how it is."

"Excuse me?"

"You're one of Henson's little lackeys, aren't you?"

Lindsey took a deep breath. She understood that Trudi was disappointed but she was not going to be bullied.

"I don't think I've ever been accused of being anyone's lackey," she said. "Now as for the room, I'm just following the procedure. If you don't like the procedure, I am happy to forward your complaint to the library board and the mayor's office."

"Don't bother," Trudi snarled. "I'll find somewhere else to have my press conference."

With a loud humph of indignation, she stomped back out the front door.

Jessica turned to look at Lindsey. "That was so not why I'm going to library school."

"I had a very wise professor in library school at Southern Connecticut State University, who told us if we were going to work in public libraries, we had better do it not because we loved books but because we loved people."

"Wise professor," Jessica said.

"How long until you graduate?"

"One more semester," Jessica said. "I'll be done by Christmas."

"Good for you. I wish I had a full-time position for you here."

"Thanks," Jessica said. She looked sheepish and added, "But I'm thinking of becoming a medical librarian."

"Really?"

"I'd finally be able to use my bachelor's in biology," Jessica said. "And I like the research element of the work."

"You'll be great," Lindsey said. "Wherever you decide to work."

"Thanks."

Jessica put the last book on the shelf and they both stepped back to admire the display.

"Fernando really makes it," Lindsey said.

The talking mechanical parrot from the children's area was hanging above the display. His voice-activated recorder had recently been shut off as he had been hanging over the area where Milton taught his young chess club members.

All had been well until one of the boys shouted, "Checkmate!" and Fernando, who repeated whatever he heard, began squawking "Checkmate!" repeatedly.

The sound could be heard all the way over at the circulation desk, which was Ms. Cole's domain, and her frown grew more and more severe with each squawk. Finally, Beth wrestled the batteries out of Fernando and he became mercifully quiet.

Although looking at him now, Lindsey could swear he was giving Ms. Cole some serious stink eye.

"I think we should put a mini eye patch on him," Jessica said.

"I'm sure Beth probably has a costume for him somewhere," Lindsey said. "Now, you must let me know if there's anything I can do to help you with graduation or with finding a hospital job when you're done."

"Thanks, Lindsey," Jessica said. "This job is what made me realize I wanted to work in libraries. I'll always owe you for that."

"Aw, pshaw," Lindsey said with a grin as she headed back to her office. She dreaded the day they lost Jessica as she had a rare combination of reference and people skills which would be tough to replace.

"Get out!" Beth said. She was back in her street clothes without her eye patch and bandanna as she and Lindsey locked up the library and walked around the old stone building to their bikes. "John's actually renting a place for the summer?"

"That's what he said." Lindsey bent over to unlock her bike from the bike rack. It was a red Schwinn cruiser that she had bought when she moved to Briar Creek in an effort to be more planet friendly.

Beth unlocked hers as well and they walked them to the corner. "How did Sully take it?"

"Fine," she said. She smiled when she remembered what he'd said about feeling sorry for John.

"Wasn't it awkward having them meet like that?"

"Only for a moment, but Sully is such a good guy that it

was really okay," Lindsey said. "Probably not so much for John but . . ." She trailed off with a shrug.

"Well, I'm glad Sully is so nice, because if I see John, I'm going to kick him in the privates," Beth said. For a second she looked like she had her scary pirate face on.

"No, you're not," Lindsey said. "It's over; he'll figure it out soon enough. We don't need to be mean or do anything that might land you in jail. You know Chief Daniels would frown on you assaulting a summer tourist."

"Arr!" Beth gave a pirate growl. "I'm really liking the pirate thing. I was thumbing through *Sea Queens: Women Pirates Around the World* by Jane Yolen and I am torn between wanting to be like Mary Read, because of her last name, of course, or Madame Ching, a nineteenth-century pirate from China, who is said to be the most successful female pirate ever."

"I think you'd better stick with Calico Prudentilla Read. Pirates make for great stories, but as Sully was telling us last night, it's hard to separate the fact from the fiction." Lindsey climbed onto her bike and smiled at Beth. "Besides, you can't be a pirate—you don't have a ship."

"That's a fair point," Beth said. She climbed onto her bike as well. "Maybe I could just take some fencing lessons?"

"I'm sure you could work it into your yoga lessons with Milton," Lindsey said as she pushed off the curb and began to pedal. "You know, warrior position, thrust and parry, etc."

Beth laughed. "I'll run it by him."

"Better than running it through him," Lindsey retorted.

"Nice wordplay," Beth said.

Lindsey led the way across the road to the bike lane. She was cruising along, passing the park, when she noticed there were more cars than usual. In fact, the park was packed with people.

She held up her hand to signal to Beth that she was going to turn and she steered her bike onto the narrow lane at the end of the park and stopped. Beth rode up alongside her. The gazebo that sat at the end of the green was full of people and a crowd had gathered around outside it as well.

Lindsey peered over the heads in front of her and saw Trudi Hargrave standing in the gazebo with Preston Riordan. The gazebo had been gussied up with pirate flags and she saw the Norrgard brothers frowning out at the crowd with bandannas on their heads and eye patches covering their right eyes.

"They have pretty good scowls for pirates," Beth said to Lindsey. "They could use some swords, though. A good sword really makes the outfit."

Lindsey gave her a dubious look.

"Just a suggestion," Beth said with a shrug.

"Trudi must have decided to have her impromptu town meeting here," Lindsey said.

She scanned the crowd and saw Milton, standing on the edge of the grass. She could tell he was doing his mountain pose, as he looked tall and strong as if he were getting ready to take on an enemy.

Lindsey got a prickly feeling of unease at the back of her neck. Milton was the town historian. She hadn't spoken to him since his tiff with Trudi in the library, but she knew he had to be unhappy about the town giving a treasure-hunting company unmonitored access to one of the Thumb Islands. It went completely against his preservationist nature.

She climbed off her bike and set her kickstand. Beth did the same beside her. Together they walked closer to the gazebo so they could hear what was being said.

"Creekers," Trudi cried and held out her arms as if to enfold them all in an embrace. "I want to welcome you to the official kickoff for the hunt for Captain Kidd's treasure."

A murmur rippled through the crowd. Lindsey caught bits of excitement and some grumbles. She glanced at Milton. He hadn't moved.

"That's right," Trudi continued. She leaned forward to speak into the mic that was attached to a small PA system. "Riordan Salvage has gotten the go-ahead to start excavating Pirate Island tomorrow. *I* invited this intrepid team of treasure hunters here, because *I* care deeply for this community and *I* know that many of you have suffered during these unstable economic times. By utilizing the resources of this uninhabited island, we will be giving a shot in the arm to our local businesses with an influx of tourists, and when the treasure is found, Riordan Salvage will be offering a substantial cut of the profit to the town, which will help us all during these uncertain times."

Lindsey saw Riordan give Trudi a small frown and she was betting he didn't like the sound of the words *substantial cut*. Ignoring the look, Trudi ushered Riordan forward toward the mic.

"And now Mr. Riordan has a few words for you," she said.

Before Riordan could greet the crowd, Milton fired a question at him. "What measures are you taking to preserve the environmental sanctity of the island?"

Riordan looked at him as if he were a cockroach that had suddenly begun speaking and looked away.

"Good evening," he said. "I'm Preston Riordan, president of Riordan Salvage. We have a long and storied history of treasure hunting all along the Eastern Seaboard."

"Mr. Riordan, when you say *excavate*, what exactly do you mean?" Milton asked. "Will you be clear-cutting the trees? Using explosives? What are your methods?"

Riordan glowered at Milton as if he'd like to use a few explosives on him. Instead, he took a deep breath and asked, "Who are you exactly?"

"Milton Duffy, president of the Briar Creek Historical Society," he said.

"Are you one of those ecozealots?" Riordan asked as if it was all beginning to make sense now. "Tell me, does keeping the island uninvestigated help your local economy at all?"

"There are more important things than money," Milton argued.

Beth visibly cringed. Nowadays very few people would agree that anything trumped the creation of jobs in an area that had been feeling the recession's pinch for the past couple of years.

Lindsey gazed over the crowd. There were several people nodding at Milton's words, but others were shuffling their feet as if they were uncomfortable, and Lindsey suspected it was because they felt that a surge in business would be good for the small town.

"That is the luxurious belief of people who are retired and living comfortably on a pension," Riordan said. "Other people have families to feed, and opening up Pirate Island to attract tourism and find a pirate's booty will do more to help this town than maintaining a rock with a bunch of trees on it."

Milton's bald head began to glow like a beacon. He opened his mouth to say something, but was cut off by a newcomer joining the group on the gazebo platform. Lindsey blinked in surprise. It was Mayor Henson.

A ripple of interest went through the crowd as they all recognized the mayor. He was wearing his best politician's smile as he stepped in between Trudi and Riordan.

"So sorry I'm late," he said. "Mayoral business can't be ignored for parties, I'm afraid."

Trudi's eyes bugged, and she forced a smile that matched the mayor's in width and insincerity.

"Mayor Henson, so glad you could join us," she said.

"I'll bet you are," he said. His smile didn't flicker in the slightest and Lindsey wondered if she was the only one to hear the sarcasm in his voice.

"Citizens," Mayor Henson said, drawing all of the attention to himself. "Let me assure you that the deepest care will be taken to preserve the natural wonder of Pirate

Island while we investigate the very real possibility that Captain Kidd may have hidden his treasure on one of our very own islands. These are exciting times for our community, and as your mayor, it is my privilege to oversee these events and make the best possible decisions for our town and its future."

Beth leaned close to Lindsey and whispered, "Look at Trudi. She's so mad, she's actually trembling."

"Well, the mayor did hip-check her out of the limelight pretty hard," Lindsey said.

Mayor Henson turned and shook hands with Preston Riordan and the two of them posed for a picture with the Swedish twins on each side. Trudi tried to pop up in between the two men, but even with her Prada stilts, she was too short and didn't make it into the background.

Mayor Henson stepped down into the crowd, and with his Clark Kent good looks, black hair, blue eyes, strong jaw and sturdy build, he looked so much the part of the mayor that it was hard to picture the petite Trudi usurping his position.

"It's almost unfair how much he looks the part," Lindsey said.

She watched as Mayor Henson approached Milton. Milton began gesturing and talking and the mayor nodded his head and asked Milton a few questions. Then he brought Riordan into their group and the three of them formed a tight circle. Trudi was shut out again and Lindsey wasn't surprised when she saw her snap at the man who was boxing up the PA system. She looked as if she wanted to do some damage to anyone unfortunate enough to cross her path.

"Well, I'm good," Lindsey said. "How about you?"

"Oh, yeah," Beth agreed. "Let's scoot before Hurricane Trudi unleashes her wrath."

Lindsey cast one last look at Milton, but couldn't tell if the conversation was going his way or not. She didn't want to interrupt so she decided to wait until she saw him again to ask him what had transpired.

She and Beth got back on their bikes and rode through town until they came to the intersection where they parted ways. With a wave, Lindsey turned onto the street that led to Nancy's house. The salty breeze teased up her hair and tugged at her clothes. There was a small hill in the road and she pedaled faster to maximize the slope that would give her bike the momentum to glide all the way to Nancy's house. She hopped off on the edge of the gravel drive and walked her bike the rest of the way.

She parked her bike on the side of the house where she usually kept it locked to the porch rail. When she came around the front, she saw someone walking up the drive, clutching a bouquet of daisies. It was John.

"Oh, no," she muttered.

She waited for him to join her. Although she was glad for the apology, she was done with the nice stuff. She did not want to keep bumping into him. Briar Creek was her town and she felt like he was invading it.

"Hi," he said. "I saw you pedal by, so I thought I'd bring you these. I meant to bring them to you at work, but I forgot."

He held them out to her and she took them with a sigh. "They're lovely, but—"

The screen door to the house opened with a squeak, and

a black ball of fur came barreling down the steps at Lindsey. She braced herself as he tended to hit hard and low and had managed to knock her down a few times when he caught her off guard.

Heathcliff slammed up against her and then stood on his hind legs and wrapped his front paws around her leg. Lindsey laughed and reached down to scratch his ears. She had never known a dog to give hugs before but he did.

John stepped back as if afraid the dog was going to maul him.

Heathcliff glanced at him over his shoulder and then spun around and dropped to all fours and barked.

"It's all right, buddy," Lindsey said. "He's a friend." She made sure to emphasize the word *friend.*

"You have a dog?" John asked, looking concerned. He was not an animal person. When he and Lindsey had lived together, he had refused to have any pets because he was worried about shedding. Heathcliff didn't shed, but she didn't feel the need to point that out to him.

"His name is Heathcliff," Lindsey said. "And we belong to each other."

Heathcliff gave one more bark and sat in front of Lindsey like a furry shield between her and John.

"Oh, sorry," Nancy said. She stepped down the stairs and joined them. "Heathcliff heard you come home. He was beside himself in there, so I just let him out. I didn't realize you had company."

"No problem," Lindsey said. "John just dropped by because he saw me on my bike. He's an old friend from New Haven."

"John, this is my landlady, Nancy Peyton. Nancy, John Mayhew," she said.

"Nice to meet you, John," Nancy said and they shook hands.

"Likewise," he said. He glanced up at the three-story captain's house. "You have a beautiful home."

"Thank you," Nancy said. She looked at Lindsey as if uncertain of whether to invite him in or not.

Lindsey was torn. She didn't want to be rude, but she didn't want John to think he could just slide seamlessly back into her life either. Boundaries. She needed to establish some boundaries and not showing up uninvited at her house was one of them.

Mercifully, the decision was taken out of her hands with the screech of a guitar riff and the pounding beat of drums.

"Charlie is having practice?" Lindsey asked.

"What?" Nancy shouted, cupping her ear.

Lindsey shook her head and gestured for them all to walk to the edge of the yard by the fence.

"What is that racket?" John asked, looking aghast.

"My nephew and his band," Nancy said. "I think they're good."

Lindsey tucked her smile into her cheek at this blatant lie. Nancy encouraged Charlie and his musical aspirations, but the truth was both she and Lindsey wore earplugs when they practiced.

"Oh, sorry, I didn't mean to offend you," John said.

"Listen, this could go on for a couple of hours," Lindsey said. It was a slight exaggeration as they usually broke it up after an hour. "So, much as I'd like to have a catch up with you, it's really not a good time."

John eyed the second floor of the house where the music was pouring forth. His eyes were wide with alarm as if he expected Ozzy Osbourne to leap out of the window at him. "Yeah, maybe another time."

"And you might want to call first since they practice a lot," Lindsey said. Again, a slight exaggeration but also necessary.

She stood holding her flowers as John departed with a wave. Nancy and Heathcliff stood beside her, and when he was out of earshot, Nancy asked, "Wild guess here, but was that the dolt you were engaged to?"

"One and the same," Lindsey confirmed.

"He seems nice, but . . ." Nancy paused as if she couldn't find the right words.

"He's a bit of a nebbish, isn't he?" Lindsey asked.

Nancy grinned. "I was thinking putz, but nebbish works."

"You know, I never noticed it when we were together, but now I can't believe I ever agreed to marry him," Lindsey said.

"Frankly, honey, me either," Nancy said.

Lindsey wrapped an arm around Nancy's shoulders and they walked back to the house, laughing.

Lindsey had settled into work and was just opening her e-mail when there was a knock on her office door. She glanced up to find Mayor Henson, standing in the doorway.

"Oh, hello," she said. She rose from her seat and gestured for him to come in. "Um, did we have a meeting scheduled?"

Mayor Henson flashed his artificially white politician's smile. "No, no, I just wanted to pop in and see how things are going at the library."

"Oh," Lindsey said. "Can I get you anything? Coffee? Water?"

"I'm fine, thanks," he said.

"Did you want to sit?" she asked.

He tipped his head as if considering it and said, "Maybe we could walk."

"Sure." She stepped out from behind the desk and let him lead the way.

Ms. Cole glanced at them as they walked past the circulation desk.

"Good morning, Ms. Cole," he said.

She gave him a flustered smile and fiddled with one of her gray curls.

"Good morning. It's so nice to see you, Mayor Henson," she gushed.

"You, too," he said.

Ms. Cole gave Lindsey a smug tight-lipped smile as if to say, "See? I'm friends with the mayor."

Lindsey would have liked to respond with a solid "whatever," but could only manage a shrug before she and the mayor moved away.

They continued through the building until they reached the far corner of the adult area, which as yet was uninhabited.

Mayor Henson paused by the window which looked over the grassy side yard to the old Briar Creek graveyard beyond.

Lindsey said nothing but waited for him to get to the purpose of his visit. She didn't know the mayor well. Usually, her dealings with his office went through his liaison, Herb Gunderson. Mayor Henson wasn't a reader; well, at least if he was, he didn't borrow his books from the library, so she had no frame of reference, no compass point, as it were, for how to start a conversation with him.

"Milton Duffy is on the library board, isn't he?" he asked.

"Yes, he's been an invaluable help to me during the past year and a half," Lindsey said.

"I appreciate Milton's desire to preserve the history of Briar Creek and the Islands," he said. "But I'm afraid he might be a bit too strident in his views."

Lindsey felt her stomach sinking toward her shoes like a life raft with a hole in it. She had a bad feeling about the mayor's interest in her and the library, which his next words confirmed.

"I would like you to talk to him about the inherent benefits of letting Riordan Salvage dig on Pirate Island," the mayor said.

"Oh, I don't know that I know enough about all of this to really have an informed opinion and certainly not one that Milton would listen to," she said.

"You were an archivist before you came to us, yes?" he asked.

"Yes," she said with a sigh.

"Then I believe he will think very highly of your opinion, don't you?"

Lindsey frowned. She didn't like feeling like she was being told to sell the mayor's message to those opposed to it, especially when the recipient was her friend. And why did the mayor care anyway? Wasn't this Trudi's dog and pony show?

"I thought Trudi Hargrave was in charge of bringing Riordan Salvage to excavate Pirate Island," she said. Just because he was the big boss didn't mean she couldn't ask the tough questions.

"Trudi was the point of contact, yes," he said. "But I'm the mayor and all business done on behalf of the town of Briar Creek is solely up to me."

"I see," Lindsey said. And she did. Trudi had hit upon a way to make some serious bucks for the town and the mayor wanted in on it, especially since his election loomed ahead and he had stated months ago that he would be running again.

"You need to call it off!" a male voice shouted. "And if you don't, then I'll—"

Lindsey glanced toward the main part of the library. The new release stacks blocked her view so she couldn't see what the ruckus was about.

"You'll what? Stop me? How do you suppose you'll manage that?" a female voice responded. Her voice was in the shrill range and Lindsey cringed. Even Charlie's lead singer was better than that.

Lindsey stepped forward and peered around the shelving unit. Her eyes went wide. Standing nose to nose, arguing in front of the entrance to the library, were Trudi Hargrave and Milton Duffy. Again!

"Well, I can see you have a situation to attend to," the mayor said, peeking over Lindsey's shoulder. "This looks like an excellent opportunity for you to do what we've discussed."

Lindsey glanced back at him. She knew she was frowning.

"You know, Herb Gunderson thinks very highly of what you've done with the library," the mayor said.

"Really?" she asked.

"You're damn right I'll stop you!" Milton yelled. "By any means necessary."

"You and what army, old man?" Trudi asked.

Lindsey felt her attention split between the mayor and the scene at the front of the library.

Herb was the mayor's liaison and known mostly for his droning voice that could lull even the worst insomniac into a deep slumber. She had a hard time seeing him wax poetic about the library.

"Yes, and I have to say I think he's right," the mayor said as he turned and began to make his way toward the exit, while keeping the bookshelves between him and the fight. "The place seems friendlier, well, usually, since you've taken the helm."

"Thanks," Lindsey called at his retreating back.

"We'll have to see about getting you a bigger chunk of the town budget," the mayor said. "In fact, I think I'll go mention it to Herb right now."

He snatched up a flier for free guitar lessons and held it over his face as he hurried past Milton and Trudi. He left Lindsey standing by the window gaping after him. What a total chicken—

"Who are you calling an old man, you pimped-out little chippie?" Milton snapped.

"Ah," Trudi gasped and clasped a hand over her chest.

Lindsey broke into a jog and threw herself into the melee before the two of them came to blows.

"Stop it, both of you, right now," she said. "I can't believe you two. I thought I made myself clear. This is neither the time nor the place for this discussion."

"He started it," Trudi accused.

"I merely wanted to have a reasoned discussion about the environmental impact to the island," Milton said with a sniff.

"Save it!" Trudi yelled. "No one cares about the environment except you. Everyone else wants money and jobs.

Go recycle some yogurt containers and leave the rest of us alone."

Milton's head turned an alarming shade of red and Lindsey feared he might stroke out on the spot.

"You give me no choice, Ms. Hargrave," Milton said. "I now see it is my duty to get rid of you any way I can."

Milton swept past Trudi and out the door without so much as a backward glance.

"He threatened me!" Trudi said to Lindsey. "You heard him. You're my witness."

"I heard no such thing," Lindsey said. She looked behind her to see Ms. Cole and Ann Marie at the circulation desk, watching her with their eyes wide and their mouths slightly agape. "And neither did you!"

They both glanced away immediately. Lindsey knew the entire situation had spun wildly out of control and she had no idea how to fix it.

"Had a nice little chat with the mayor, did you?" Trudi asked.

Lindsey blew out a breath. She so did not want to get involved in departmental politics, but she wasn't going to lie either.

"Yes, Mayor Henson came to see me," she said.

"And you just can't keep your horsy nose out of things, can you?" Trudi shouted.

Lindsey resisted the urge to feel her nose with her hand. She knew it wasn't a little turned-up button nose, but she felt the horse comparison was a little harsh.

"Trudi—" she began but Trudi cut her off.

"No! Don't bother trying to talk me out of it. You're not

as smart as you think you are," Trudi said. "We'll see what Chief Daniels has to say about it. I'm going to file a restraining order against that yoga-loving lunatic."

Trudi stomped toward the front door.

"Stop right there!" Ms. Cole barked.

Trudi spun on her lethal heel and glared. "What? Don't tell me you have a soft spot for that wrinkled-up bendy straw, too."

"You are not allowed to leave the library with our materials until you've checked them out." Ms. Cole sniffed and then held out her hand.

Trudi glanced down to where she had three rather large map books tucked under her arm.

"Fine," she said, and she slammed them onto the counter.

Ann Marie took her card and swiftly checked out the books to her while Trudi tapped her toe and muttered about town employees having to follow the procedures. As soon as the checkout machine cleared the last item, she snatched back the stack of atlases and dashed out the door, leaving her card behind.

Lindsey blew out a breath. She remembered being at a cocktail party recently where one of the guests, upon hearing what she did for a living, said, "Oh, a librarian, how nice it must be to sit in a quiet place reading all day."

Yeah, right.

Lindsey watched while Milton ran his young chess club through their strategy lesson. She had muscled Milton into starting the chess club a few months ago, and to everyone's delight, the club had taken off with ten regular members and frequent drop-ins.

A week had passed since the mayor's visit to the library, and she still hadn't been able to drum up the courage to talk to Milton. Not that she planned to do as the mayor asked. She had no intention of trying to sway Milton one way or another, especially after his scene with Trudi, but she felt the need to tell him about the conversation just so he would know what was going on.

The chess club held their meetings in a small conference room on the side of the library. Its glass walls made it easy to see through and she watched Milton walk around the ten players all with chess boards set up between them so that five matches could go on at the same time. She watched while he drew one of his complicated diagrams on the rolling white board. Somehow, she could not find the inner strength to interrupt him.

Trudi had gone through with filing an order of protection, much to everyone's chagrin. As Emma, Officer Plewicki, told it, Chief Daniels had been very reluctant to do the paperwork but felt he had no choice, given Trudi's insistence.

Milton had not taken it well at all. A Creeker from birth, he had lived his entire life in Briar Creek and had never had so much as a speeding ticket. Trudi's maneuver rankled to say the least.

"Ms. Norris." A voice called her name and Lindsey turned to find Preston Riordan standing there with her neighbor Charlie Peyton. "Sorry to interrupt but I was wondering if I might have a word with you."

Lindsey looked at Charlie, who looked sheepish and said, "I told him you knew about old stuff."

"I was hoping you'd take a look at my map. As the town librarian, I thought you might have some insight since, well, we're having a heck of a time trying to locate what we're looking for."

Lindsey felt dazed. He was going to let her look at the map?

"Will my office do?" she asked.

Riordan nodded and she noticed he had a leather satchel hanging from his shoulder. She led the way, mindful of the stares their odd group got from several library users and staff.

Lindsey opened her door and the men trooped in. She cleared off a space on her desk and Riordan opened his leather bag and pulled out a piece of thick paper, no bigger than a dinner plate, which was inside an acid-free clear plastic casing.

Lindsey's first thought was that it was smaller than she had imagined and also much plainer. It was an ink sketch on what looked like thick paper and it was minimalist in detail as if the person drawing it had been pressed for time.

She knew that William Kidd had spent over a year in prison and she wondered if some intrepid guard had snuck him a quill and paper so he could jot down the location of the treasure. Did the guard promise him his freedom or did Kidd do it just to spite his captors so that someone else would dig up his gold long before they found it?

They all leaned over the map. There were latitude and longitude markings on the bottom in a scrolling script and a rough compass sketch in the upper-right-hand corner.

"If this is truly William Kidd's map, it's worth a fortune all on its own," Lindsey said. "Has it been verified as authentic?"

"The British Museum offered, but I turned them down," Riordan said. "I don't want anyone touching it except me, at least until I've gotten the treasure."

"There's no '*X* marks the spot,' " Charlie said.

"Are the coordinates specific to Pirate Island?" Lindsey asked.

Riordan gave her a sharp glance.

"I've been studying maps of the islands for the past year," she said. "I know that those coordinates could mean any number of islands out in the bay. There are over one hundred of them, you know."

"Yeah, I've noticed," Riordan said. "Especially if you count the rocks."

"We've trekked all over Pirate Island," Charlie said. "There is no sign of anything resembling a place to bury treasure."

"The few spots we tried didn't pan out," Riordan said bitterly. "I'm beginning to think this might have been a wild-goose chase."

"Which is why it might have been wise to verify the authenticity of the map before you started looking for treasure," Lindsey said. "I believe I have a contact who may be of assistance."

She flipped through the notes on her desk until she found the one from Patti Fulton with Dr. Harris's phone number on it. Since Riordan hadn't let anyone see the map, she hadn't followed up on calling the curator, but now with the map in front of her, she realized she needed professional advice.

The phone rang four times and then made a clicking noise as if it had been automatically forwarded.

"Map collection, Dr. G speaking," a voice said.

"Hello, this is Lindsey Norris calling from the Briar Creek Public Library. I was hoping to speak with Dr. Harris."

"Sorry, he's on sabbatical," Dr. G said. "Try back in three months."

"Wait," Lindsey cried out before he could hang up. "I have a patron here with a map that is purported to have belonged to Captain Kidd. Is there anything you can tell me that might help me verify that?"

There was a put-upon sigh on the other end of the line.

"The old treasure map found in Grandma's attic story," the man said. "I love that one. It's right up there with the old stock and bond papers found in the basement. You know, the ones people always think are worth a fortune but are for companies that haven't existed in over fifty years."

Lindsey had met a few of those patrons, so she could empathize, but still, treasure hunting was happening right here. It would be good to verify the map at least.

"I wouldn't have called if I didn't think there might be something to it," she said.

Another sigh sounded. "Fine. Hold it up to the light."

She put the phone on speaker and picked up the map and examined it under her desk lamp. "What am I looking for?"

"Without equipment, the best you can do is a visual assessment," Dr. G said. "Is it parchment or paper?"

"What's the difference?" Charlie asked.

"Paper is made of wood pulp, parchment is from stretched animal hide," Lindsey said.

Charlie squinted at the map. "How can you tell?"

Lindsey turned the lamp and held the map in front of it. It wasn't like the equipment she would have once had access to in her old job, but it was enough to confirm what she suspected.

"If it is animal in origin, like parchment, it will have a hair follicle pattern and there will be some veining as well as some traces of scars that no amount of stretching and thinning can make go away completely," she said.

"Does it?" Charlie asked. He shoved his head in between Lindsey and the parchment to get a closer look.

"Yes," she said. "See here?"

"Whoa," Charlie said.

Riordan raised an eyebrow at her, looking impressed in spite of himself.

"But if it's made from animal hide, shouldn't it be tougher than paper?" Charlie asked. "Why is it all wrinkled on one side?"

"Parchment is hygroscopic," Dr. G said over the speaker phone.

Riordan and Charlie gave both the phone speaker and Lindsey blank looks.

"*Hygroscopic* means it absorbs moisture, which makes it dimensionally unstable. Changes in moisture levels allow the fibers, which were stretched under strain, to change shape, which causes the wrinkles you see."

"Please tell me they're not carting it around in an old

shopping bag," Dr. G said. No one answered, which seemed to be answer enough for him. "In order to preserve it, this map needs to be kept under pressure constraint."

Riordan scratched his gray head with one hand while he cupped his chin with the other. Lindsey had a feeling she had lost him at *hygroscopic*. She decided to address his wallet.

"Dr. G is right. If this is Captain Kidd's map, it needs to be properly preserved. You know, if you did have the British Museum verify the handwriting, well, the map alone could be worth a small fortune."

"So you keep saying. I'll keep that in mind if I can't find the treasure that is supposed to be at the end of this map. Of course, the way it's going on that damn island, we may never find the blasted treasure."

"Don't tell me there is an actual treasure hunt happening?" Dr. G asked. "Fabulous. Well, if you manage not to lose the map or destroy it, please bring it to us for further testing. If you'll excuse me, it's time for my lunch break."

"Thank you for your time, Dr. G," Lindsey said.

There was a grumble and then the sound of the dial tone filled the room.

"Jolly guy," Charlie said.

"It runs in the business," Lindsey said. She wondered if her mentor, Patti, had met Dr. G. Given that they both lacked people skills, they could be the off-putting couple of the century.

There was a knock on the door and Lindsey went to answer it.

"Having a meeting?" Sully asked. "I don't want to interrupt."

"Actually, you may be the perfect person to offer some help," she said. She glanced back at Riordan and Charlie. "No one knows the islands better than you."

She stepped back so Sully could enter. With three large men in her office, Lindsey felt as if the walls had moved in, making the tight space a bit claustrophobic.

"Hi, boss," Charlie said.

"Hi," Sully returned. He glanced at Riordan and then at the map. "How goes the treasure hunt?"

"Not well," Riordan said. "But as Ms. Norris says, you may be able to help."

Sully raised his eyebrows and then looked at Lindsey.

"Not you, too?" he asked.

"Me what, too?" she asked.

"Treasure-hunting fever," he said.

She grinned. "No, not me. You can keep your rubies, silks and bars of gold. I'm more excited about this old map."

He smiled. "That's my girl."

"Speaking of this old piece of paper," Riordan said. "Would you mind taking a look and telling me if this looks like an accurate rendering of Pirate Island? Of course, there might be changes as it was drawn three hundred years ago."

Sully leaned over Lindsey's desk. She admired his strong profile while he frowned in concentration. He turned the map one way and then another.

"That's not Pirate Island," he said.

They all groaned and Riordan cursed.

"Are you absolutely sure?" he asked. His jaw was clenched and he looked like he was bracing for news of a loved one's death.

"Yes," Sully said.

They all exhaled in disappointment. Lindsey glanced at Charlie and saw him sag in defeat.

"However," Sully said, bringing all their attention back to him, "it is a spot-on rendering of Ruby Island."

Lindsey gasped. Charlie gaped. Riordan frowned.

"Ruby Island?" he asked. "The one where the family died when lightning struck their house and burnt it down?"

"That's the one," Sully said. "See this?"

He pointed to the eastern edge of the drawing of the island. Lindsey looked and saw what appeared to be a sketch of a rocky outcropping.

"Those rocks are on the eastern side of Ruby Island," Sully said. "My sister and I played on them with the Ruby kids when we were young. The thing is, those rocks are only visible during low tide. Whoever drew this map had to be familiar enough with the island to know that and probably drew it as it would look at low tide, so it would be more difficult to find."

"Excellent!" Riordan said. "So all we have to do is get the town to give us access to Ruby Island. Thank you, Mr. Sullivan, you have been a huge help."

He scooped up his map and tucked it back into his satchel. "Come on, Charlie, let's go have a chat with the mayor."

"Wait! You can't just go out there and start digging around," Lindsey protested. "That island was inhabited once. It's the scene of a terrible family tragedy."

But Riordan was already heading out the door, taking Charlie with him.

"Well, this should prove interesting," Lindsey said to Sully. "Riordan is going right to the mayor. Trudi is not going to be happy about that."

"It'll be interesting to see what the mayor and town council decide about letting Riordan on Ruby Island," Sully said.

"Do you think they will?" Lindsey asked.

"Probably," he said. "It seems like treasure fever has swept the entire town. I saw Ann Marie and her boys on the beach when I walked through the park. Those two looked like they were trying to dig to China, but I'd be willing to bet they just have treasure fever."

"Ann Marie was okay with it?"

"Are you kidding? With the two of them occupied by digging that hole, she was reclined in her beach chair, reading. She looked thrilled not to be chasing after them for a change," he said.

Lindsey smiled. She imagined it had been a nice break for Ann Marie. "Maybe she should send them to work for Riordan."

"I don't know," Sully said. He looked past her and out the far window that gave a view of the bay and the innermost islands. "Honestly, there are too many ghosts on Ruby Island for me. Mary and I used to play with the Ruby kids, and even back then when I was eight, I didn't like their father, Peter Ruby. He was odd. I never believed that Mrs. Ruby and the two kids perished in a house fire set by a lightning strike. It was just too convenient that they died and Peter was never found."

"You told me once that you thought he murdered his family and fled. Do you still think he did?"

"I don't know, but I have a bad feeling about all of this," Sully said. His face looked grim and Lindsey felt a sense of foreboding brush by her like a passing shadow.

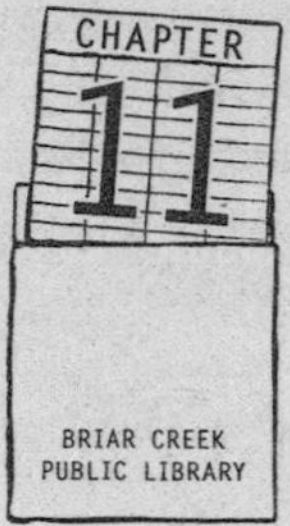

Riordan Salvage had been on Ruby Island just three days when they discovered what they were looking for, or more accurately, Charlie Peyton fell into a hole while surveying the island and Preston Riordan declared it the location of the buried treasure. The news had brought treasure seekers, the media and the merely curious into Briar Creek much like a horde of locusts on a field of crops.

The media frenzy was in its fourth day, but despite the crowds in town, Lindsey agreed to join Sully for breakfast at his office on the pier. It was her day off and she refused to let the crush of reporters stop her from enjoying the beautiful day. She was just walking across the street when the first of the day's news crews arrived. The Channel 8 van stopped at the base of the pier right in front of the Blue

Anchor. Three more news vans followed, and the cameramen and intrepid reporters made a messy knot of people clogging up the pier and making it impossible to navigate the way to Sully's tour boat office.

Lindsey stopped and watched the mayhem. One of the reporters, Kili Peters, Lindsey had met before and she was not a fan.

As Lindsey watched, she saw Ronnie, Sully's secretary, step out of their office. Ronnie was well into her eighties but she was fit, smacking back the years like a hockey player doing a slap shot in sudden-death overtime.

Ronnie's cranberry red hair was in a Motown-style updo that added at least five inches to her petite stature, and her hands and neck were sporting big chunks of turquoise stone in ornate silver settings.

Kili Peters was trying to maneuver around her, and Lindsey was pretty sure Ronnie was going to use her rings like brass knuckles if Kili didn't back off.

Thankfully, Preston Riordan arrived with his good-looking Swedish backup team. As they parked their truck at the edge of the pier, one of the reporters spotted Riordan and began the mad dash down the thick wooden planks toward him. The others followed, and Lindsey ducked to the side to avoid being trampled.

Riordan stood answering their questions, looking immensely pleased with himself.

Lindsey took the opportunity to hurry down the pier to Sully's office before the cameras returned. Ronnie was still standing out front when she got there.

"Hi, Ronnie," she said.

"Hi." Ronnie was still glaring at the throng. "That man is turning this place into a circus."

"Well, now that they've found a place to dig, maybe it will settle down."

"You don't really believe that, do you?" Ronnie asked.

"No." Lindsey shook her head and they both chuckled.

"Sully's down at the water taxi," she said.

"Thanks," Lindsey said. She turned and hurried down the steps to one of the smaller docks, where Sully kept his small canopied water taxi.

"How about breakfast on the open water?" he asked. He held out a hand and helped her onto the boat.

"Sounds nice," Lindsey said. "What's the occasion?"

"Nancy asked me to run some things out to Charlie on Ruby Island," Sully said. "Apparently, Riordan is paying him and the Norrgard brothers extra to watch over the island at night. Charlie forgot his toothbrush and some other necessaries."

"Are we going onto the island?" Lindsey asked.

"'Fraid so," Sully said. He didn't sound happy about it, and she wondered if he dreaded confronting the memory of the childhood friends he'd lost.

"Are you sure?" she asked. "Maybe you could have Ian make the run."

"He's got a tour," Sully said. "Besides, with the crowds of tourists and media, Mary will need him in the restaurant. No, it's better if I go."

Lindsey put her hand on his as he motored the boat carefully through the no-wake zone. He looped an arm around her and pulled her close as if bracing himself with her nearness.

Once he could open up the engine a bit, Sully grabbed a small cooler from the floor of the boat. He handed it to Lindsey and she unpacked their breakfast while he drove the boat.

They ate big flour tortillas stuffed with sausage, eggs and cheese. Lindsey wasn't sure if it was eating on the open water that made her so hungry but she did know it was one of the best burritos she'd ever tasted.

She was just balling up the wax paper that had wrapped it when Sully pulled up alongside a dock that looked to have seen better days.

Lindsey scrambled out of the boat and tied it up, watching where she put her feet in case one of the old boards gave way beneath her. Sully had cut the engine and was hoisting a backpack over his shoulder and stepping out when Charlie appeared on the rocky outcropping above them.

"Sully!" he cried. His voice was high and quavered as if he was about to lose his power of speech. He sucked in a breath and yelled, "Come quick! I think I found, oh man, I think I found a body!"

"Wait here!" Sully said, and he dropped the backpack and scrambled up the steep, rocky incline to the island above.

Lindsey picked up the backpack and tossed it into the boat, then she followed. It wasn't that she was stubborn or didn't want to listen; more accurately, it was that she didn't want to be left below on a rotting dock not knowing what was happening. Besides, maybe she could help.

Sully glanced over his shoulder at her as he reached the top of the rocks. The wooden staircase that was once there was nothing more than a frame. Lindsey scrambled up the rocks, relieved that she had worn jeans and sneakers today.

Sully reached down and pulled her up the remaining few feet until she was standing beside him. She met his searching blue gaze and said, "You didn't really think I was going to stay down there, did you?"

"I, yeah, what was I thinking?" he asked. "Come on."

Charlie was already tromping through the overgrown brush ahead. An aluminum scaffolding had been erected over the pit and Charlie was bracing himself on the lower rung while he looked down into the pit below.

His hand was shaking as he shone a Maglite into the hole, and Sully and Lindsey hurried to the edge of the work area to see.

Lindsey grabbed a rung of the aluminum structure and leaned forward.

"Please tell me I'm seeing things," Charlie said.

"You're not," Sully said. "That definitely looks like a head of hair."

"Maybe they're just unconscious," Lindsey said. "Charlie, how can we get down there?"

"They use a harness and pulley system," Charlie said. "They're trying to dig it out, but right now they can only go down one person at a time, so Steig and Stefan have been taking turns. It's tricky because you have to work with the tide. When the tide is high, the pit fills up, but when it's low, it empties out."

"Have you called the police?" Sully asked.

Charlie looked pained. "I dropped my phone—down there."

"Okay, here's what we're going to do," Sully said. "I'll go down in the harness. Lindsey, you spot me. Charlie, you can run the winch, right?"

"I think so," Charlie said.

"Lindsey, call the police and tell them to send an EMT."

"Got it," she said as she took the phone he held out to her.

"Shouldn't I go down there?" Charlie asked. "I'm smaller than you and it's a tight space."

"True, but I think my naval training will come in handy down there, especially if the person is injured."

Lindsey listened to the phone ringing at the police station while Sully buckled into the harness and Charlie slowly lowered him into the pit.

"Briar Creek Police, Officer Plewicki speaking."

"Emma, it's Lindsey Norris, I have an emergency."

"What is it?" Emma asked.

"I'm on Ruby Island with Charlie Peyton and Sully," she said. "Emma, there appears to be a person trapped in the hole that they're excavating."

"Are they injured?" Emma asked.

"We don't know for sure, but Sully said to get an EMT out here as fast as possible," she said.

"I'm calling it in right now. Stay on the line," Emma ordered.

Lindsey felt her chest spasm as Sully's head disappeared below the edge of the pit. She glanced at the pulley that held his weight as Charlie turned on the electric winch that lowered him. The steel cable looked strong; still, she felt nervous.

"Lindsey, are you there?" Emma asked.

"Yes," she said.

"Chief Daniels and the EMTs are on their way. They're

meeting at the pier. They should be there in twenty minutes."

"Stop!" Sully yelled from below and Charlie switched off the motorized winch. "I need more light."

"Emma, I'm putting the phone down, Sully needs light," Lindsey said. She didn't wait for a reply but put the phone on a nearby board and took the extra Maglite that Charlie handed to her.

Together they aimed their beams down into the hole, trying to give Sully as much illumination as possible.

The hole was narrow, maybe three feet across, and Sully filled it pretty well. He was twenty feet below the surface, and as Lindsey watched, he braced himself on a narrow ledge and slipped out of the harness. It hung slack for a second and he glanced up and shouted.

"Let it down. I'm going to try to get them hooked in," he shouted.

Charlie lowered the harness by several feet until Sully gave him the okay. He then rejoined Lindsey at the edge with his light.

They couldn't see much except Sully's back as he tried to maneuver in the narrow passageway. Lindsey couldn't imagine how he was going to get out of there. But as she watched, he braced his feet and his back against the wall and used the steel cable to hoist himself up.

Charlie grabbed him above the elbow and hauled him out. Once Sully had rolled clear, Charlie turned on the winch and Sully and Lindsey braced themselves to grab the person as they neared the top.

The long, multihued hair was marred by a dark spot near the temple that Lindsey realized was caked blood. Although her power suit was streaked with dirt and torn in places and she was missing one of her platform pumps, Lindsey knew without looking at her face that the person being hoisted out of the hole was Trudi Hargrave.

"Easy," Sully ordered. They reached out as one and gently grabbed the slumped figure. Charlie shut off the winch and together they got her out of the harness and hefted the body to a spot of grass just outside the scaffolding.

Sully quickly checked her vitals, but Lindsey could see that her color was bad and her chest wasn't rising or falling. She was as still as a clock that had stopped marking time.

Sully's shoulders dropped in defeat. He reached out and put a hand on Charlie's shoulder.

"She's dead, isn't she?" Charlie asked.

"I'm afraid so," Sully said.

Trudi's eyes were closed, and blood caked the side of her face, which was misshapen as if it had been hit by something hard.

Lindsey glanced up at the sound of retching to see that Charlie had crawled over to a nearby bush and vomited.

"I've got a blanket in the boat," Sully said. "I'll go get it."

"I'll stay with her," Lindsey said. She didn't know why she felt that Trudi needed someone to watch over her, but she did.

Sully met her gaze and nodded. "I'll take Charlie with me."

Lindsey saw Charlie rise to his feet. He was shaking from head to foot and still looked green around the edges.

"Good idea," she said.

"I'll be right back," he said.

He brushed her cheek with a fingertip and their gazes met. Lindsey was struck by the compassion in his blue gaze and it hit her anew that Mike Sullivan was a remarkable man.

She watched as they disappeared into the undergrowth of the island that had been uninhabited for so long. A small part of her wanted to run after them, but it wouldn't feel right.

A breeze rustled the leaves of the trees above, but other than that, there was no noise on the small island. It was almost as if the birds had decided to stop singing in the wake of such a tragedy. Lindsey knew it was more likely that the motor of the winch had scared them all into silence, but still.

She glanced at the scaffolding nearby and at the island around her. She could just picture Captain Kidd and a band of pirates breaking through the trees, hauling a chest of gold, rubies and silks up onto the island to be buried until they could come back to reclaim it.

Kidd would be wearing the captain's dress of the day—boots with cuffs at the top, a big powdered wig under a wide-brimmed hat, maybe with a feather in it. His coat would be of velvet or maybe an embroidered brocade. He would carry a sword or perhaps a musket.

His men would be much less well dressed, in cotton and wool with no fancy hat or coat. They would fear him and they would do as they were told for a cut of the treasure later. But if that was true, why hadn't any of them come back when Captain Kidd was hanged?

Three hundred and thirteen years had passed since Captain Kidd had been here. Surely, someone should have found his treasure by now. She glanced at Trudi's body and then quickly away. Her gaze lingered on the ruins of the Ruby house just visible through the trees. Maybe the island was cursed. Maybe anyone who came too close to the treasure of Captain Kidd was cursed to die for their efforts.

A shudder went through her from her head to her feet.

Sully reappeared through the trees and she had to resist the urge to run and wrap herself around him like a peel on a banana.

"Are you all right?" he asked.

"Sure," she lied.

After he placed the blanket over Trudi, Lindsey tucked her hand into his and gave it a squeeze. He squeezed back. It was enough. They sat and waited, without speaking.

* * *

"But what was Trudi doing out there?" Beth asked.

They were sitting at a corner table in the Blue Anchor. Lindsey had spent most of the afternoon at the police station, and she and Sully had come over to the Anchor to grab something to eat when they ran into Beth, who joined them for dinner.

"No idea," Lindsey shrugged. "From what Charlie told us, Riordan had them watching the island in shifts in case any would-be treasure hunters showed up and messed with their dig."

"So Charlie was out there alone all night?" Mary asked.

She was sitting in Sully's seat since he was over at the bar talking to Ian about Charlie. Since Charlie worked for their tour boat company, they were wondering if they'd need to scrape up bail money to spring him if Chief Daniels decided to formally arrest Charlie.

"He was," Lindsey said. The three of them exchanged a grim look. "He said he slept through the night, never saw anyone or heard anything. But this morning, his boat was missing. He knew someone must have untied it, so he went back up to the dig to see if someone had messed with the excavation. That's when he saw Trudi in the hole. He tried to call for help, but he was so jittery, he dropped his phone."

"It was lucky you and Sully went out there," Beth said. "Where's Charlie now?"

"At the police station, being questioned by Chief Daniels," Lindsey said. "Nancy and Violet are over there now."

Mary gave a low whistle. "I actually feel sorry for Chief

Daniels. If he decides to lock Charlie up, well, it won't be pretty."

A reluctant smile tipped the corner of Lindsey's lips. "Do you think they'll go straight for a shot to the groin, or will they start with the eye gouge first?"

"I'm betting on an over-the-back full-body slam," Beth said.

Nancy and Violet had recently signed up for self-defense classes in New Haven. They liked to give demonstrations of what they'd learned, and so far they had managed to maim just about every able-bodied male in Briar Creek that they'd come into contact with since their first class.

"They got Ian in the privates," Mary said. "Poor guy, when he could speak again, he made me promise to never let him volunteer to help them ever again."

"They got Sully on his instep," Lindsey said. "He limped for two days."

"I think Milton is too crafty for them," Beth said. "I found him hiding behind the new bookshelves when they came in for crafternoon last week."

"I can't say I blame him," Lindsey said. She sipped her crisp white wine and picked at the peach cobbler in front of her.

"Are you okay?" Mary asked. Her blue eyes, so like her brother's, were full of concern.

"I've been better," she said. She squeezed Mary's arm. "It was a rough day, but I can't really complain given that I'm here and Trudi—isn't."

Both Mary and Beth nodded.

"Don't look now," Beth said. "But we're about to enter the awkward zone."

"What do you mean?" Lindsey asked.

Beth jerked her head in the direction of the door, and Lindsey felt a sigh escape her. John had just walked into the restaurant. She was so not in the mood for this.

"What?" Mary glanced between them. "What am I missing?"

Beth looked at Lindsey, letting her make the call whether to tell or not.

"Not a big deal," Lindsey said. "My former fiancé just walked in, that's all."

Mary's head whipped around to stare at John, who was, of course, staring back at them.

"Mary," she hissed. "You weren't supposed to look!"

"You're kidding, right?" Mary asked. "The former fiancé of my crafternoon buddy, who is dating my brother, walks into my restaurant and I'm not supposed to look. Am I made of stone?"

Lindsey laughed. She had to concede the point. But her laugh was unfortunately seen by John as an invitation to join them. He got halfway across the room when Beth spun around in her seat and gave him her best scowl. John paused, Lindsey shook her head, and John made an abrupt turn toward the bar. Luckily, he chose the opposite end from where Sully was standing.

"Did you see that?" Beth asked. "I was channeling my inner pirate. I may have to consider a career on the high seas. I'm telling you I am bad-a-s-s."

"It sort of loses something in the translation when you spell it," Mary said.

"Arr," Beth growled.

"Is it just me, or has this small town gotten even smaller?" Lindsey asked.

"And getting smaller every time the door opens," Mary said.

Lindsey glanced at the door to see Riordan and the Norrgard brothers enter. No sooner had they taken seats at the bar than a gaggle of twenty-something girls followed in their wake, draping themselves around the twins like kelp on a pair of beach boulders.

Mary rose from her seat. "I'd better go give Ian a hand since we seem to be getting busier."

They watched her leave with a wave.

"Why do you suppose Charlie isn't with them?" Beth asked.

"If I know Nancy, he is home eating a pile of chocolate chip cookies and washing them down with a glass of cold milk."

"You don't think Chief Daniels will lock him in the brig, do you?" Beth asked.

Sully resumed his seat at their table and said, "If by that, do you mean was Charlie arrested? No, he wasn't."

"Phew," Lindsey said with relief. "What about Riordan and the brothers? How is it that they are here?"

"Well, the brothers have a solid alibi," Sully said. "Apparently, both had company in their rooms last night."

Beth and Lindsey exchanged an understanding glance.

"Riordan, I'm not so sure about. Chief Daniels hasn't charged them with anything but they're not to leave town until the investigation is complete. I doubt they'd abandon their dig in any case," Sully said. "Riordan is unhappy because they've halted his treasure hunting until the crime scene investigators are done and that could be several days."

"Well, surely he wants to know how and why Trudi Hargrave ended up dead on his excavation site, doesn't he?"

"You tell me," Sully said. He nodded his head in Riordan's direction. "Does he look like a man who is wracked with concern?"

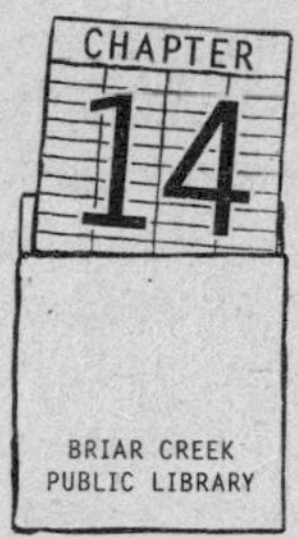

Riordan had his arm around one of the girls. He threw his head back and laughed at something she said. No, he didn't look concerned. In fact, if Lindsey had to choose a word to describe him, she would have said he looked relieved.

"So I noticed your former fiancé made a quick exit stage left," Sully said.

"Beth gave him her best pirate scowl," Lindsey said.

"Arr!" Beth chimed in.

"You know you're my favorite children's librarian, right?" Sully asked. His grin was slow and sweet and made Lindsey's heart hammer hard in her chest.

Beth smiled back at him and they exchanged a knuckle bump.

"Seriously," he said to Lindsey. "If you want to invite him to join us, I'm fine with that."

Lindsey glanced over at John, who was sitting alone at the bar, studying a menu. Ian was keeping him company, because he was good like that. Lindsey saw the way his blond hair fell over his forehead. He wore his polo shirt tucked into his khaki shorts with a belt and he'd hooked his loafer-clad feet, sans socks, on the lower rung of his stool.

He looked a little out of his depth in this small town of odd characters. It would do him some good to navigate the people and their eccentricities without Lindsey smoothing the way for him.

She had changed since that fateful day when she'd been let go at work and came home to find John buck naked with a writhing grad student beneath him. Because his schedule had been more demanding than hers, she had always taken up the slack. She did the cooking, the cleaning and the laundry. She ran the errands. It was the sort of labor division that had crept up slowly over the years they were together, with John being harried with his full schedule and asking, "Would you mind . . ."

Lindsey was crazy in love with him, or so she had thought; of course she didn't mind. And slowly, it wasn't so much a request for her to do these many things but an expectation.

Lindsey always tried to do what was expected of her. It was a flaw in her character she had never recognized until the day she came home and found him and his little friend sullying the sheets she had laundered in the room she had dusted and vacuumed just the day before. It was illuminating, especially as she had seen John from a side she had never had reason to observe before. It wasn't his best.

But Lindsey wasn't bitter anymore, and she wasn't holding a grudge. She also didn't feel the need to make his life easier for him either. As her mother liked to say, "He made his bed, let him lie in it." Of course, Lindsey mentally added the other tried-and-true cliché, "Lie down with dogs and wake up with fleas." She had to admit she hoped he had gotten bit by a nice, itchy swarm of them.

"He seems fine," she said. "Besides, I think I'm going to head home. I want to check on Charlie."

"I'd like to check on him, too," Sully said. "Poor kid, I think that was his first dead body."

The three of them exchanged a glance. Last year, they'd all shared the experience of finding a different dead body. Only this one had been the man dating Beth at the time. It was the sort of bonding experience a person never forgot even though they'd rather.

"Well, I'm off, too," Beth said.

"Can I give you a lift?" Sully asked.

Beth drained her glass of wine. "Absolutely."

Sully met Lindsey and Beth back across the street at the library. They loaded Beth's bike into the back of his ancient truck and they set off. Beth's small house, called "A Shore Thing," was nestled among a small neighborhood of cottages. Some were summer houses only, but most were for year-round residents.

While Sully parked and got Beth's bike out of the back, Lindsey glanced at the front window and saw Beth's two cats, Slinky Malinky and Skippy John Jones, named for cats in children's picture books, sitting in the window as still as statues. They didn't move until after Beth had locked up her bike and was climbing the steps up to her deck.

Sully climbed back into the cab of the truck. He waited until Beth was inside before he put the truck in reverse and backed out of her driveway. This was one of the many reasons Lindsey liked Sully. It wasn't just good manners with him. He watched out for those around him. He didn't consider it an inconvenience to make sure a woman was safely inside before he sped off. It would just never occur to him to be any other way.

He glanced at her. "You're staring."

"I am?" she asked. She glanced away.

"It's okay," he said. "I find I stare at you a lot, too."

"You do?" she asked. "Wow, I sound about as intelligent as Beth's mechanical parrot Fernando."

Sully laughed. "I like him, although I'm pretty sure I heard him drop an F-bomb the other day."

Lindsey blew out a sigh. "Yes, Beth put his batteries back in and Ann Marie's boys felt the need to test him. They like to broaden his vocabulary."

"I can't see that going over well with Ann Marie," Sully said. He stopped at the intersection and then turned down the road that led to Lindsey's apartment.

"Beth caught them, and not only did they have to sit there and teach Fernando nice phrases, but then she had them wipe down all of her story time toys with disinfectant wipes."

"And they went for that?" Sully asked.

"She told them they could do all that or she could talk to their mother about their language," Lindsey said.

"So they chose hard labor instead of facing the warden—smart boys," Sully said.

"Indeed," Lindsey said.

Sully pulled up onto the gravel drive in front of Lindsey's house and parked.

They walked hand in hand up the front steps. Nancy was sitting on the front porch, rocking in her favorite wicker chair.

"Hi, Nancy," Lindsey said. "How's Charlie?"

"Rattled," she said. "I gave him some cookies, milk and a shot of Jack Daniels and put him to bed."

"He had a rough day," Sully said. "That was a big dose of reality to take in."

"So what's the word in town?" Nancy asked. "Do the police have any idea what Trudi was doing out on the island?"

"If they do, they're not talking," Lindsey said.

She found herself leaning into Sully, as if the feel of his warmth and strength could ward off the tragedy they had witnessed that day. Sully must have felt the same because he pulled her close and rubbed his hand up and down her arm as if her presence reassured him.

"Well, I'm sure it'll come out in time," Nancy said. She stood and stretched and then paused and gave the two of them a fond look. "Feel free to leave your truck parked in the drive as long as you like, Sully."

Lindsey saw her wink just before she disappeared into the house.

"Subtle as a box of rocks, isn't she?" Lindsey turned to ask Sully. The words caught in her throat.

He was giving her *that* look. The one that was so steamy it about set her hair on fire.

"Race you up the stairs," he said.

With a grin, Lindsey took off running.

Three e-mails and a voice mail message all from John were waiting for Lindsey the next morning when she arrived at work. He wasn't going away and avoiding him did not seem to be giving him a clear enough message. She sighed. She so didn't want to deal with this. She had enough work to do already.

She holed up in her office planning to work on the staff evaluations that were due to the town's human resources department by the end of the month. She had to evaluate the job performance of each staff member and then meet with them to discuss the evaluation and go over the goals they'd set last year, determine whether they'd met their goals and then assign new ones for the next year.

She was confident that most of her staff would exceed expectations. They all had their quirks. Ann Marie tended to run late, but was always willing to cover for others. Jessica occasionally did her homework at the reference desk, but she was studying library science so it seemed to Lindsey that she should get a pass if the rest of her work was done. Beth's exuberance sometimes leaked over into the quieter areas of the library and she needed to work on containing herself a bit. Ms. Cole, well, her people skills were seriously lacking but she knew the patron records and the library's holdings as if all of thc information were tattooed on the insides of her eyelids.

Library school had not really prepared Lindsey for the supervisory portion of her job. Whenever she found herself wondering what to do, she called on Carole Towles, a library board member and former librarian from Phoenix, who had become a mentor to Lindsey over the past year.

She picked up her phone and decided to give Carole a call. Maybe she could help her brainstorm some new goals for her staff.

The phone rang twice and Carole answered with a chipper "Hello."

"Hi, Carole, it's Lindsey," she said. "I was wondering if you'd be available sometime in the next few days."

"I'm available right now," Carole said. "In fact, I'm out in the new book area with my friend Sheila. She's visiting from Phoenix. I'd love for you to meet her."

"Excellent, I'll be right out." Lindsey hung up the phone.

She stepped out of her office and crossed the workroom. She came out the door behind the circulation desk and glanced across the library. Sure enough, standing by the new books, Carole was putting her phone away in her purse. Beside her was a dark-haired woman Lindsey had never seen before.

Carole waved her over and Lindsey joined them.

"Lindsey, this is my friend Sheila Levine. We started our library careers together," Carole said. "Sheila, this is Lindsey, our new director."

"Nice to meet you," Sheila said, and she shook Lindsey's hand. "Welcome to public librarianship."

"Thanks," Lindsey said. "You work in the public sector, too?"

"Yes," Sheila said. "That's where Carole and I met, oh, a few years ago."

"No more than five," Carole said with a dimpled grin.

They exchanged a chuckle, and Lindsey could tell the two friends had a long history between them.

"Ten tops," Sheila joked. She had shoulder-length, dark brown hair, and behind her glasses her eyes were a sparkling pale green. Her smile was as contagious as her laugh.

Lindsey noticed they were both in tennis shoes, jeans and windbreakers, and they had the flushed cheeks of people who had spent some time outside.

"I just took Sheila on the Thumb Island boat tour," Carole said. Her dimples deepened as she added, "Sully was in rare form today."

"Was he?" Lindsey asked, trying to look innocent.

"You know, in all the summers that I've lived here, I don't think I've ever seen him this happy," Carole said.

Lindsey felt her face grow warm and she was hard pressed not to smile, so she didn't even try. She grinned.

Sheila glanced between them. "Is this relationship talk? I'm so down with that, unless of course it's private, in which case, I'm happy to go browse books."

"No need," Lindsey assured her. "It is relationship talk, but I think I'm getting used to small town living and having my life be common knowledge. I've been dating Sully for a few months now."

"And things are going well?" Carole asked.

"Very, but I have one small complication," Lindsey said. "My former fiancé is in town, and he wants to get back together."

Carole and Sheila exchanged a look. They each had an eyebrow raised as if to say *Uh-oh.*

"How do you feel about that?" Carole asked.

"Vindicated," Lindsey said, her own honesty making her cringe. "I mean he was the one who ended it, so it's nice to see that he realizes what he lost."

Sheila gave her a warm smile. "I think that's pretty normal. At least you didn't say you were feeling vindictive; then there'd be something to worry about."

"I suppose," Lindsey agreed. She paused to see if she did feel vindictive toward John but was relieved that no, she was just done.

"So what was it you wanted to see me about?" Carole asked.

"Setting goals for staff," Lindsey said. "You know, to play to their strengths."

"How much time do you have?" Sheila asked.

Lindsey laughed. "I think the question is how much time do *you* have?"

"We're taking in a show at the Long Wharf Theatre in New Haven this evening," Carole said. "But other than that, our day is pretty unstructured."

"How about some tea in the crafternoon room?" Lindsey suggested. They exchanged a look that she couldn't read, so she upped the ante. "I happen to have some cannoli from Lucibello's that Sully and I picked up for a staff meeting. They are so rich my entire staff couldn't finish them off."

"I'm in," Carole said.

"Me, too," Sheila agreed.

"Excellent. I'll just go get the refreshments and meet you back there."

Ten minutes later they were ensconced in the small room off the main library, and Lindsey happily spent the next hour talking shop and figuring out how to motivate her staff. Ms. Cole did present a challenge for all three of them, but by the end of the meeting, both Sheila and Carole had given Lindsey enough ideas to fill several sheets of notebook paper.

They talked a little bit about Trudi Hargrave's death and what might happen to the treasure hunt on Ruby Island, but since no one knew whether her death was a tragic accident or something more nefarious, there really wasn't much but speculation to go on.

When the two librarians left with a promise to visit again before Sheila returned to Phoenix, Lindsey was sad to see them go. There was a kinship in public librarianship that Lindsey loved. The public library existed to serve the needs of its patrons, and the librarians were dedicated to the people they served. It was a noble profession, and Lindsey felt pleased to be a part of it.

She was returning to her office when she saw John standing by the newspaper rack. He was leaning casually against the wall, and every now and then he glanced up from the paper and scanned the room. When he caught sight of her, he lowered the paper and smiled. She had a feeling he'd been waiting for her.

"Lindsey," he said. His voice was more jovial than normal for him, and it made her put her guard up. "Just the person I was hoping to see."

"Hi, John."

"I've been trying to get in touch with you," he said.

"I noticed," she said. "I'm sorry, but I really—"

"I was wondering if you'd like to grab dinner one evening, you know, for old times' sake," he said.

Lindsey looked at him. His blond hair fell over his forehead. He looked like he had just stepped off the tennis court. She felt a pang, remembering how they used to play doubles on the weekends at their club.

He threw that life away. He threw her away. And now that she had someone good and kind in her life, someone who valued her, here John was looking for another chance and working all the angles.

She knew she was going to have to spell it out for him in no uncertain terms.

"All right," she said. "Let's have dinner."

He looked so pleased that Lindsey frowned.

"Let me be clear," she said. "This is just as friends and it is solely so that we can find closure and move on with our lives. We are not getting back together. I have moved on with my life. But if it will make it clear to you that we're through, we can talk it out once and for all."

John's face fell, but he quickly rallied. "But it's still dinner, right?"

Lindsey wondered if she should make it lunch. No, dinner would be okay. Much better to bury the past over three courses than a soup and sandwich combo—at least she hoped so.

Lindsey was bicycling home that evening when she passed the police station and saw Emma Plewicki escorting Milton Duffy up the stairs into the building.

She hit her brakes so hard that her bicycle locked and she left a streak of rubber on the pavement. Both Emma and Milton snapped their heads in her direction. Milton gave her a wry smile.

Checking both ways, Lindsey shot across the street, putting her bike in the rack in front of the police station and hurrying through the front doors.

"Emma, what's going on?" she asked.

"Lindsey . . ." Emma's voice held a note of warning.

"It's all right," Milton said. "They just want to ask me a few questions."

"About?" Lindsey asked.

"Trudi's death," Milton said. His voice was low as if weighted with the grim reality of his situation.

"Surely you can't think that Milton had anything to do with her death," Lindsey said. She stared at Emma, looking for a sign that this was all just a horrible mistake.

"I'm not at liberty to discuss the case," Emma said. She tossed her black hair over her shoulder as if trying to toughen herself up for a battle.

"What's happened?" Lindsey asked. Neither of them answered her. "Did the medical examiner figure out what happened to Trudi?"

"What do you not understand about 'I'm not at liberty to discuss the case'?" Emma asked. She looked annoyed.

"You may as well tell me," Lindsey said. She gestured through the front window at the reporters who had taken up residence over at the pier. "It's going to get out one way or another."

"Well, it's going to have to be another because it's not coming from me," Emma said.

"Lindsey, I appreciate your concern," Milton said. "But I'll be fine. Go home. There's nothing you can do here."

"I'm not leaving," Lindsey said.

"I'm not asking," Milton retorted.

They stared at one another for a few moments. The steadfast calm in Milton's gaze told her that she was not going to be able to make him see reason.

"If you need—" she began but Milton shook his head, dismissing her.

"Shall we, Officer Plewicki?" he asked.

Emma cast Lindsey a regretful glance as she led Milton toward the back of the station, where Lindsey knew the interview rooms were located since she had logged some time in one of them herself.

She turned and left the police station, feeling disoriented. Milton? How could they take Milton in? Sure, he and Trudi had tiffed over permitting the treasure hunters on the island, but Milton was the institutional memory of the town, the resident historian and a certified yogi—not a killer.

Lindsey stood on the front steps and stared out at the water. She had a feeling her dinner with John was going to happen sooner rather than later, because now she needed him and his criminal law skills to help defend Milton.

"No, no, no." Violet La Rue looked Lindsey up and down and shook her head. "You just trot back up those stairs and find something less, well, I don't know, but less."

"Suggestive?" her daughter, Charlene, offered.

Lindsey glanced down at her khaki skirt and white blouse. The girls were firmly secured without even a hint of cleavage showing. Her skirt stopped just above her knees and flared at the edges. Her shoes were her sensible loafers, not her please-ogle-my-legs pumps. Her outfit screamed kindly-spinster-aunt, so the ensemble was anything but suggestive.

"Really?" she asked. "What would you have me wear?"

"A nun's habit?" Nancy offered.

Heathcliff chose that moment to come bounding down

the stairs, holding one of her rubber mud boots in his mouth. He dropped it at her feet, as if suggesting a change in footwear making Lindsey suspect that he, too, didn't approve of her plans for the evening.

"Don't you start," she said to him and scratched his ears.

He gave her a shrewd glance from under his bushy eyebrows and trotted into Nancy's apartment, as if fully aware that she had agreed to be his babysitter for the evening.

The three women were crowded in Nancy's doorway and Lindsey suspected they'd been lying in wait for her. She knew her friends were very concerned that she was going to have dinner with her ex-fiancé, which was precisely why she was meeting him at the end of the driveway instead of letting him come anywhere near the house, for all the good it did her.

"Listen, I need to clear the air with John once and for all," she said. "I appreciate your concern, but Sully knows that I'm having dinner with John and he's fine with it. Besides, since Milton has managed to make himself suspect number one, and John's specialty is criminal law, I might be able to get John to help Milton."

"It's not Milton's fault he has no alibi," Violet said. She looked grumpy. "Living alone makes it very difficult for anyone to have an alibi. They could question Nancy and I like they have Milton and we'd look just as guilty."

"True, except for the small detail that you didn't threaten to stop Trudi by whatever means possible," Lindsey said.

There was a honk outside and Lindsey peeked out the door to see John waiting in his car for her.

She glanced back to see three disapproving frowns pointed in her direction. She sighed.

"Don't wait up," she said, knowing full well that they would.

John held open the passenger door for Lindsey and she slid into her seat. He shut the door and circled the car, and as Lindsey watched him, she wondered how many times had she sat in this exact same spot. How many times had John held the door for her before they'd cruised off to one Yale function or another?

She glanced at Nancy's three-story captain's house as they pulled away from the curb. She'd left a light on in her upper apartment, like a beacon to lead her home.

"I thought we might not want to eat at that quaint little café," John said. "The food is excellent, but it seems to be the only restaurant in town, and given that you seem to know everyone . . ."

"It's fine," she said. "Wherever you'd like to eat is okay with me."

John looked surprised and relieved. "Great, then I have just the place."

Lindsey wondered if he would drive into New Haven to go to Ibiza, his favorite restaurant on High Street, but she was surprised when he turned and headed east, away from the city. They were quiet as he drove along the shoreline. Lindsey studied him out of the corner of her eye. He was dressed in slacks and a dress shirt, but he didn't have on a tie or jacket. For John, that was downright casual. She felt herself relax. Maybe he had taken to heart what she said about the purpose of this dinner being about closure for them. She certainly hoped so.

"I went with seafood," John said as he pulled into a gravel parking lot that was full to bursting with cars. He maneuvered around several trucks and a van and tucked his Prius in with the big boys.

Lindsey glanced around them. The sun was beginning to set, and as the purple hue of twilight settled over them, the sharp edges of the place in front of her seemed to soften.

John opened her door, and she walked beside him toward the small restaurant, which was little more than a kitchen housed in a red, wooden shack on the edge of the wetlands that were separated from the beach beyond by a thick line of trees. Picnic tables, full of diners, were scattered all around the grassy slope surrounding the small shack.

"No offense, but this doesn't seem like your kind of place," Lindsey said.

"I've been experiencing some personal growth over the past year," he said. "New experiences and all that, you know."

Lindsey stared at him and he smiled. He looked pleased that he'd caught her off guard.

"Why don't you grab us a table while I order?" he said.

"How do you know what I want?" Lindsey asked. Now this seemed like the old John she knew. He had always liked to order for her as if she might muck it up on her own.

"They only serve two things here," he said. "Soft shell crab and beer."

"Oh, then by all means," she said. "Have at it."

He escorted her over to an empty table at the edge of the slope that had a hurricane lantern on it. She could hear the murmuring voices of the diners around them, interrupted by the occasional burst of laughter.

John arrived back in minutes, bearing a tray loaded down with two plates heaped with crabs and a pitcher of beer. It looked so amazing that Lindsey almost took a picture of it with her phone, but the person she most wanted to show it to was Sully, and really, did the man want to see the food from her nondate with her ex? Yeah, probably not.

As night settled in, the lanterns on the tables were the only light other than the glow coming from the windows of the tiny kitchen. As the warm spring air moved across them, Lindsey could hear the distinctive trill of the gray tree frog.

John tucked into his crab and she did the same. It seemed by unspoken mutual agreement, they would eat before they delved into any heavy-duty conversation. As Lindsey savored a mouthful of salty crab meat and washed it down with an icy beer, she realized that if things had been more like this between them when they were a couple, maybe they wouldn't have gone off track as much as they had.

They destroyed their pile of crab with Lindsey giving John the last of hers. The pitcher was running pretty low and Lindsey knew that now it was time to get to the meat, as it were, of their reason for being here.

She opened her mouth to start the conversation with the line she had been practicing all afternoon. It was a variation on the old chestnut "It's not you, it's me," which was a complete lie, because it was most definitely him. After all, he was the one who had ended it to pursue the young cutie pie. But now that Lindsey had Sully and had moved on, she really didn't feel the need to give John the swift kick in the privates that Violet and Nancy had been coaching her on since they had become the dynamic duo of self-defense—at least not like she had once fantasized.

She paused. This was harder to phrase than she'd thought.

"I don't know where Trudi put it," a voice hissed from behind Lindsey. It was a man's voice, low and gruff, and she thought she recognized it.

"Well, you'd better find it," another man's voice hissed back. "If you want me to invest in this little project of yours, I'm going to need a whole lot more than your say-so that this map is real."

Forgetting all about her conversation with John, Lindsey turned her head surreptitiously toward the sound of the voices. She kept her napkin at her mouth as if dabbing her lips while she glanced at a table behind her and to the right. She recognized the head of gray hair immediately. Preston Riordan.

He was sitting with another man. There was an empty pitcher between them but only one glass, which was in front of Riordan, and Lindsey wondered if he'd drunk the entire pitcher himself. She couldn't see the other man. He didn't have an accent and he wasn't large enough to be one of the Norrgard brothers. He was sitting with his back to her, and in the pale lamplight the only thing she could make out was his gold and black sweater, which looked familiar but she couldn't place it.

"Lindsey, are you listening to me?" John asked.

She turned back around to see John, looking at her with a frown.

"Huh?" she asked.

"I'm pouring my heart out here," he said. "Do you think you could pretend to listen?"

"Oh, I'm sorry," she said. "I thought I recognized someone . . ."

She let her voice trail off as she tried to pick up Riordan's conversation again.

"How long until you're allowed back on the island?" the stranger asked.

"I don't know," Riordan said. Then as if aware that he might be overheard, he lowered his voice. "The police chief said when they're done investigating, they'll let us back out there."

"The dead woman—you knew her?" the man asked.

"She arranged for us to come here," Riordan said. His voice was reluctant as if he didn't want to talk about it.

Lindsey wondered why. Did he feel guilty?

"Do they know how she died or why she was out there?"

"How the hell should I know?" Riordan snapped.

"Well, it's your show, isn't it?" the man asked. "You want me to invest in this excursion but all you've got to show for it is a dead body. Not the most stable investment, is it?"

"I'm sure it was just a freak accident," Riordan said. His voice sounded nervous. Lindsey felt the hair prickle at the nape of her neck. Riordan was lying. She was sure of it.

"Well, I'm not giving you one damn dime until you can show me the map and you have the go-ahead from the mayor's office to find the treasure," the voice said. "Honestly, I'm not sure why I even agreed to this meeting, except morbid curiosity. As far as I can tell, your ambition has gotten ahead of you."

"What are you saying?" Riordan snapped.

"That you will do anything to get what you want, even mur—" The other man's voice was abruptly drowned out by a raucous shout of laughter from a woman at a neighboring table.

"Lindsey, clearly you're more interested in what's happening elsewhere," John snapped. "I mean we came here to talk about us and our future, not to listen in on the conversations of others, which I have to say I find to be very poor manners."

Startled, Lindsey felt as if she'd been forcibly yanked out of the other conversation. Without thinking, she shushed him with a firm "Shh!"

When she turned back, however, it was to find that the two men were gone. She would have thought she'd imagined the entire thing except when she glanced over toward the parking lot, she saw Riordan's truck fire up and careen out of the lot onto the main road, leading back to Briar Creek.

Lindsey jumped up from her seat. "Come on, we've got to go."

"What?" John looked dismayed. "But we haven't talked about us and our future."

"There are more important things happening," she said. "Come on."

She was off and hurrying toward the parking lot, giving John no alternative but to follow. He grumbled while he unlocked his car and opened the door for her.

As he pulled out of the lot, Lindsey glanced down the road, but any sign of Riordan's truck was long gone.

"I suppose we're headed back to town?" John asked.

"Yeah, and if you could manage to catch up to the truck that was ahead of us, that would be great."

"Lindsey, have you lost your mind?" John asked. "I'm not going to risk our lives on these back roads, pretending to be in some high-speed chase. I'm sure your testosterone-laden boat captain would be happy to oblige you, but I'm—"

"Oh, shut it!" Lindsey said. "Look, I can see his taillights, it really isn't going to kill us to keep him in sight."

John cast her a sullen look, but Lindsey was too busy fumbling with her phone to pay him any notice.

"Hi, gorgeous," a deep voice answered on the first ring.

"Hi," she breathed, completely forgetting the purpose of her call at the sound of his voice. You had to give it to a man who was not afraid to make a woman feel good about herself.

"Are you calling *him*?" John asked. His outrage brought Lindsey back to her reason for calling.

"Sully!" Lindsey said. "I think I heard something about Trudi's death that might be important."

"Hang on," he said. She heard the raucous background noise dim and his voice came back to her as he said, "Okay, I'm outside the Anchor, what did you say?"

"I think I heard something about Trudi's death that might be important," she said.

"Where?"

"At dinner," she said.

"So the big convo went well?" he asked.

Lindsey glanced at John, whose jaw was clenched while his hands gripped the steering wheel at ten and two.

"Not exactly, no," she said.

"I can't wait to hear about it," Sully said. She wasn't sure but she thought she heard the faintest chuckle in his voice. "So what did happen on this date of yours? And how did Trudi's name come up?"

"It wasn't a—oh, never mind," Lindsey said, realizing that he was teasing her. "Listen, Riordan and another man were sitting at a table nearby. I heard Riordan say that his map is missing and I heard the other man accuse him of, well, murder."

"What?" Sully asked. The amusement fled from his voice as if chased out by concern.

"We're following him right now," Lindsey said. "I can't tell if the other man is with him, but it sounded like Riordan was asking the other man to invest in his treasure hunt. The man refused until Riordan produced the map and got the go-ahead to resume excavating the island."

"Where are you exactly?" Sully asked.

"Just outside town," Lindsey said. "Listen, I called because I want to see if the other man is with Riordan. I suspect Riordan will stop by the Anchor as he seems to haunt the place. If he gets there before we do, I'm hoping you can get a look at his companion and see if he's a resident of Briar Creek. I didn't recognize his voice and I couldn't see his face because he had his back to me."

"I'm on it," he said. "Have John circle the block before he drops you off. I don't want Riordan to think you were following him. If he is involved in something bad, he could be armed and dangerous."

"But—" Lindsey protested.

"No buts," Sully said. "I'll stay outside waiting for you."

"Isn't that a little—" Lindsey began but he cut her off by saying, "Paranoid? Yes, but when it comes to you, I can live with that. Circle the block."

"Fine, but I want a full report."

Lindsey ended the call and glanced at John. "Sully asked you to circle the block before dropping me off at the Blue Anchor."

"The Anchor? I thought I'd be taking you home," John said.

"Change of plan," Lindsey said. "Look, I'm truly sorry for the rude end to dinner. I know we never got a chance to talk things out, but we'll have to reschedule. I wanted to ask your professional legal opinion on behalf of my friend Milton. The police aren't saying as much but I think the medical examiner has declared Trudi's death a murder, and I think Preston Riordan had something to do with it."

"That was Preston Riordan we were following?" John asked.

"Yes!" Lindsey said. She knew she sounded exasperated, but honestly, had John always been this thick? "Who did you think we were following?"

"I don't know," John said with a shrug. "I thought maybe he was a library patron with an overdue book."

Lindsey shook her head. "No. Riordan is hiding something and I want to know what."

"Why?" John asked. "What does any of this have to do with you?"

"Well, Milton is the president of the library board and a friend," she said. "I have a responsibility to help him out."

"Lindsey, you've only lived here a little over a year," he said. "How good a friend can you be with these people?"

Lindsey was looking out the window. She saw Riordan turn into the parking lot of the Anchor. She could see by the light of a streetlamp that he was alone in his truck. Damn it. She really wanted to know who he'd had dinner with.

"Lindsey, did you hear me?"

"Yeah, sure," she said. Blatant lie. She had no idea what he was talking about.

"So you're not that invested in this community, right?" he asked. "I mean you couldn't be. You haven't been here that long."

Lindsey thought about the town. Was she invested? She thought about her library staff, her crafternoon group, her third-floor apartment and her dog.

She thought about the sound of the waves that she could hear at night when she slept with her windows open, the smell of the sea, and the cries of the seagulls who swooped up and down on the air currents in the bay. She thought about her daily bike rides, her walks on the beach with Heathcliff and even her boring monthly department head meetings.

She was astonished to discover that she had sunk her roots down deep into this small town. The way she felt, it was going to take one tough John Deere backhoe to get her uprooted again. She smiled.

John had circled around and pulled over to the curb. Before he could climb out to get her door, she pushed it open and sprang from the car.

"Thanks," she said. "But you're wrong. I'm completely invested in this town, these people and this community."

Before he could say a word, she slammed the door and hurried across the parking lot toward her tall sea captain, who stood leaning against the wall waiting for her.

Sully had barely opened his arms when Lindsey threw herself at him. He grabbed her close and hugged her tight.

"I missed you," she said, and she kissed him.

When they pulled apart, he rested his forehead on hers and said, "I'm going to have John take you out more often if this is how happy you are to get back."

A couple pushed out the doors of the restaurant. Lindsey and Sully both smiled and nodded at them, moving aside to let the couple pass.

"Come on." Lindsey grabbed his arm and led him out onto the pier and away from the café.

She paused beside a tall piling and leaned against it. "We ate at this small crab shack over in Guilford."

"I've heard of that place," Sully said. "Good crab?"

"Really good," she said. "We have to go there sometime."

Sully smiled as if he liked the sound of that.

"But it's also where I overheard Riordan talking to another man about how Trudi took his map and now he can't find it," she said.

"Are you positive?" Sully asked.

"Absolutely," she said. "That's why I had John follow Riordan, although he got a bit ahead of us because John drives so slow. I forgot how much that used to annoy me. Anyway, Riordan was alone, huh?"

"Yes," Sully said. "And he looked pretty upset when he arrived. We need to tell Chief Daniels about this. If Trudi did take Riordan's map, that would certainly be reason enough for him to kill her."

"That's what I thought, too," she said. "Let's see if he's in now."

They stepped off the pier and headed across the parking lot. Sully put his arm around her shoulder as they walked, and Lindsey leaned into him.

"So how did your talk go with John?" he asked.

"We never got to it," she said. "Seeing Riordan and hearing about the map sort of took over my purpose. I suppose I'll have to find another opportunity to clear the air."

"How do you feel about that?" he asked.

"Like it's overdue," Lindsey said. "I realized tonight that although I may not have been born here, I am Creeker through and through. I love this town."

It was the first time the *L* word had been used between

them, and even though she'd been talking about the town, Lindsey knew that Sully was a large part of the reason she loved Briar Creek, and she felt the teensiest bit awkward that she'd said it first.

"I feel the same way," he said. He squeezed her close and Lindsey glanced up at his face, trying to figure out if he meant that he loved the town or if there was more to it.

As they climbed the steps to the police station, she shook her head, trying to shake the thought away. She was being silly. Yes, she and Sully were dating exclusively, but they were mature adults and declarations of love would happen when they were ready, and they would be straightforward and not coded as if they were talking about something else.

As Sully pulled open the door to the station, however, all thoughts of their relationship status fled as Lindsey took in the spectacle before her.

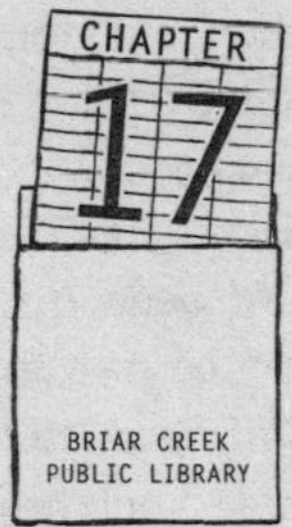

Chaos would best describe the scene that greeted Lindsey and Sully as they stood staring at the flock of women who filled the lobby. They ranged in age from fifty to ninety, from the gray-haired and pleasantly rounded of figure to the well-maintained and dripping in diamonds, but the one thing they all had in common was that they looked mad.

"You let him go, Chief Daniels!" Jeanette Palmer said. She was a petite lady who wore her white hair in a tidy bun on the top of her head.

Jeanette owned the local bed-and-breakfast and was partial to steamy romance novels, preferably featuring vampires. Lately, she'd been on a Laurell K. Hamilton kick.

"What's going on?" Lindsey whispered to the woman

beside her. It was Mrs. Holcomb, a matronly widow, who was known around Briar Creek for her rum cake.

"Chief Daniels arrested Milton for the murder of Trudi Hargrave," she whispered back.

"What?" Lindsey asked, shocked.

She had known he'd been questioned. After all, his scenes with Trudi over the past few weeks had been the talk of the town. But still, arrested for murder? That had to mean that the police had some evidence and that it pointed to Milton.

She glanced at Sully. He was frowning, too.

"Are you thinking what I'm thinking?" she asked. Sully didn't get a chance to answer.

"Let Milton out!" one woman at the front shouted. The rest of the room took up the chant. "Let Milton out!"

Lindsey saw the door to the office open in the back of the room. She knew it was Chief Daniels because she could just see the top of his head, which boasted a distinctive receding hairline that always reminded her of the outline of Africa on the globe at the library.

"Ladies, please," he said. "I know that you're upset, but this sort of demonstration is not helping matters. If you want to help Milton, you should all go home."

This was, apparently, the wrong thing to say. The chanting grew louder, and the ladies looked like they were considering doing some damage to the police station.

"Uh-oh," Lindsey said to Sully. "Looks like we've got a mob mentality going on here."

"What on earth?" a voice from behind Lindsey said.

She spun around to see Emma Plewicki pushing her way through the door.

"What's going on?" she asked them.

"A rally to set Milton free," Sully said.

"Oh, for Pete's sake!" Emma snapped. She took her nightstick off her belt and used it to nudge a path through the crush of women. "I don't want to club you, Mona, but if you don't step aside, I'll take you out at your knees."

Mona Turley, a spry octogenarian, with hair dyed so black it practically absorbed light, glared at Emma through her bifocals. "Police brutality!"

Emma rolled her eyes, but it was too late. The women that filled the lobby dropped to the ground as one and there they lay in full protest mode.

"Well, that made it easy," Emma said as she picked her way over the bodies to get behind the desk with the chief, who looked out at his station house in equal parts consternation and fascination.

Lindsey and Sully followed Emma, hoping to find out what was happening.

"What is it about Milton that brings out the love of the ladies?" the chief asked Emma.

"At a guess?" she asked. "He listens when they talk, he brings them flowers and he's never late."

"Wow, that's overkill if you ask me," Chief Daniels said. "Hey, how do *you* know this?"

"He's a gentleman friend of my aunt Mitsy," Emma said.

"Isn't she . . ." Chief Daniels pointed to the corner and Emma sighed.

"Yes, she's on the floor by the fake ficus. My dad is going to be so unhappy if I have to arrest her."

"Sully, Ms. Norris, how can I help you two?" Chief Daniels asked as they worked their way toward him. "Unless, of course, you're about to lie down, too."

"How are you doing, Chief?" Sully asked and held out his hand. The two men shook, and Chief Daniels seemed reassured by Sully's gesture.

"Sorry, I'm a little out of sorts," the chief said.

"It's all right," Lindsey said as she glanced behind her. Someone in the crowd began humming and it was beginning to surge in volume. "We were hoping to talk to you about something."

The chief's eyebrows lifted with interest and not a little relief. Lindsey had a feeling she could have said she was here to squabble about a parking ticket and he would have jumped at the chance to leave the room to discuss it.

"Well, that sounds serious," he said. "Emma, start calling these ladies' families to come and collect them. I'll be in the back with Sully and Lindsey."

Lindsey noticed that he used her first name. She and the chief had gotten off to a rocky start when she first moved to Briar Creek. She had accidentally set off the alarm at the library and had been greeted by the chief with his gun drawn as she had exited the building. He had always called her Ms. Norris after that, especially when her children's librarian, Beth, had been accused of murder and Lindsey had butted into the investigation determined to prove her innocent.

Things had slowly begun to change between them when

the president of the Friends of the Library, Carrie Rushton, had found her husband murdered. The chief had gone out of his way to help Carrie, a nurse who had taken care of his mother when she died, and Lindsey realized there was more to the chief than met the eye.

"Now wait just one minute," Emma protested. "You're going to leave me here by myself with them?"

"What could possibly happen?" Chief Daniels asked.

"They could overpower me," Emma said. "Then they'd take my gun and shoot up the joint while trying to free their man."

"Yeah!" a lone woman in the crowd cried.

Chief Daniels leaned over the desk and frowned. "The first one who moves so much as an inch in your direction gets hit with the Taser. Got it?"

"Does that hurt?" Mitsy by the ficus asked.

"Yes," Chief Daniels said. "You'll probably pass out and pass gas. It'll be the talk of the town for weeks, maybe months."

The group of women blanched as one.

Emma took the Taser that he handed her and put it prominently on the desk while she began making calls.

"Follow me," Chief Daniels said, and he led Lindsey and Sully to the back of the station.

They went right into his office. Lindsey had never been in there before. The chief's office was pleasantly cluttered but not sloppy. Cushy leather chairs took up one corner while his desk and two large bookcases filled the other half of the room. Lindsey was impressed to see that he had a copy of the Connecticut State Statutes as well several current titles on law enforcement. She turned to look at him with some surprise when she saw a row of cookbooks on the bottom shelf.

"I didn't know you liked to cook," she said.

The chief shrugged, looking embarrassed. "Reading recipes relaxes me, although I don't get as much time in the kitchen as I'd like. I've really been obsessed with making my own pasta lately."

"You should try his barbeque," Sully said. "Ian's been trying to get his sauce recipe out of him for years."

"He'll never get it," the chief said. He tapped his right temple with his index finger. "The secret ingredient is up here and I'm not sharing."

The chief gestured for them to sit, so Lindsey and Sully took the small couch while he took the lone chair.

"So what do you have to tell me?" he asked.

Lindsey recounted her dinner at the crab shack. The chief listened without interrupting.

Lindsey concluded by saying, "So right there, I would say Riordan is a greater suspect than Milton. I mean if Trudi took his map and this investor pulled the plug on the project because there was no map, well, Riordan could have been desperate."

Chief Daniels rubbed his chin with the back of his hand.

"Milton isn't officially under arrest," he said. Lindsey and Sully exchanged a look. "Don't get me wrong. He's a person of interest, given the antagonism of his relationship with the victim right before her murder."

"Why is he here then?" Sully asked. "What about the protestors?"

"Yeah, we really didn't anticipate that," the chief said. "Milton's been taking a pounding by the media, particularly that Kili Peters woman. They won't leave the poor guy alone. When I had him in for an interview, he commented on how quiet it was, so I told him he was welcome to spend the night in the jail. Well, one of the ladies saw him coming in with his toothbrush and everything just went squirrelly from there."

"So why didn't you tell them the truth?" Lindsey asked.

"Milton asked me not to," the chief said. "Honestly, I think he's a little afraid of them, too."

He looked so flummoxed that Lindsey laughed. Sully joined in, too, and the chief gave them a sheepish smile.

"You know," she said. "I have a few Italian cookbooks that you might find interesting. I'll put them aside for you at the library."

He beamed at her. "I'd like that. Thanks."

"So what will happen now?" Sully asked.

The chief put a hand over the back of his neck and tipped his head back as if trying to ease a knot of tension.

"It looks like I'll be bringing Riordan in for questioning—again," he said. "It might make it more interesting if I ask him to produce the map."

"And he can't," Lindsey added.

"I'd appreciate it if this went no further," Chief Daniels said. "I'd like to have the element of surprise on Riordan."

"Of course," Sully said and Lindsey nodded.

"Do you think Emma's got them cleared out now?" Chief Daniels asked.

"I can go check for you," Sully said.

"Thanks," the chief said.

"Would it be all right if I just popped back to see Milton?" Lindsey asked. "And I'd like to tell him what I overheard. I'm sure he won't tell anyone, especially since he's isolated at the moment."

The chief thought about it for a moment and then nodded. "I don't see why not."

They rose from their seats and the chief walked them to the door. Sully went toward the lobby while the chief led Lindsey to the section of the station which had a small block of jail cells.

He opened a security door and ushered Lindsey through.

"Just press that button when you want to come out," he said. "The buzzer will sound and I can unlock the door from up front."

"Thanks, Chief Daniels," Lindsey said.

Milton's cell was in the back corner. He was standing in the center in warrior pose. His eyes were shut. Lindsey didn't want to interrupt his concentration, so she waited quietly.

"Hi, Lindsey, what brings you here?" he asked. He didn't open his eyes.

"How did you know it was me?" she asked.

"I could smell your perfume," he said. "Yoga declutters the mind and opens up our other senses. My olfactory knew it was you, because you always smell like sunshine."

"I didn't know that sunshine had a smell," Lindsey said.

Milton slowly released from his posture and opened his eyes. His smile was warm as he regarded her.

"Like my new digs?" he asked. He stepped forward and

pushed open the door. A chair was propped in the doorway to keep it from locking. "Care to come in?"

"I think I'd rather you came out," she said. "I've spent my entire life out of jail and I'm pretty sure I'd like to keep it that way."

"Understood," Milton said. He stepped out to join her in the hallway, keeping the chair in the door so he could get back in. "Ironically, that Kili Peters, the barracuda reporter, has staked out my house so it feels more like a jail than this cell."

"Not to mention your groupies," Lindsey said. "There were over twenty women in the lobby protesting for your release."

Milton smiled. "That's nice of them."

"You have quite a fan base," Lindsey said. "You know, if Kili Peters gets wind of it, she'll twist it to make you look like an octogenarian Lothario."

"They're just friends," Milton said. "I am still and always will be faithful to my Anna."

"I know," Lindsey said. "I'm just bracing you for the possibility."

Lindsey knew that after his wife, Anna, had passed, every single woman in Briar Creek over the age of fifty had set her sights on Milton. He was kind to them all and treated them all exactly the same, but he never led anyone to believe that she was more than just a charming dinner companion. Lindsey liked that he was very democratic about it, but given the circumstance, it really didn't look good for him.

"I can't live my life worried about what other people say

about me," Milton said. "My heart is pure and that is all that matters."

"Is there anything I can bring you?" Lindsey asked. "Books, magazines, snacks, anything?"

"Thank you, but I have found that the sterility of my accommodations is very conducive to reflective meditation," he said. "When I get out of here, I may go home and throw out all of my stuff and become a minimalist."

"Milton, you know you are a person of interest," Lindsey said.

"I am and not necessarily in the way they mean," he said. His green eyes sparkled and Lindsey smiled.

"I'm glad you haven't lost your sense of humor, but this is worrisome," Lindsey said. "Especially if the media—"

"Lindsey." Milton raised his hands in a stop gesture. "Sometimes you just have to trust the Universe to take care of things."

Lindsey wished she had his inner peace, but she just didn't.

"Milton, you don't have an alibi, do you?" she asked.

"No."

"That's not helpful."

"So I've been told," he said.

For the first time he looked a bit forlorn, and Lindsey knew he was thinking that if only his Anna were still here, he wouldn't be in this fix.

"We'll figure it out," she said. Then she told him about seeing Riordan at the restaurant and hearing him discuss the map with the mystery man.

Milton looked infinitely cheered by this news. But then he frowned.

"What is it?" Lindsey asked.

"Well, it doesn't seem likely that Riordan murdered Trudi, does it?" he asked.

"What do you mean?"

"If he was going to murder her, wouldn't he do it after she gave him the map back?"

"Unless it was an accident," Lindsey said. "Or it was someone else."

"Curious and more curious," he said.

The door behind them opened and Sully poked his head in. "Hi, Milton, nice place you have here."

Milton smiled at him and nodded.

"Lindsey, the lobby is clear for the moment. Are you ready to go?"

"Yes," she said. She turned and put her hand on Milton's arm. "You'll call me if you need anything."

"I promise," he said.

"Good night then." Lindsey left him with a quick hug.

As Sully closed the door behind her, he asked, "How's he doing?"

"Pretty well, all things considered," she said.

Suddenly the day caught up to Lindsey. The adrenaline surge she'd felt while they were following Riordan and then confronted with the protest in the lobby left her and she felt drained. All she wanted now was to sink into her bed with Heathcliff beside her.

"Come on, I'll take you home," Sully said.

He wrapped an arm about her and together they walked over to the Anchor to his truck. The cool night breeze felt good against her skin. Lindsey glanced out across the water at the islands beyond.

It seemed that, like so many years before, when tragedy struck Ruby Island the first time, the only witness to what had really happened was the island itself.

"You know, if we get caught, we are going to be in so much hot water, we won't be able to bail ourselves out, and by that I mean pay our bail, not use a bucket," Beth said.

"Could you talk louder, Beth?" Lindsey asked. "I don't think they heard you all the way down the hall. Besides I brought the printout of the books Trudi checked out, so if anyone asks, we're merely getting our books back."

"And we're doing it this early because—"

"Librarians are like vampires; we don't sleep," Lindsey said.

"Oh, I can't wait to see you use that one," Beth said. "Kili Peters would have a field day if she heard that."

It was early morning. Unable to sleep, Lindsey had

biked over to Beth's house to tell her what she and Sully had found out the night before.

Beth had been impressed but then asked the question that had been nagging Lindsey all night. "So if Trudi did take the map, where did she hide it?"

Lindsey remembered the last time she saw Trudi alive. It was the day she'd taken a restraining order out on Milton. It was also the day she'd checked out three books from the library.

Before they decided to visit Trudi's office, Lindsey had stopped by the library and looked up Trudi's record. The books were still on loan to her and they were all books about treasure maps, including Ferris La Verne Coffman's 1957 *Atlas of Treasure Maps.* What could Trudi have wanted from that?

Lindsey and Beth had both concluded that there were only two possibilities where Trudi might have hidden the map, her house or her office. Since they didn't want to break into her house, and because Trudi lived for her job, they both agreed her office was the likelier bet.

And so here they were in the town hall, hours before it actually opened, trying to break into Trudi's office.

Lindsey was crouched on the floor while Beth kept watch. It was five o'clock and it wasn't likely that anyone would be in the town hall until the cleaning crew arrived at six.

Beth was hopping from foot to foot, which was ruining Lindsey's concentration.

"Beth, could you please stand still?" she asked.

"I can't help it. I have to go to the bathroom."

"No, you don't, it's just nerves," Lindsey said. "Like when we were in grad school and you had to wait to make your presentation. You always had to go."

"Can we talk about something else?" Beth asked. "This is so not helping to take my mind off of this."

"Why don't you do one of your story time poems," Lindsey suggested.

Beth was silent for a moment and then she busted into "Boa Constrictor" by Shel Silverstein.

" 'Oh, I'm being eaten by a boa constrictor,' " she recited.

Lindsey smiled. Beth was always very dramatic when she performed this piece. With Beth occupied, Lindsey turned her attention back to the door. She had spent the morning on the computer, looking up ways to open locked doors, fascinating stuff, with the added bonus that she no longer felt secure in her own home.

" 'Well, what do you know? It's nibbling my toe,' " Beth said.

Because the town hall had similar door hardware to the library, Lindsey had found a wiki on how to unlock a door with a credit card. She had taken the advice of the website and was using a long strip cut from a plastic soda bottle as it was more flexible. Of course, it was still proving to be a lot harder than it had looked.

" 'Oh, fiddle, it's up to my middle,' " Beth recited while glancing back and forth along the deserted hall.

Lindsey ignored her and focused on her task. She slid the strip of plastic in so it was perpendicular to the door. Then she pushed on the doorknob while she tried to use the plastic to leverage the lock back.

"'Oh, dread, it's upmmmmmmmmmmfffffffff . . .'" Beth finished.

With a click, the door popped open and Lindsey opened it wide.

"I did it!" she cried.

Beth gave her an astonished look and they hustled into the small office and closed the door behind them.

"I can't believe you did it!" she whispered.

"Neither can I," Lindsey admitted. Now she felt like she needed to piddle. "Okay, let's find the books first. But think if you were Trudi, where would you hide something valuable that you stole from Riordan?"

They scanned the office. It was cluttered but not untidy. The large wall calendar was covered in sticky notes, listing things to do. And there on the corner of the desk were the library books. Lindsey picked them up and put them by the door.

It was obvious that the police had already been here to search for clues as black fingerprint kit residue covered most of the surfaces.

"It looks like it's already been thoroughly gone over," Beth said. "What makes you think we can find something that the police couldn't?"

"Because they only found out last night that Trudi had the map, which means they weren't looking for it before," Lindsey said. "And besides, we're librarians. We know how to find things."

"If you say so," Beth said.

"Try not to touch anything," Lindsey said. "We don't want to leave prints behind."

"You're kidding, right?" Beth asked. "How are we supposed to open drawers then?"

"Use the bottom of your shirt," Lindsey said.

"What was that?" Beth hissed.

"What?" Lindsey asked. She was standing over Trudi's desk trying to figure out where to start.

Beth held up a finger to her lips and then Lindsey heard it, too. It was the sound of footsteps coming up the hall toward Trudi's office. The steps were stealthy as if the person was trying not to be heard.

Lindsey glanced at the door. It was shut and thank goodness she had relocked it. Unless the person had a key, in which case—

The door handle jiggled. Beth gently put her hand over her own mouth as if to keep herself from making any noise, which Lindsey suspected would have been a whimper as she was choking back a few of her own.

There was a grunt from the other side of the door, as if the person outside was trying to use their weight to open the door.

The knob jiggled more noisily this time. Beth sent Lindsey a wide-eyed terrified look. Lindsey swallowed and it sounded horribly loud in her own ears.

"Hey, you, what are you doing by Ms. Hargrave's office?"

Lindsey knew that voice. It was Herb Gunderson, the mayor's liaison to the department heads.

Whoever was outside didn't answer Herb, but the knob stopped rattling and Lindsey heard the sounds of footsteps pounding away from the door.

"Hey, wait! I want to talk to you!" Herb cried and Lindsey heard his feet stomp past the door as he trailed after the man.

Beth and Lindsey both strained to hear what was happening. There was a yell and then the sickening sound of someone falling down a staircase.

"Oh, my God!" Beth cried. She yanked open the door and hurried out. Lindsey was right behind her. She paused only to snatch up the library books as she went.

She raced after Beth, slamming the door behind her. She ran down the hall and bolted down the staircase to find Beth crouched beside Herb. He was propped up on the bottom step, his face twisted in pain, while he held his shin. The ankle below his hand looked to be at an odd angle and Lindsey cringed.

Beth was already on her cell phone calling an ambulance. Lindsey dropped the books and hurried across the lobby to unlock the door. The paramedics would want to come right to the front to collect Herb. She then went back to sit beside him with Beth and await their arrival.

As the EMTs got Herb on the stretcher and began to wheel him to the door, he grabbed Lindsey's hand and said, "Tell the mayor what happened, okay?"

"Sure, but what did happen?" Lindsey asked.

The gurney was lifted over the door frame and Herb winced. Then he looked at Lindsey and said, "I saw someone trying to get into Trudi Hargrave's office. I caught him at the stairs but he knocked me down and took off. I think it has something to do with her death."

"I'll be sure to tell the mayor and the police," Lindsey said.

"Hey, what were you doing here so early?" Herb asked.

"I came to collect some overdue library books," Lindsey said.

Herb nodded as if this made sense and Lindsey wondered if it was just that his pain medicine was kicking in. She walked with them until he was lifted into the ambulance. Beth was behind her, having retrieved the books.

The ambulance jetted out of the parking lot and Lindsey felt a trickle of sweat run down her back. She didn't know if she was sweaty from nerves or the day's humidity, but there was no question that a shower would be in order.

"Do you think he knew we were in Trudi's office?" Beth asked.

"No, I was vague and I think he was in enough pain that he didn't question it."

"We didn't get much of a search done."

Lindsey glanced at the time on her cell phone. It was after six and the cleaning crew would be here soon. She took the books from Beth and said, "How about coffee and a muffin? My treat."

"Make it a double," Beth said.

"Coffee or muffin?" Lindsey asked as they walked toward the bakery that was nestled at the back of the Briar Creek grocery store.

"Both," Beth said. "This B and E stuff really gives a girl an appetite."

It wasn't until after her shower that Lindsey remembered the books. She had combed out the tangles in her long, curly blond hair and was letting them air dry. Since the day promised to get even stickier, she had dressed in a red sleeveless blouse and a fitted jean skirt with red sandals for the library.

The windows were open in her apartment, but the air was so heavy outside that the curtains were utterly still as if weighed down by the somber events of the past few days.

She twisted the damp strands of her hair up into a loose bun and shoved two wooden hair sticks in it to hold it in place. This was the sort of day that tempted her to cut her hair short, but she knew she'd regret it. When it was short, her hair went to frizz and she looked like a man, an unattractive man.

She grabbed her purse and was just about to leave for work when she saw the books by the door. She scooped them up and put them in her Friends of the Library tote bag.

Probably, she needed to tell the chief about taking the books from Trudi's office. She didn't think he'd mind. In her defense, with pirate fever sweeping the town, these books could go back on the display, which was pretty well picked over right now.

Reassured, Lindsey took the bag with her and called to Heathcliff, who was wrestling with his squeaky pig toy, to follow her out.

She played fetch with the puppy in the yard until her arm felt about ready to give out. Nancy appeared in the back door and called for Heathcliff to come in and he went at a run. Nancy always seemed to have a treat in her apron for Heathcliff, and he knew it.

Lindsey wasn't sure when Nancy had become her unofficial pet sitter, but she was delighted that the situation seemed to suit everyone. Nancy said Heathcliff was good company during the day, and he made her feel more secure. For his part, Heathcliff had his own bed at Nancy's house, and he seemed quite content to spend his days in the yard and the kitchen with her.

"Thanks, Nancy!" she called.

"My pleasure." Nancy waved and closed the door behind them. "So I thought I heard Sully's truck pull into the driveway last night."

"Yes, you did," Lindsey said. She did not, however, elaborate.

Nancy seemed satisfied as she gave Lindsey a blinding grin. "Have a great day!"

"You, too."

Lindsey hurried over to where she kept her bike locked up. She dumped Trudi's books in the back basket and set off for work. Her early morning adventure with Beth had knocked her mentally off her schedule. Today was her day to go in late and work the evening shift. Normally she would have spent the morning running errands or lazing in bed reading a good book. As it was, she'd gotten up so early to get to the town hall, it was only late morning and yet she felt as if it were midafternoon.

She pushed off on her bike and headed down the lane to the center of town. The air was still thick and heavy. By the time she got to the library, she was coated in a sheen of sweat. Knowing that the air conditioner would feel great for about a half hour and then would freeze her to the bone for the rest of the day, Lindsey had tossed her sweater into the back of her bike as well as Trudi's books and her purse.

She locked up her bike and unloaded her stuff. She was just closing the back door behind her when she turned and found Ms. Cole standing there waiting for her.

"Mr. Tupper was never—" Ms. Cole began but Lindsey cut her off.

"Late. I know, I'm what—a minute and a half late?" Lindsey asked. "Is there an emergency that needs tending?"

"That's not what I was going to say." Ms. Cole frowned.

Lindsey glanced at her in surprise. Today's monochromatic color of choice was brown. Lindsey refused to dwell on the endless list of things Ms. Cole could be likened to with such an unfortunate choice of dark brown shoes, light brown hose, dark brown skirt and a mud brown blouse.

"Oh," she said. "I'm sorry. What were you going to say?"

"There is a gentlemen waiting for you in the meeting room," she said. Then she glanced at Lindsey and sniffed. "But since you mentioned it, no, Mr. Tupper was never late."

Ms. Cole turned on her sturdy heel and headed down the hallway toward the circulation desk. Lindsey blew out a breath and followed, pausing by her office to drop off her purse and the book bag.

As she glanced through the glass wall of the meeting room, she recognized the neatly trimmed head of blond hair. John.

She tapped on the glass door and pushed into the room. He glanced up from the magazine in front of him and gave her a small smile.

"Hi, Lindsey," he said. "Sorry to bother you so soon after . . ."

"Yeah, it's hard to say what that was last night, isn't it?" she asked.

To John's credit, he laughed. "*Debacle* comes to mind."

Lindsey laughed, too. "The crab was excellent."

"As was the company," John said. "Listen, I know I was slow on the uptake when you had me following Riordan. Multitasking is not my gift."

"I remember," she said. "After the third kitchen fire, I think we both caught on that the ability to scramble an egg while trying to grade papers was not in your DNA."

He smiled and Lindsey felt the bond of friendship they had once shared strengthen at the memory. She wasn't sure how to feel about that, so she quickly brought them back to his purpose.

"So what brings you here today?" she asked.

"When I got home last night, I started thinking about what you heard Riordan say and why you had me follow him."

"Oh?" Lindsey asked.

"Lindsey, I think I know who your Mr. Riordan was talking to at the crab shack."

"Who?" Lindsey asked.

"My landlord," he said. "Paul Gavin."

Lindsey felt her eyebrows snap up like blinds on a window. "I thought he was away for the summer."

"So did I," John said. "But when I woke up this morning, there he was on his dock, taking his boat out into the bay."

"What makes you think he was the man with Riordan?" Lindsey asked.

"That's what he does," John said. "He invests in art and antiquities."

"Do you think the news of the treasure hunt is what brought him back early?" Lindsey asked.

"Could be. I mean, if Captain Kidd's treasure is really

here, it would be the most significant find of the decade, if not the century."

Lindsey nodded. She had to agree. It made sense that an investor would want to be near the excavation. Of course, she remembered that the investor had accused Riordan of murder. Did he know something? Should she tell Chief Daniels what John had told her or was it just speculation?

"Well, I just wanted to let you know that when I thought about it, I recognized his black and gold sweater from Pierson College. I saw him wearing the same one this morning when he went out in his boat."

"Pierson College is one of the residential colleges at Yale," Lindsey said.

"I know," he said.

They exchanged a grave glance and she asked, "Is he an alum?"

"Must be," he said. "I can't imagine why he'd wear it otherwise."

"Thanks, John," Lindsey said. "For letting me know about this and for dinner."

They stood awkwardly for a moment. John looked as if he wanted to say more but thought better of it, and with a quick nod, he left the room.

Lindsey made her way back to her office. She felt as if there was just too much to take in. The stark reality couldn't be avoided, however. Trudi had taken Preston Riordan's treasure map and then she had been found dead on Ruby Island in the midst of the excavation. Had the person who killed her stolen the map? Or had the person she'd stolen the map from, Riordan, killed her?

Lindsey saw Beth sitting at her desk in the children's area. She looked as drained as Lindsey felt. Obviously, breaking into someone's office took more out of a gal than she had supposed.

Lindsey sank onto the chair behind her desk and opened her book bag. She stacked the books one by one on top of her desk. They would have to be checked in before they could go on display. She wondered why Trudi had checked them out. What was she trying to learn about treasure maps and why?

Lindsey lifted the stack into her arms when she noticed a corner of plastic sticking out of the Coffman atlas of treasure maps. Her heart began to pound and her fingers were shaky. She knew before she opened the book what she would find.

Yes, tucked in behind a detailed map of all of the shipwrecks around Florida was Captain Kidd's treasure map just as she remembered it.

She glanced at the door to see if anyone was looking toward her office. She held the map by the corner so as not to smudge any fingerprints that might be on its acid-free plastic casing.

The safe where they kept the library's cash was in the corner of her office. She hurried over to it and quickly turned the dial to the correct numbers. When the safe door unlatched, she turned the handle and pulled. She took out an empty canvas money bag and slipped the map inside.

Her heart was pounding and the blood pulsed in her ears. This was ridiculous. It wasn't as if she'd stolen the map. Okay, well, technically, she had taken it from Trudi's office, but it wasn't as if she had known the map was in there. Yes, she'd been looking for the map, but taking it had been purely accidental.

"Lindsey."

"Ah!" Lindsey fell back onto her heels, slamming the door to the safe shut as she went.

"I'm sorry, did I startle you?" Violet asked.

"A little," Lindsey said as she rose from a graceless heap on the floor.

Violet reached out and helped her up. "Girl, you are a terrible liar."

Lindsey smiled at her. "I know."

"I came to ask you to put in a request for our next craft-ernoon book," Violet said. "Nancy and I decided that we really should read *Treasure Island*."

"Good idea," Lindsey said. She forced her lips into a facsimile of a smile and hoped Violet didn't notice how hard her heart was beating. "I know Beth will enjoy it. She's certainly gotten in touch with her inner pirate."

"Is that Calico Prudentilla Read thing going to last long?" Violet asked. "I heard she was considering a tattoo of an anchor on her bicep."

"No idea," Lindsey said.

"Ah, well, this, too, shall pass," Violet said. "I'm off to the community theater. I'm trying to talk them into opening this fall's play season with *A Midsummer Night's Dream*."

"Starring 'that shrewd and knavish sprite called Robin Goodfellow,' " Lindsey quoted from the play.

" 'I am that merry wanderer of the night,' " Violet recited the next line.

"One of my favorites," Lindsey said. "I can't wait to see it."

"I'm holding you to that. In fact, I may have you and the rest of the crafternooners help with the production. We could use some new blood," Violet said. It wasn't a question.

She swept out of the office, leaving Lindsey staring after her. Even offstage the woman had a presence that was positively electric.

Lindsey turned back to the safe to make sure it was shut. Now what should she do? She had the map. She should tell the police about the map and the identity of the person Riordan had been talking to. Yes, that's exactly what she should do.

She would walk over right now and tell Chief Daniels what happened—well, mostly. She'd leave out the part about the strip of the plastic soda bottle being used to encourage the door to open.

She stopped by the circulation desk, where Ms. Cole was checking in a stack of books. She was about to tell her that she had to step out for a moment when the sliding doors to the library slid open and Preston Riordan walked in.

His gaze met Lindsey's and he lifted an eyebrow as he studied her.

"Ms. Norris, you're just the person I'm looking for," he said.

"I am?" she asked.

"Yes, I believe you have something that belongs to me, and I want it back," he said.

Lindsey sucked in a breath and felt the blood drain from her face. How did he know? He couldn't. She decided to bluff.

"I think you must be mistaken," she said.

"I assure you, I am not," he said. "In fact, I see it in your office from here."

"What?" Lindsey's head whipped back toward her office. She glanced through the windows of the backroom and into her office window, but the safe wasn't visible from where she was standing.

Riordan was already striding past her toward the room. Lindsey hurried after him. She couldn't let him take the map. It was evidence.

Riordan walked into her office.

"Now, wait just a minute," she said. "You can't just go barging into people's offices and touching their—"

Riordan grabbed a denim jacket off the coatrack by the door, and Lindsey felt her words dry up in her throat like dirt under a hot summer sun.

"Oh," she said. "That's your jacket."

"Yes, what did you think I was talking about?"

Lindsey looked at him, and before she could think to hold them in, the words flew out of her mouth.

"The treasure map."

Now he looked stunned.

"Why would you think that?"

His gaze darted around the room as if he expected to see it lying about.

"It's not here," she said. Her voice was too high. She cleared her throat. "But I know that Trudi took it from you, and I know you want it back."

Very quietly, Riordan closed the office door, shutting them in together.

"You seem to know an awful lot," Riordan said. Despite the gray hair and wrinkles and beer belly, there was no question that Riordan could overpower Lindsey physically if he chose to. She wondered if that was what he'd done to Trudi.

She felt her breathing speed up, and her heart thumped hard in her chest as if trying to decide between flight or fight. Did anyone know Riordan was here? Surely, he wouldn't do anything stupid here. She tried to gauge how desperate he was feeling. By the set of his jaw, she decided he looked more determined than desperate, a fact that managed to make her feel even more uneasy.

"How do you know about my map?" he asked. His voice was low, almost a growl.

Lindsey moved so that her desk was between them in what she hoped seemed a nonchalant walk but what she suspected looked like a leap to safety.

She couldn't tell him she had overheard him at the restaurant. Well, she could but it wouldn't give her any more information. No, it was better to let him think she'd found out another way.

"Trudi called me before she died," she said. She made sure to maintain his gaze. She didn't want him to suspect that she was bluffing. His eyes bored into hers. He seemed to accept it as the truth.

"What did she say?"

"She wanted me to authenticate the map," Lindsey said.

"I don't believe you," Riordan said. He turned as if to leave, dismissing her.

"She wanted to use it as leverage to get a bigger cut from the investors you were courting."

"Why would she tell you any of that?" he asked. He was clutching his jacket so tightly that his knuckles were white.

"She had to offer me something to get me to agree, now didn't she?" Lindsey asked.

"What do you want from me?"

Lindsey shrugged. The blood pounding in her ears made it hard to hear. "The same thing Trudi wanted."

"Ha! Well, you're as much of a fool as she was. When

she showed up on the island with her meaningless threats, I told her it was a no-go," he said. "Why would I give her any more money? If she had just given me the map back, I wouldn't have had to hurt her."

Lindsey sucked in a breath. "So you did kill her."

"No!" Riordan protested. "She came after me when I refused to give her a bigger cut. She started punching me and I had to get her off."

His eyes glazed over with the memory and he shuddered. "I didn't mean to hit her in the head so hard, but I swear she was conscious and cursing at me when I ran to get the first aid kit. When I came back, she was gone."

"I don't believe you," Lindsey said.

Riordan glowered at her. "Fine. Don't believe me—I don't care. You know, what you don't seem to realize is that I don't need that map to find the treasure."

"No, but you do need it to prove to your investors that your scheme is legitimate."

"Why I ought to . . ." Riordan snarled, but he broke off. He glanced around the room, looking like he wanted to ransack it.

"What?" Lindsey goaded him. "Kill me like you killed Trudi?"

"I didn't—"

"Aw, come on," Lindsey said. Sudden fury overrode her fear. How could he stand there and lie about killing Trudi when he just admitted she was on the island with him and that they'd fought and he hit her?

"What did you do? Knock her into the pit when she wouldn't give you the map? Or did you hit her first, and when you realized you'd killed her, you dropped her into the pit, hoping Charlie would be blamed?"

"I didn't—"

"Stop lying," Lindsey snapped. "I was there when she was found. I was there when we pulled her out. She was killed and you did it!"

The door to Lindsey's office banged open and in strode Officer Plewicki and Chief Daniels.

"Preston Riordan, you're under arrest for the murder of Trudi Hargrave," Chief Daniels said.

"You can't be serious!" he protested. "You can't listen to her."

He pointed at Lindsey, who was huffing and puffing as if she'd just run a race.

"I didn't do it!" Riordan shouted.

"We'll discuss it further down at the station," the chief said. "Officer, please escort Mr. Riordan to the jail and read him his rights."

"Yes, sir," Emma said.

Riordan looked like he would bolt, but Emma blocked the door and palmed the Taser strapped to her hip.

"I have eighteen watts, and I'm not afraid to use them," she said.

Riordan took her at her word and was still as she cuffed him and told him his rights.

With her anger spent, Lindsey sagged into her chair with relief. "How did you know?"

"Well, we've been watching him since you told me what you overheard at the crab shack," he said. "Also, Beth called to tell me he was in your office with you."

"Oh," Lindsey said. She'd have to thank Beth later.

"Interestingly enough," Chief Daniels said as he settled into the chair across from hers, "I spent my morning reviewing the security tapes from town hall to see if we could ascertain who knocked Herb Gunderson down the stairs."

"Security tapes?" Lindsey asked. She felt a trickle of sweat ease down her neck to slide in between her shoulder blades.

"Yep," he said. "Now who do you suppose was on my tape just moments before a man in a dark hooded sweatshirt sent Herb tumbling down the steps?"

"The mayor?" Lindsey asked.

The chief gave her a hard stare.

"It was me," Lindsey confessed. "And it was my idea. I take full responsibility. Beth just came along because I forced her to."

"Uh-huh," he said.

"How much trouble am I in?"

"That depends," he said. "What did you take from Trudi's office?"

"Well, at the time, I thought it was just a stack of library books that I could put back on our pirate display," Lindsey said. She rose and crossed the room to the safe. "When I got back to the library, however, I found something else tucked into the books."

She opened the safe and pulled out the money bag with the map in it. She unzipped it and held it open for the chief to see inside.

"It's the map. I was on my way over to tell you, I swear, when Riordan showed up," she said.

The chief studied her face. "I believe you."

"I only touched a corner of it, so if there are any prints, they should be intact."

The chief smiled and shook his head. "You're a big fan of mysteries, aren't you?"

Lindsey hung her head in embarrassment. "It started with Nancy Drew when I was nine, then I moved on to Agatha Christie. Now I read them all, you know, Tess Gerritsen and Kathy Reichs, oh, and I've never missed an episode of *Masterpiece Mystery*."

"Maybe there's a twelve-step program for this sort of thing," the chief said. "I'm going to pretend you have a disorder and that it's not because you think I'm an incompetent boob."

She smiled. "I don't think that."

"But you did once," he said. Lindsey glanced down at the floor. The chief sighed and shook his head. "It's all right. I've been forced to do a lot of growing over the past two years. My sleepy little town where my biggest issue was a loud party on Saturday night has become a place of murder and mayhem."

"Sign of the times?" Lindsey asked.

"Maybe," he said. He took the money bag and rose from his seat. He hitched up his pants, securing them around his girth. "Between you and me, I think this dog is too old for these new tricks."

Lindsey didn't know what to say so she just nodded. It was disturbing that there had been so many murders in Briar Creek in the past year. If she had Chief Daniels's job, she didn't know if she'd want the responsibility of solving the crimes either.

"I'll need you to stop by the station and make a statement about finding the map, and I'd like your version of your conversation with Riordan."

Lindsey nodded.

"Chief Daniels, how long were you listening at the door?" she asked.

"We just caught the tail end," he said. "I was afraid you were pushing him too hard and he might harm you."

"Did you hear him say that Trudi was on the island with him?"

The chief's eyebrows shot up. "Maybe we could take that statement now."

Lindsey nodded and grabbed her purse from the lower-right-hand drawer of her desk.

As they left her office, they found the staff of the library huddled around the door.

"Are you all right?" Beth asked. "I saw Riordan in there with you and I just panicked and called the police."

"No, that was perfect," Lindsey said.

Beth looked relieved and then in a lower voice she asked, "Are we in trouble?"

"A little bit, but nothing serious," Lindsey assured her. "I'm just going to the station to give a statement about what Riordan said. I won't be gone long."

At this, the rest of the staff nodded and headed back to their stations. Ms. Cole was the last to leave, and when she did, she gave Lindsey a withering glance.

"She really doesn't like you, does she?" the chief asked as they headed out the main doors.

"Not even a little," Lindsey said.

Lindsey left the police station a couple of hours later. Riordan had not gone quietly into his cell. In fact, he had made so much noise that Milton had come flying out of his cell, clutching his toothbrush and looking alarmed.

Lindsey was reading over her statement and signing it when Riordan's attorney arrived. He was wearing a Rolex and carrying a Vuitton attaché case, both of which matched his charcoal Brooks Brothers suit. He glanced at Lindsey as he passed the interview room. She noticed he moved with the lithe grace of a shark, or maybe that was her imagination.

She signed her statement and handed it to Emma, who looked it over.

"I'll have the chief call you if he needs to see you again," she said.

"Thanks, Emma."

Lindsey was happy to let the doors of the station close behind her. She glanced out at the pier as she made her way back to the library. She noticed all of Sully's boats were out, and she felt a little disappointed. She would have liked to have told him about the day but didn't want to call him to tell him. She wanted to see his face when she told him that Trudi's killer had been caught.

A part of her couldn't believe that it was Riordan. To throw away all he had built and the opportunity to find Captain Kidd's treasure over a map that he hadn't even authenticated.

She glanced out over the bay, trying to imagine what this cove had looked like during Captain Kidd's time. Had he really buried treasure here? With so many islands to choose from, it didn't seem out of the realm of possibility.

Now with the map being logged in as evidence in a murder case, would anyone ever find the treasure or would it remain buried just as it had been left three hundred and thirteen years ago? A strong gust of wind tugged at the hem of her skirt and pulled a thick strand of hair out of the knot she had wound it in. Lindsey took a deep breath of the salty air.

It seemed the oppressive humidity was being swept away. Now that Trudi's killer had been caught, maybe things could get back to normal, or so she hoped.

"Something isn't sitting right with me about this," Lindsey said to Sully over breakfast. Two days had passed since Riordan had been arrested.

They were eating on the patio outside the Blue Anchor, which overlooked the islands and the bay. A seagull was perched on the railing near Lindsey, and he cocked his head to the side as if to slyly determine whether she was done with her toast and if she might throw some his way.

Ever the sucker, Lindsey ripped off some of her crust and flung it out over the water. With a happy cry, the seagull dove after it, snatching it before it hit the surf.

"What do you mean?" Sully asked. He put aside the paper and took a fortifying sip of his coffee.

"Murder isn't neat and tidy," she said.

"No," he agreed. He watched her as if he had all the time in the world for her to gather her thoughts. She loved that about him. There was that silly *L* word again. She felt her face grow warm as if Sully could read her thoughts. With a shake of her head, she forced her attention back to the topic.

"Trudi taking Riordan's map and Riordan killing her," she said. "It appears neat and tidy but then it isn't. It's sort of like when you go visit someone and their front room is immaculate, but then the rest of the doors in their house are shut. You know it's because those other rooms are a disaster."

Sully grinned at her.

"What?" she asked.

"I love the way your mind works," he said.

Lindsey felt trapped in his blue gaze and it was exhilarating like a sailboat catching a strong breeze and flying across the surface of the sea.

"Thanks," she said. Her voice was rough and she swallowed hard.

"Charlie and the Norrgard brothers have been given permission to return to the island and retrieve their things," he said. "I'm taking them this morning. Do you want to come out there with us?"

Lindsey was covering the night shift for Jessica and was going into work late. She had the time to go out to the island but she wondered why Sully had invited her.

"Do you think I should?" she asked.

He gave her an understanding look. "You've been very preoccupied since Riordan was arrested. Maybe going out there will give you some closure."

"Maybe," she agreed.

She wondered if she really wanted to revisit the scene of Trudi's death. It seemed so gruesome and grisly, and yet it bothered her that there was something too convenient about Riordan being the killer—not that she didn't think he couldn't have done it.

She'd seen his temper. There was a ruthlessness within him that made her think he was a perfect treasure hunter because he was very much like a pirate. That being said, she couldn't reconcile that he would have killed Trudi without getting what he wanted from her first.

"All right, count me in," she said.

The Swedish brothers were like having two towers in the back of the water taxi. Lindsey sat between them while Charlie sat up front with Sully. She hadn't had much of a chance to get to know them over the past few weeks, so she tried to break the ice by asking where they were from in Sweden.

Steig, or maybe it was Stefan, answered for both of them. His deep voice was melodic as he said, "Gothenburg."

"A port city," she said.

The other brother smiled and said, "Very good. Most people have only heard of Stockholm."

"One of your American lovelies actually asked if we had indoor plumbing," he said.

"No," Lindsey said, feeling embarrassed on behalf of her country.

The brothers laughed. "We told her we didn't."

Lindsey laughed, too. She could see why the two of them had managed to charm every single girl in Briar Creek with their brilliant smiles and terrific humor.

"Your library carries a nice number of Swedish authors," Stefan, or maybe it was Steig, said. "Mankell, Larsson, Sjöwall and Wahlöö."

"I've always been a fan of Nordic mysteries. *The Laughing Policeman* was one of the first Swedish books I ever read. I loved it."

The brother on her right nodded. "It's a classic."

They were silent for a moment as the small boat bounced over the waves that would lead them to Ruby Island.

Lindsey had to raise her voice to be heard over the wind. "How long have you two worked for Riordan?"

"What is it now, Stefan, almost five years?" Steig asked. "We signed on when he was just starting up his salvage company. He needed divers and we needed work."

"Sounds like a good match," Lindsey said.

"It was until now," Stefan, who was on her right, said.

Lindsey hesitated then she asked anyway. "Do you think he killed Trudi Hargrave?"

The brothers exchanged a look over her head and Lindsey wondered if she'd gone too far and was no better than the dim-witted girl who'd asked if they had indoor plumbing.

"Honestly?" Stefan asked. "I don't know."

"Nor do I," Steig said.

They both looked away out across the water as if they were shamed by a gross betrayal.

"I'm sorry," Lindsey said. "That was rude of me to ask and put you on the spot like that."

"It's nothing we haven't asked ourselves," Steig said. "You just said it out loud."

Sully cut the engine and the brothers rose to their feet, preparing to leap from the boat onto the rickety dock. Lindsey grabbed a handrail to steady herself as she braced for the boat to stop. Sully slid the boat into place without even a bump.

"Nice," Charlie said.

Sully gave him a small nod.

Stefan hopped out first and tied off the boat. One by one they clambered out. Sully turned and gave Lindsey a hand out and she was grateful. Now that they were here, she was nervous about returning to the scene of Trudi's murder. A quick glance at Charlie confirmed that he was feeling the same.

His pasty skin was paler than usual and he was staring up at the rocky slope as if trying to find the will to climb.

"All right, Charlie?" Sully asked.

Charlie gave a stiff nod and began to follow the brothers up the slope.

"You can wait here if you want," Sully said, giving Lindsey a concerned look.

"No, in for a penny, in for a pound," she said.

He nodded in understanding and together they made their way up to the excavation site.

As soon as she saw the scaffolding, Lindsey started to have flashbacks. Remembering Trudi's body coming up out of the ground made her flinch, and Sully took her hand in his and gave it a squeeze of reassurance. Lindsey squeezed back.

The brothers and Charlie were all standing near the hole. Lindsey wondered if they were having a moment of silence because of the tragedy, but no, when she and Sully joined them, Charlie whipped around and looked at Sully with a frown.

"Someone's been here and they've been digging."

"I'm sure it was just the police during their investigation," Sully said. "They would have had to examine where her body was found."

"No." Steig shook his head. "This isn't the digging of evidence. It looks as if someone's been trying to fill the hole."

"What?" Sully and Lindsey said together as they stepped forward to look down into the pit.

Stefan gestured to where there had been a pile of dirt and rock they had been digging out in the course of their treasure hunt. There was nothing left of it. Charlie found one of the Maglites they had used when lifting Trudi's body out. Sure enough, the pit was nowhere near as deep as it had been.

"Could Chief Daniels have done this as a safety measure?" Lindsey asked.

"I suppose, but I can't see him tampering with anything that might have been considered evidence," Sully said. "By pouring dirt in over where the body was found, well, that could damage the investigation."

The others were silent and Lindsey knew they were thinking the same thing she was. That someone didn't want the excavation to continue. Since Riordan was in jail, it wasn't him. Lindsey didn't want to think about the person most likely to try to stop their work, but there it was. Milton.

It was a somber group that packed up their belongings and tools. The only thing left behind was the scaffold and the winch because they were too big to fit in the water taxi. They would take a while to disassemble and they would need a bigger boat to get them to shore with.

On the ride back to the pier, Lindsey sat up front with Sully.

"Do you know when the police finished up with the island?" she asked.

"Sometime yesterday," he said. "Charlie and the brothers were given permission to go back to get their things yesterday evening."

"So if it wasn't the police who filled in the pit, then whoever did it had to have done it last night," she said. "I don't see Milton going out there in the middle of the night, do you?"

"No, and I don't see someone doing that just to stop an excavation. It had to be someone who is trying to hide something," Sully said.

"Like Trudi's murderer?" she asked.

"Yes." Sully's tone was grim.

"Riordan is still in jail," she said. "That rules him out."

"Unless he isn't working alone," he said.

"They had to know that someone would have noticed," she said.

"Maybe they don't care."

Lindsey turned this over in her mind, but she couldn't make any sense of it.

Once they had docked, she still had a half hour until she was to be at work. She decided to stop by Milton's house on her way to the library just to see how he was doing. Okay, yeah, and to see where he was last night.

She knew he had vacated the jail once Riordan had taken up residence, but she hadn't seen him at the library and she wondered if he was keeping a low profile at home until the furor died down.

She gave Sully a quick hug, but when she would have hurried off, he held her back. He brushed a long curly strand of hair away from her face and his gaze ran over her features as if to reassure himself that there was no harm done from their trip to the island.

"Did it help?" he asked.

"In some ways," she said. "In others, not so much."

"You're going to check on Milton's alibi, aren't you?"

Lindsey frowned at him. "Exactly when did you get to know me so well?"

"Must have been during all those months that I was pining for you to notice me," he said.

Lindsey saw the honesty and the humor in his gaze, and

she wondered what she had done to deserve such a good man. Sheer force of will made her pull her gaze away.

"What we found out there is worrisome. Be careful," he said. He kissed the top of her head and added, "Call me."

"I will on both counts," she agreed. She left the pier, trying to remember if she had ever known a man like Mike Sullivan before, a man who accepted her for exactly who she was and seemed to like her anyway.

Milton lived in the oldest house in Briar Creek. It sat on the bay just past the center of town. Lindsey was pleased to see that there wasn't a gaggle of admirers parked out on his lawn. Now that he'd been freed from jail, it appeared they had given up their protest on his behalf. Thank goodness. She didn't want to have a smack down just to ask him a few questions.

She knocked on his door, and after a moment, it swung wide and there was Milton in his usual track suit. He looked tired but otherwise fine.

"Lindsey," he said. "This is a surprise."

"Sorry to intrude without calling first," she said.

"Not at all," he said. "Come in."

"Actually, I can't stay as I have to get to work, but Milton, I need to ask you a question," she said.

"It sounds serious," he said.

He stroked his silver goatee and then crossed his arms over his chest as if bracing himself for a blow or an insult of some sort. Lindsey thought about not saying anything but reasoned that if it wasn't her asking, it would be Chief

Daniels. She might as well prepare him for what was coming.

"I went out to the island with Charlie and the brothers to gather their things."

Milton uncrossed his arms and gave her a sympathetic look. "That had to be hard. I'm sorry, Lindsey. I hope it doesn't need to be said, but I'll say it anyway. Although Trudi and I had our differences, I certainly wished her no harm."

"Oh, Milton, I know that," Lindsey said. "You're the most peaceful person I know, but—"

"*But*s are never good," Milton said with a raised eyebrow.

Lindsey laughed in surprise but then grew serious.

"Milton, someone was out on the island last night, and it looks like they were tampering with the excavation site."

"What do you mean?" he asked. He looked bewildered. Lindsey knew Milton was too much of a straight shooter to feign surprise.

"I mean someone is filling in the site, and I think it's either to hide evidence or to stop the excavation," she said.

"Well, the crime scene investigators are done, aren't they?" he asked.

"Yes, so the hiding of evidence seems unlikely," she said.

"Which means it's someone who wants to stop the excavation, which means you're thinking of me," Milton said. His electric green eyes dimmed with hurt. Lindsey instantly felt regret. How could she accuse an eighty-two-year-old man of sneaking out onto an island in the middle of the night and tampering with an excavation site? She was an idiot.

"I'm sorry, Milton. Of course, the idea that you had anything to do with it is simply ridiculous." Impulsively, she hugged him.

Surprised, he patted her back awkwardly. Then he laughed. When Lindsey pulled back, she was relieved to see the sparkle back in his eyes.

"I know you had nothing to do with it," she said. "But maybe you know someone who might have?"

"What do you mean?" he asked.

"Well, you do have a pretty rabid fan base," she said.

To her surprise, Milton's face flushed bright red and he cleared his throat.

"Maybe if you put the word out to your groupies . . ."

He sighed but she ignored him.

"It's a network," she said. "Let's use it."

"I'll do my best," he said. "But I can't make any promises. Usually the most I get out of my 'groupies' is a hot dish."

Lindsey gave him a wide-eyed look and he chuckled.

"I meant a casserole."

"Oh," Lindsey said with a snort.

Milton stroked his goatee. "There are a few, however . . ." His voice trailed off and Lindsey knew he was thinking of his more zealous admirers.

"Thanks, Milton," she said. "Maybe we'll get lucky and find out it was just a big misunderstanding."

"Maybe," he said.

But Lindsey could tell that neither of them believed it.

* * *

When Lindsey closed the library that night and walked around the building to the bike rack, she found Sully standing beside his truck, waiting for her.

"Is there any news?" she asked when he enfolded her in a hug.

"No. Riordan denied any knowledge of anyone being on the island while he's been in jail," Sully said.

"Do you believe him?"

"Given that he can't even scratch an itch without an officer seeing him right now, yeah, I believe him," Sully said.

"Is he still claiming that he's innocent of murder?" she asked.

"Yep," Sully said. "He says the last time he saw Trudi, she was alive."

Lindsey stepped back to study his face. The sun was just beginning to set, and the reddish hue that lit the sky brought out the red in Sully's mahogany curls. She wondered if he found this whole situation as perplexing as she did.

"What if she was alive?" Lindsey asked. "What if there is someone out there who wants the treasure hunting stopped so badly that they're risking exposure by filling in the excavation site?"

"But why?"

"To hide the evidence that they are the real murderer?" she asked.

"Do you really think Riordan is innocent and that someone else killed Trudi?"

"I don't know, but someone else was on that island last

night. Maybe when Riordan left to get the first aid kit, the real murderer demanded the map from Trudi. When she refused to give it up, they threw her into the well," Lindsey said. "Maybe Riordan was telling the truth."

"He still hit a woman," Sully said. "He should do time for that alone."

"Agreed," Lindsey said. "But what if he didn't kill her?"

"Then there's still a murderer out there," he said.

"But who?"

"Peter Ruby," he said.

Lindsey looked at him. She knew he wasn't just throwing the idea out there. He had been thinking about this ever since they'd been on the island the first time and found Trudi.

"Do you really think it could be him?" she asked.

"They never found his body," Sully said. "If he discovered there might be treasure on his island, don't you think he'd want to come back and claim what is his?"

Lindsey glanced away from him to the cemetery on the opposite side of the library. She knew the Ruby family had a plot there and she knew that the mother and two children were buried there. Could it be true? Could Peter Ruby be back?

"How can we find out?" she asked.

Sully gestured to the back of his pickup truck. "Care for a dive?"

Lindsey glanced over the side—fins and wet suits. She could easily think of five million other things she'd rather do than swim at night. She had never mentioned to Sully that she had an irrational, or in her mind quite rational, fear of water over her head as well as water that she couldn't see in.

She felt her insides spasm as she asked, "At night?"

"It's the best way," he said. "We can park the boat out in the water and sneak onto the island. If Ruby is out there, he will never see us coming."

"Shouldn't Chief Daniels and his officers be in charge of this?"

"Charlie and I tried to mention the possibility to him, but he's resisting," Sully said. "I can't really blame him. I'm really hoping that I'm wrong."

"Can I ask you something?"

"Sure."

"Why is this so important to you?" He gave her a sideways glance as if unsure of her meaning. "I mean, why do you care if Ruby is back?"

Sully was silent for a moment. Lindsey didn't press. She knew he would tell her when he was ready.

"Kevin Ruby was my best friend," he said. "He was a funny, freckled kid with big ears and he knew everything about the sea. Crazy facts like the heart of a blue whale is the size of a compact car or the United States could fit into the Pacific Ocean eighteen point two times. He taught me to love the ocean and he was a big part of the reason I became a sailor."

Sully turned and glanced over the bay. It was bathed in the purple hue of twilight, and the islands were barely visible against the horizon.

"His sister, Kayla, was shy and quiet. She and Mary were always together. She was good at tempering Mary's impulsive nature, and Mary taught Kayla to take some risks." He paused. "I can't explain it, but I think there's more to what's happening on Ruby Island than Captain Kidd's treasure. I feel like I owe it to them to find out the truth. Does that make sense?"

"Yes, it does," she said. She squeezed his arm. "Let's go."

"Are you sure?" he asked. "You know, I'm fine going by myself. I just figured you'd never forgive me if I didn't give you the choice to go."

The clucking chicken in her was ecstatic to bow out, but Lindsey looked at him and then at the equipment. She gave herself a mental face slap. She was being silly. This was Sully. She knew she would be perfectly safe with him.

"No, I'm good," she said. "Let's do it."

The water was black. Lindsey felt her insides quiver at the thought of willingly sliding into the murky depths. She must be out of her mind. Sully had anchored the boat beside a nearby island, which meant they were going to have to swim a far stretch just to get to the island.

The wet suits would keep them warm, and the fins would give them some speed. She could do this. Sully slipped into the water with hardly a splash. Lindsey took a deep breath and realized that following this man into the water was a bigger leap of faith than she'd ever taken with any man. He held out a hand to her, and without hesitation, she followed.

The shock of the cold made her gasp and a wave caught her on the chin, sending a small spray of salty water into her mouth. She spat and tried to acclimate to the cold.

"Are you all right?" Sully asked.

She could feel his hand on her waist, steadying her, and she nodded.

"I'm good."

"If you get into trouble, call me," he said.

"What if someone hears me?"

"I don't care if anyone hears you. You're more important."

His curls were slick against his head, and Lindsey could just see his shape in the darkness. Still she smiled. He was one of a kind.

"Let's go," she said.

With Sully in the lead, they made their way toward Ruby Island. They had timed it so that they could approach the rocky side of the island at low tide and slip ashore from a side where they wouldn't be expected.

Following in Sully's quiet wake, Lindsey could feel her panic begin to rise. She felt something brush her leg and it was all she could do to bite back the scream, knowing full well it was probably seaweed.

She knew they were supposed to ease their way to the island and not draw attention to themselves, but the cold black that surrounded her terrified her, and she felt herself pick up the pace until she was practically on top of Sully. He turned and treaded water, catching her around the middle.

"All right, Lindsey?"

"Panicking," she admitted. She clutched his shoulders. She would have climbed on top of him if she could have.

She thought it spoke well of her that she didn't have a stranglehold around his neck.

"I'm here," he said. "I won't let anything hurt you."

Lindsey sank a bit in the water. Man, she hated being such a wimp.

"Why didn't you tell me?" he asked.

"I thought I could handle it," she said. The disappointment she felt in herself tasted bitter.

"Come here," he said. He pulled her up alongside him. "Swim right beside me."

Lindsey let him guide her until she was tucked into his side and together they managed an awkward side stroke. They moved slowly but her panic ebbed as she was completely enfolded by him and felt completely safe.

In no time at all they were nearing the rocks. The waves pushed them into the partially submerged boulders, and Lindsey let go of Sully and grabbed on to a sharp edge covered in the bubble-shaped seaweed called rockweed. It was slippery under her fingers, but she was so relieved to be on shore she didn't care. Sully hauled himself up beside her and they carefully scrambled over the boulders until they reached the grassy surface of the island.

"Nicely done," he said.

"I couldn't have done it without you," she said.

Sully reached out to pull a strand of sea grass out of her hair and brushed the sodden mess that was her hair off her face. Then he kissed her.

It was salty and tenderly sweet and made Lindsey wish she could just melt right into his wet suit with him. He pulled away to take off his flippers so she slipped off hers and put them next to his.

They clasped hands and made their way through the trees at the edge of the slope toward the site of the excavation. The cadence of the waves hitting the shore and the whisper of the night breeze were the only sounds to be heard. Well, that and her thumping heart.

"I hear something," Sully whispered.

His voice was just a breath in her ear. She tightened her grip on his fingers so that he knew she heard him.

They stole up to the edge of the trees. The same trees she'd imagined Captain Kidd striding out of just days before while she'd sat next to the still body of Trudi Hargrave. A shiver coursed through her.

The moon was a bright crescent and it shone down on the aluminum scaffolding, making it gleam. Lindsey stared hard, looking for movement. There was nothing except for a noise that sounded out of place in the peaceful island. Like the sound of metal scraping against a rock.

A head popped out of the hole of the excavation site. Startled, Lindsey jumped. Sully pulled her closer into the shadow of the trees.

They observed as a man with a slight build pulled himself up out of the hole. As they watched, he began to walk away from them toward the dock on the opposite side of the island. He was unraveling a spool of something as he went. He disappeared out of sight and Lindsey looked at Sully.

"Did you recognize him?" she asked

"No, did you?"

"No. What do we do now?"

"I'm going closer," he said. "You stay here."

Lindsey knew that despite his larger size, Sully could move much more silently and gracefully than she could. She leaned against the rough bark of the tree trunk while he crept closer to the excavation site.

She stared at the spot where the man had disappeared, hoping he didn't come back and catch Sully. Sully had reached the pit and was examining whatever the man had been doing. Silently, she willed him to hurry.

Her heart was hammering in her chest and she could feel her palms itch with sweat. She tapped her bare foot in the grass.

Abruptly, Sully shot up from the hole. He ran toward her in a full-on sprint and yelled, "Lindsey, run!"

Too stunned to move, she gaped at him. He was halfway to her when an ear-deafening explosion sounded, knocking her off her feet. Her last glimpse of Sully was of him making a leap for the safety of the trees.

She hit the ground hard on her back, knocking the air out of her lungs like a punch to the gut. Sucking in shallow breaths, Lindsey lifted her head. Fire shot out of the pit, igniting the trees in the surrounding area. She was mesmerized by the sight of the flames until the breeze brought the searing heat toward her. Like a slap, it shook her out of her stupor.

She rolled to her side and rose up onto her knees. She had to find Sully. She crawled across the ground. The light from the flames illuminated the crumpled form of a man just twenty feet away.

"Sully, are you all right?" she cried.

He was facedown and nonresponsive. Carefully, she ran her hands over his skull but she felt no gashes or bleeding.

An acrid smell assaulted her nose and she saw that the back of his wet suit had been burned and looked to be seared to his skin. She knelt down close to him and called his name again. This time his eyes blinked open. He looked as dazed and disoriented as she felt.

"Sully, we have to get out of here," she said. The heat from the flames was growing stronger. "Can you move?"

He rose up slowly as if making sure that he could.

"Are you all right?" he asked.

"Yeah," she said. "What happened?"

"Explosives," he said. "Whoever that was, he's trying to shut down the excavation for good."

"But why?" she cried.

A tree cracked from the heat of the fire and they both jumped. Sully rose to his feet and pulled Lindsey up with him.

"Get to the rocks," he said. "I'll meet you there."

"Where are you going?" she asked.

"I'm going to check out the dock and see if he's still there," he said.

"No, don't," she said. "It's not worth the risk."

"I have to. I have to know if it's him," he said. He turned her around and pushed her in the direction that they'd come. "I'll meet you. Now go."

Lindsey ran a few feet. Then she stopped and swiveled to watch him. She wanted to make sure he was okay.

Sully dodged around bits of flame as he made his way to the rocky slope that led to the rickety dock below. The fire was getting worse, leaping from tree to tree. If he didn't turn back soon, he wasn't going to make it at all.

A tree fell down with a roar of flame, blocking Sully's way back. Lindsey yelled. Surely, he would jump in on the far side of the island and swim around. But what if the person who started the fire was still over there and saw him?

Lindsey hopped up and down on her bare feet. She didn't know what to do and she was terrified by what might happen to him. It hit her like a tree bursting into flame how much she cared about Mike Sullivan.

Damn it. She couldn't stand not knowing. She scurried a bit forward trying to get a better view. A dark shadow was making its way toward her. She held her breath. It couldn't be the person who'd set the island on fire. No, she recognized the broad frame. It was Sully. Relief almost took her out at the knees.

"Lindsey, look out!" he shouted.

She glanced behind her and saw another wall of flame as the island's dry grass caught like tinder for a bonfire.

"Come on!" He grabbed her hand and together they ran.

Lindsey felt smoke burn her throat as she gulped in a breath. They weaved their way through the trees, trying to get back to the place where they had left their flippers.

It was no use. The fire was ripping through the island like lightning shooting across the sky. There was no escaping the lick of the flames. Lindsey could feel the fingers of the fire reaching out to grab and burn her in its searing embrace.

"We can't outrun it!" Sully cried. "Hold your breath!"

In one swift motion, he hefted Lindsey into his arms and tossed her out toward the black waves. Lindsey just had time to gasp in a breath of air before she hit the cold water with a full-body slap. She plunged below the surface, feeling the forest of seaweed around her grabbing at her limbs as if it would hold her under.

She kicked upward and broke the surface just in time to see Sully engulfed in flames make a running dive into the water beside her.

Panic thrummed through her. This time it wasn't fear of the water. It was terror that Sully had been burned. She struck out toward where she'd seen him hit. He wasn't coming up. She took a deep breath and dove.

The narrow moon above was no use in illuminating the darkness of the water. Her hands grasped all around her but came up empty. She popped up, took a huge breath and dove back down.

She could feel the pull of the water. She followed it, hoping it was pulling Sully, too, and she'd be able to find him. She kicked hard. Then her hand brushed something soft. Hair. Sully's mahogany curls.

Her lungs burned but she pushed forward until her fingers found his shoulders. She clutched at his wet suit until she could wrap her hands around his chest. She pushed upward, letting the water buoy them to the surface.

She sucked in a huge gulp of air as soon as she broke the surface. Sully was dead weight in her arms, but she maneuvered his head up onto her shoulder, trying to get him to breathe. She didn't know how long she could hold him.

By the blaze of the fire behind her, she knew she wasn't far from the rocky edge of the island. Her fingers were stiff with the cold but she clutched Sully as she half swam, half let the waves push her toward the rocks. Finally she bumped one with her shin. She got her feet onto its smooth top. The water was at her shoulders, so she could brace Sully against her and keep both of their heads up.

"Sully, come on, don't leave me," she whispered. She noticed her teeth were chattering but she didn't know if it was shock, fear or the cold water that seemed to have penetrated her wet suit. She held him around the middle, rocking with the waves so as not to get knocked off her feet. She knew the tide would go out eventually. With any luck, they'd find themselves on the rock in the morning when someone came looking for them.

She didn't know how long she stood there, feeling Sully's breath against her cheek, her only reassurance that he might be okay, when a light swept over the water.

It was a searchlight. It swept back and forth across the dark depths. Lindsey wanted to wave an arm or cry out, but her voice came out as little more than a croak and she couldn't risk letting go of Sully. She wanted to sob with frustration but it was no use. She watched as the boat moved away.

Exhaustion slapped her, buckling her knees, as the adrenaline that had kept her going ebbed, leached away by the cold water that rocked her in its chilly embrace.

She pressed her face against Sully's. His damp cold cheek gave her purpose, and she took a deep breath. She would not let go, she would not sink, and she would not fail.

The soft drone of an engine was like the insistent buzz of a mosquito. Hope flared within her, higher than the flames of the island behind her. She glanced up to see a boat coming her way. For one second, she was afraid it might be the arsonist coming back to check on his handiwork, but no.

The shiny, bald dome of the driver was unmistakably Ian Murphy. He maneuvered the boat to within feet of her and cut the engine. Another man, with scraggly black rock and roll hair, jumped into the water. Charlie!

In moments, he was beside her, helping to support Sully. As one, they lifted him and handed him off to Ian. Then Charlie was lifting Lindsey into the back of the boat, where Ian wrapped her in a towel.

Lindsey collapsed onto the floor of the boat beside the bench where Sully lay on his side. Charlie draped a blanket over him while Ian checked his vitals.

"He's breathing," Ian said. His voice was gruff with relief. "Nasty knot on his head, though, and his wet suit is scorched. It looks like he's been burnt through to the skin. We need to get him to a hospital."

"Please, hurry," Lindsey said.

Ian gave her a quick nod and then fired up the boat's motor. They went rocketing back to the shore while the island burned behind them.

Lindsey slept in a chair beside Sully's hospital bed.

He was being monitored for a concussion and some bad burns on his back. The doctors wanted to keep him under observation. Lindsey felt the same way and was determined not to let him out of her sight.

She had told Chief Daniels and Officer Plewicki everything that had happened. The chief had not been thrilled that Sully and Lindsey had gone out to the island, but he said little about it, obviously deciding that what was done was done.

Lindsey shifted her cramped position in the hard chair she'd slept in and her blanket fell off. She reached to get it when she realized someone was sitting at Sully's bedside. She jumped to her feet as if to protect him from harm, but she recognized the two gray-haired people immediately and put on the air brakes.

Too late. Her momentum caused her to bang into the bed, and the man and the woman turned to look at her. It was Mr. and Mrs. Sullivan, Sully's parents.

"Lindsey," Mrs. Sullivan said as she rose from her seat on the edge of the bed. She came around the end and held out her arms, hugging Lindsey close. "I am so glad you're all right."

"I'm sorry, we shouldn't have—I'll never forgive myself if—" Lindsey's words tumbled over themselves in their rush to get out.

"It's all right, dear," Mrs. Sullivan soothed her. She held her out at arm's length and met Lindsey's eyes. "Sully is a grown man. If he decided to go out to that island, there was not much you could do to stop him."

Mr. Sullivan joined their group and put his arm around his wife. "She's right. We know how Sully felt about that island. What happened to the Ruby kids never sat right with him. I'm not surprised he wanted to investigate. I'm just glad you're all right and he's going to be okay, too."

"Is he?" Lindsey asked.

"Yes, the doctor was here an hour ago, and said he expects that Sully will make a full recovery," Mrs. Sullivan said. Her voice was light with relief.

"Did he wake up then?" Lindsey asked.

"Yes, for a minute," Mr. Sullivan said. "First thing he did was ask for you, but he wouldn't let us wake you."

Lindsey felt as if a concrete block had just dropped off her shoulders. She had been so worried. It was then that she glanced down and realized she was still wearing her wet suit.

Mrs. Sullivan gave her a small smile. "I think it would be all right if you went home and changed. I can watch over him, and I'll call you if he even flutters an eyelash."

The door to Sully's room swung open and there stood Mary, Beth, Nancy, Violet and Charlene. As one, they tiptoed into the room.

"How's he doing, Mom?" Mary asked as she hugged her parents.

"He's going to have a thumper of a headache, but there's no sign of any permanent damage."

"Good," Mary said. She approached her brother's bed and leaned over to place a soft kiss on his head.

Lindsey wondered if Mary would be angry with her for the state her brother was in. She wanted to say something to her to apologize for what had happened. She swallowed and forced the words out around the lump in her throat.

"Mary, I—" she began but Mary cut her off.

"Don't bother," she said.

Lindsey sucked in a breath. Mary was angry. She couldn't blame her. If something like this had happened to her brother, Jack, Lindsey would be livid.

Mary moved to stand in front of her. She took Lindsey's hands in hers and said, "He's going to be all right, because you were there to save him. If you hadn't been, well, I can't even think about it."

She pulled Lindsey close and hugged her tight.

"You mean you're not mad?" Lindsey asked, hugging her back.

"Lindsey, you saved his life," Mary said. "Ian told me how you held him up and kept him safe. I can never thank you enough."

"We feel the same way," his mother said.

Lindsey felt like crying. She knew it was exhaustion and relief and the fact that she was still wearing her wet suit, but still the knot in her throat burned like a lump of burning coal.

"Come here," Beth said. "I brought a change of clothes for you. Let's get you home so you can rest."

Lindsey nodded. She moved to the side of the bed and kissed the top of Sully's head. She felt him lean into her and she rested her cheek on his head.

"I'll be back later," she said. "I promise."

She glanced up to see if anyone was listening, but they were all looking away, intently studying the chart with the smiley faces used by the patients to describe the level of pain they were feeling, one being a happy face and ten looking like the circular head was about to explode. Lindsey was pretty sure she was hovering at a seven.

With everyone turned away, she took the opportunity to whisper, "Get some rest, Sully, I . . . I love you."

She kissed his curls one more time and quickly hopped off the bed. Even though he was unconscious, she couldn't help feeling she was taking a huge emotional risk by telling him how she felt.

She stopped by Mary on the way out. "You'll call me."

"Absolutely," she promised.

Lindsey nodded and let the rest of her crafternoon buddies take her home.

* * *

Lindsey slept for eight hours with Heathcliff burrowed into her side. When she woke up, it was early evening. She reached for her cell phone. There were three texts from Mary, status updates on Sully, all of which were good.

She crawled out of bed and took a hot shower. She hadn't had the energy to do it earlier. She felt as if she was washing off salt water, soot and smoke all at the same time.

She dressed in jeans and sneakers and a T-shirt. Her first thought was to get back to the hospital to visit Sully. Unfortunately, she didn't own a car. She supposed she could borrow Nancy's, but judging by the time, even if she left right now, she'd have only a few minutes with him before visiting hours were over.

Heathcliff needed to go out, so she wound her way down the stairs with him at her side. It was as if he was afraid to let her get too far away from him. She reached down and rubbed his ears. He was her fuzzy little barnacle.

Once in the yard, she had to encourage him to go do his business. Finally, he trotted off, leaving her to think about the events of the past twenty-four hours.

The thought that she and Sully could have wound up as people crisps made her shake a bit in her shoes. Her gaze moved over the bay to Ruby Island. Violet and Nancy had told her that the fire had been put out, and that it had definitely been arson. No surprise there.

An inspector with the fire department was said to be conducting an investigation. Lindsey wondered if they would find evidence of who had done this and why.

That's what she couldn't figure out. Why had someone tried to raze the island? Did they not want Captain Kidd's treasure found? Why not? More important, who had done it? Was it Peter Ruby? Had he returned? If so, how had he gotten out to the island? He had to have had a boat.

Heathcliff finished his patrol of the yard and came trotting back to her side. Lindsey turned to head back to the house when the front door opened and Nancy came outside.

"Are you feeling better?" she asked. She crossed the yard and stood beside Lindsey, studying her as if she expected her to fall over.

"I'm fine," Lindsey said. "I was hoping to go and see Sully, but I'm afraid I've missed visiting hours."

"He'll understand," Nancy said. "After a night like that, you needed your rest."

"I suppose," Lindsey said. She couldn't help the restlessness that was snapping inside her. She was worried about Sully, she felt bad about the island and she was afraid of whoever had set the blaze. She knew she was missing something, but for the life of her, she couldn't think what it was.

"Lindsey!" a voice called from the street.

She glanced up to see John, making his way toward her.

"Are you all right?" he asked. He stopped in front of her and studied her face. "I heard about what happened. You could have been killed."

"I'm fine," she said. "But thanks for the concern."

"Concern?" he asked. "Where's that boyfriend of yours? I have a few words for him, too. How could he put you in danger like that?"

"Sully didn't put me in danger," Lindsey said. "We just went out to look around. We had no idea something like this would happen."

John still looked grumpy.

"John, Sully saved my life," she said. "He's still in the hospital. I don't want to hear any words against him."

John heaved out a breath. "Fine, but that doesn't mean I won't think them."

Lindsey rolled her eyes. She supposed, were the situation reversed, she would feel the same.

"Can I get either of you a glass of sweet tea or lemonade?" Nancy asked.

"None for me, thanks," Lindsey said.

"Me either," John said. "But I appreciate the offer."

A buzzer sounded from the house and Nancy said, "Oh, that'll be my almond cookies. Excuse me."

Both John and Lindsey nodded. As she watched Nancy hurry into the house, Lindsey marveled at the other woman's hostess skills. No matter what was happening, even during last winter's blizzard, she always had refreshments on hand. It was a gift, truly.

Lindsey thought about her own barren refrigerator and pantry and shook her head. After living next door to Nancy for over a year, she would have thought she'd have improved but no. Unless a visitor wanted Cheez-Its or Snausages, they were out of luck in Lindsey's apartment.

"Nice lady," John said.

"The best," Lindsey agreed.

An awkward silence fell between them. Heathcliff was sitting on her feet and Lindsey reached down to scratch his ears. She glanced back at John, who showed no sign of leaving.

"Well, I guess I'd better . . ." Her voice trailed off and she hoped he picked up her meaning that it was time for him to go.

He looked at her with an expression akin to Heathcliff's when he wanted something.

"What?" she asked.

"Well, we never did get to have that conversation about us," John said. "So how about I buy you dinner?"

Lindsey looked at him and tipped her head to the side. When they'd been together, she'd been aware that John was mostly about John. But given that she'd just escaped a lunatic with her life, she found it hard to believe that he would think she was up for relationship talk now.

Then she realized that John wasn't going to be able to move on until they had the big talk and that the best thing she could do for him, for them both, was to let him say what he had to say.

"All right," she said. "I can't do dinner, because I have some errands to run, but if you want to come with me, we can talk on the way."

He looked like he might argue and lobby harder for dinner, but Lindsey must have looked determined because he gave a quick nod and asked, "Okay, where to first?"

"The boatyard," she said.

"How about I drive?" he offered.

"Even better," she said.

John went to get his car while Lindsey took Heathcliff inside and grabbed her purse.

Nancy met her in the foyer and offered to watch Heathcliff while she was gone. Lindsey gratefully took her up on her offer. Nancy gave her a concerned look, but she did not explain where she was going or why.

How could she tell her that she was going to the boatyard to see if they had rented a boat out to anyone yesterday? It was the ultimate in not minding her own business, and she really didn't want to be lectured right now.

John pulled up in his Prius and Lindsey slid into the passenger seat. He drove through town following her directions to the boatyard nestled on the far side of the bay.

To Lindsey's surprise, John didn't talk on the ride over. She had really thought he'd start right in about them and why they should try again and how it would be different. She had even expected him to use the added leverage of how Briar Creek was obviously too dangerous a place to live, but he said nothing.

This was fine with Lindsey as she was too preoccupied with how she was going to ask to see the records at the boat office to converse about anything.

John slid into a parking spot and Lindsey hopped out of the car, not waiting for him to come around and let her out.

The boatyard was huge. The summer residents who were gone all winter housed their boats here, and the place did a booming business getting boats ready for summer and storing them for winter.

Lindsey saw several large vessels up in the air on what looked like giant cradles, while their undersides were being refinished for the boating season, which was just getting under way.

The office was built into a corner of the warehouse and she headed for it. John walked beside her, still not speaking.

The glass door opened into a small cramped office. A narrow counter separated a tiny waiting room from the receptionist. A very tan and very blond young woman was working behind the counter. She looked to be about eighteen. She was on the phone but smiled at Lindsey and John in greeting.

While she finished her call, Lindsey glanced at the calendar on the wall. It featured glossy pictures of boats.

"I always thought I'd like a boat," John said.

"Really?" Lindsey asked.

"Sure, why not?" he said.

Lindsey wondered if he was saying that just because Sully owned boats and he was trying to compete or if there really was a part of him that would like a boat. She could see him in leather Top-Siders and a cheesy cloth captain's hat with an anchor embroidered on it. The image made her smile.

"Why not, indeed," she said.

"Hi, sorry about that," the receptionist said from behind the counter. "I'm Marley. Just to let you know, we're about to close. Is there something I can help you with?"

Lindsey blew out a breath. It was the moment of truth.

"I need to know who rented a boat from you last night," she said.

Marley raised her eyebrows. She glanced from side to side as if hoping someone would appear and give her backup.

"I can't tell you that," she said. "We have privacy rules."

"I think it was the same person who burned down Ruby Island," Lindsey said.

"Are you with the police?"

"No, I'm with the library," Lindsey said. She studied the girl closer. She recognized her now. Marley was a fan of young adult paranormal. "How did you like the *Iron King*?"

Marley blinked at her and then smiled. "I loved it."

"There are three more in Kagawa's series," Lindsey said.

"I know. I'm working my way through them," Marley said.

John glanced between them as if they had started speaking a new dialect. Lindsey could have told him it was book nerd talk, but she didn't. Instead, Lindsey waited quietly, letting Marley think.

"I suppose if I happened to be reading aloud and you heard me, then I really wouldn't be giving out private information," Marley said.

"Nice," Lindsey said with a nod. "Tell me, have the police been by?"

"Yes, Chief Daniels was in earlier today," she said. "I gave him a printout of all of our boat rentals."

Lindsey wasn't surprised. She hadn't really thought that

she'd be the only one to think that the perpetrator might have rented a boat.

Marley sat at her desk and opened up a file on her computer screen. She began calling out names.

"Let's see, Harry Cooper, the Marr family, Stephen Briggs . . ."

Lindsey didn't recognize any of them. She frowned as the list went on. She didn't know what she'd expected—yes, she did. She'd thought she'd hear a name that meant something.

"David Burch, P. Ruby . . ." Marley said.

Lindsey sucked in a breath.

"Could you repeat that?" she asked.

"P. Ruby," Marley said. "I remember him. He wasn't a regular. He was tall and thin, too thin, and he had a scruffy gray beard."

"Do you know what the *P* stands for?" Lindsey asked.

"No," Marley said. "He put a deposit down in cash and paid in cash. Because his deposit was more than the cost of the boat, we didn't make him show ID, which he was reluctant to do."

Lindsey felt her heart pounding in her chest. "Thank you, Marley. You've been a huge help."

Lindsey left the office in a daze. It couldn't be. It was just a coincidence, she told herself, but the hair standing on end on the back of her neck refused to lie down.

"Lindsey, are you okay?" John asked as he followed her outside. "You look like you've seen a ghost."

"Maybe I have," she said.

"What do you need to do?" he asked.

"Go to the police," she said. "I want to know if Peter Ruby is alive."

John gave her a curious look, but Lindsey had no time to explain. They climbed into his car and he obligingly drove back around the bay to the station house.

Together they made their way into the small building. Lindsey glanced at the front desk. No one was there. She paced the waiting area, craning her neck trying to see if anyone was in back.

Finally, she heard voices. They sounded as if they were coming to the front.

"I'm going to see Sully," a voice said. "Maybe he got a good look at him. Maybe he recognized him."

Lindsey stepped forward. That was Chief Daniels's voice. He was going to see Sully. That meant that what she suspected might be true. The man who had rented the boat was Peter Ruby.

Officer Emma Plewicki appeared first. She was fretting her lower lip between her teeth. Her dark, glossy hair was pulled back and she wore her summer uniform of a short-sleeved light blue shirt over navy-colored pants.

Chief Daniels was right behind her, and he was shoving his hat on his head as he walked forward. At the sight of Lindsey, his steps slowed. Lindsey gave him a small smile.

"Is it true?" she asked. "Is Peter Ruby alive?"

Chief Daniels and Officer Plewicki exchanged a quick look as if they were trying to decide how much to tell her. It made Lindsey feel as if she were still an outsider in Briar Creek, a stranger who wasn't allowed in on the town's secrets yet.

John broke the tension by asking, “Who is Peter Ruby and why are you acting so weird?”

“He’s a man who had been missing for over twenty-five years,” Lindsey said. “But suddenly he’s renting boats and appearing on islands right before they get blown up.”

Chief Daniels removed his hat. “How do you know about this?”

“I just came from the boatyard,” Lindsey said. “I was listening while the girl who worked there was going over who rented boats yesterday.”

The chief frowned. Lindsey had a feeling he wasn’t happy with her butting in, but given that she had almost been blown into another hemisphere, he couldn’t really deny she had a vested interest.

“Was it him?” she asked.

The chief sighed. “We don’t know. The only pictures we have of him are really old and we weren’t on the island. That’s why I was going to see Sully. I wanted to know if he saw the person and if he recognized him.”

Lindsey thought back to the horrible scene the night before, the fire and smoke and the explosion that rocketed out of the excavation site. If Sully had gotten a good look at the man and recognized him, he hadn’t said so. Of course, they’d been fleeing for their lives, so it may have been lower on his priority list at the time.

“He didn’t say anything,” she said. “But then again, he did get knocked unconscious.”

“For the love of Pete, why do you care about Peter Ruby?” John asked.

Officer Plewicki was the first one to speak. "If he is who we think he is, then he is the man responsible for the deaths of his wife and two children in the worst case, the only case, of mass murder Briar Creek has ever suffered."

"Whoa," John said. He looked at Lindsey with wide eyes. "And he was on the island with you?"

"Maybe," she said. "Honestly, I don't know. I don't know what he looks like."

"Did you get a good look at the man on the island?" Chief Daniels asked. "We could get a sketch artist in here and have them do a drawing."

"We're going to have Marley at the boatyard do it," Emma said.

"It was so chaotic," Lindsey said. "I saw an outline of a person but nothing more specific than that."

They looked disappointed but nodded in understanding. Still, Lindsey felt that she had let them down.

"The security cameras on the boatyard have about

thirty seconds of footage of this 'P. Ruby' taking his boat out. It's pretty grainy, but if you could match it to the person you saw on the island, it would help," Chief Daniels said.

"It can't hurt to look," Lindsey said.

"Come around here," Emma said. "I have it on my computer."

Lindsey walked past the main desk to Emma's area. She had a desk pushed up against the window that overlooked the parking lot. It was littered with paperwork and had pictures of her many dogs on it. Lindsey particularly liked the one of the dogs in their Halloween costumes. Emma had dressed them up as a hot dog, a hamburger and a can of beans.

As if unwilling to let her get too far away from him, John came with her. She wondered if it was nerves or curiosity that drove him.

Emma opened the media player on her desktop and then clicked on a file. She skipped the film ahead to where she wanted it to start and then hit Play.

Lindsey leaned close while John looked over her shoulder. It was a terrible bit of film. A constant buzz was the only noise and the images were grainy.

"No way to zoom in?" Lindsey asked.

"Not without better equipment," Emma said and gave the chief a chastising look, which he ignored.

Lindsey saw a man getting into a boat and then driving it out to the open water. It was a small craft and he handled it with the familiarity of someone who knew boats. There was no close-up of his face. His body appeared to be tall and thin. It could have been anybody.

She sighed and stood up straight. She had been hoping she could say that it was the man on the island, but no.

Emma and Chief Daniels were watching her. She shook her head.

"Well, that's odd," John said from behind her. "My landlord has a boat. Why is he renting one?"

All three of them spun to look at John.

"Excuse me?" Chief Daniels said.

"That's my landlord," John said. "I'm renting his guest house for the summer. He moves exactly like that guy on the film, all stoop-shouldered and gangly."

John bent over and did an impression of his landlord. The three of them stared at him.

"What?" he asked. Then he seemed to realize what he'd said. "I'm not saying it is him. It's just that the similarities are uncanny."

"Who is your landlord?" Chief Daniels asked.

"Paul Gavin," he said.

"Address?" Emma Plewicki grabbed a piece of paper and a pen.

"It's on Rose Court," John said. He frowned and Lindsey knew the street number was eluding him. "Brown house, white trim, summer roses all along the white picket fence."

"I know the one," Emma said. She grabbed a set of keys off the top of her desk. "Do you want me to bring him in?"

"Yes," Chief Daniels said. "I'm going to call the state investigator and have him meet you out there. I don't want you going near this guy without backup. If he's our arsonist, we don't want to do anything to jeopardize the case."

"Roger that," Emma said and she headed out the front door.

Lindsey looked at John. His eyes were round. He glanced back at the still frame on the computer screen and narrowed his gaze. Then he gave a slow nod. Lindsey knew the lawyer in him was double-checking what he thought he'd seen.

Chief Daniels turned back to John. "Don't go home until after we've brought him in. If he's dangerous, I don't want him to figure out that you're our lead."

John nodded. Lindsey was surprised that he didn't look more alarmed.

"Now I need the two of you to get out of here before they bring him in," Chief Daniels said. "Lindsey, if you remember anything that you think might help, call me."

"There is one thing," she said. "John and I overheard Riordan meet with his landlord, Paul Gavin, before over at a crab shack in Guilford a few nights ago. They were arguing about Gavin's investment in Riordan's treasure hunt. Gavin wanted Riordan to produce the map, but Trudi had stolen it and he couldn't. Gavin was pretty unhappy with him."

"Are you absolutely sure it was Gavin?"

"Yes," John said.

"Listen, no more going off and asking questions on your own, Lindsey," Chief Daniels said. "Until we know who burned down Ruby Island and why, you're not safe." He glanced at John. "No one is."

"All right," Lindsey agreed. Mostly because she didn't have any other choice.

She led the way out of the station with John beside her.

He started up the car and turned out of the parking area toward Lindsey's house.

"So it looks like we'll be bunkies," he said.

"What?" she asked. She was sure she must have heard him wrong, because if he thought he was staying with her, then the boy was seriously mistaken.

"Well, I don't know anyone else in town," he said. "Obviously, I'll need to crash with you."

"Um, no," Lindsey said. "That is not an option."

"Why?" he asked. He sounded just the teensiest bit petulant.

"Well, first of all, there's a lovely bed-and-breakfast right in town that you can stay at," she said. "And second of all, you're only a half hour from your apartment in New Haven. If you really need a new place to sleep, that would be the place—not mine."

"I can't go home," John protested. "What if my landlord is the arsonist and he finds out that I identified him? He'll come after me and he has my home address on my rental papers."

"Then it looks like it's the Beachfront B and B for you," Lindsey said. She had a twinge of guilt but she knew better than to let it show, lest John use it to manipulate her into letting him stay with her.

She could just see how it would go. She'd give in, he'd take her bed because of his bad back and she'd be relegated to her couch. Not to mention the complication this would cause if anyone found out that John had spent the night at her place. Sully was the nicest guy in the world, but she imagined even he would be hard pressed to accept that his girlfriend had her ex-boyfriend spend the night in her apartment.

"I really think that as mature adults—" John began but Lindsey cut him off.

"We know what is acceptable and what isn't," she said.

John parked in front of Nancy's house and Lindsey hopped out.

"The Beachfront is less than a mile away," she said. "The road will curve and then fork. Stay to the left. There's a sign. You can't miss it. Good night, John."

She shut her door before he could reply. Lindsey hurried up the stairs to the porch. She wanted to call Sully and hear his voice. She didn't know if she should tell him what they had learned—that Peter Ruby was alive and well and renting boats, oh, and he also happened to be John's landlord, Paul Gavin, who'd been living in Briar Creek for years. It made her head hurt to think about it.

No, she didn't want to tell him anything that would alarm him. If Nancy would let her borrow her car tomorrow, she'd go into New Haven and see him early in the morning. This was the sort of thing she wanted to tell him in person.

She felt a pang of guilt as she heard John's car pull away, but she didn't turn to look as his taillights disappeared around the corner. Maybe this was exactly what he needed to know that whatever was between them was over once and for all.

* * *

Lindsey couldn't sleep. Sleeping the day away had ruined her for a good night's rest so she catnapped in between working on her cross-stitch, watching late-night movies and sitting up in bed, searching the Internet on her laptop for any information about Peter Ruby and Paul Gavin and whether they were, in fact, the same man.

There was a St Peter's Ruby Red Ale that kept coming up and there were several people listed under the name but no one with ties to Briar Creek—at least none that she could see. She then searched the name *Paul Gavin*, John's landlord. There were over 47,000 hits. She couldn't imagine searching them all, so she went onto the local tax assessor's property site.

She went into the land records section and typed in the name *Paul Gavin*. She wanted to know how long he had owned the house on Rose Court. Oddly, the search brought up the record but it listed the name as *Gavin Paul*, who had owned the house for ten years.

She supposed it could be a typo—having a first name for a last name was bound to cause errors—but she couldn't shake the sense that something was off. Then again, so much was off about the whole situation. Why had Paul Gavin rented a boat under the name *P. Ruby*? Especially in Briar Creek, where Ruby had been missing for almost thirty years. If Paul Gavin was a phony name for Peter Ruby, why would he use the old name now and risk being discovered? Unless he didn't care anymore.

The thought gave her the shakes, and she wondered if

the police had managed to pick up Peter Ruby aka Paul Gavin. She closed her laptop, knowing that she needed to try to sleep.

Heathcliff was on his back with his feet in the air, his paws twitching while he dreamed of chasing rabbits. Lindsey gently stroked his soft belly and hoped he caught one.

Lindsey was up with the sun. She took Heathcliff for a brisk walk and then came back to borrow the keys to Nancy's car. She planned to get into the library later in the day. Beth had promised to cover for her, knowing that she wanted to go and check on Sully.

Lindsey had another errand she wanted to run in New Haven as well. She had to do both before her shift began so that Ms. Cole would not feel the need to document her absences to Personnel. Not that she particularly cared what the lemon did, but she had missed her library and couldn't wait to get back to it.

Nancy sent her off with a tin of cookies for Sully. She had made his favorite, which was the classic chocolate chip. The drive was light on traffic and so mercifully shorter than usual. She took the I-95 over the Quinnipiac River Bridge, locally known as the Q Bridge, into downtown New Haven, which after several turns led to the hospital parking garage that straddled York Street.

Lindsey checked at the Information desk that Sully hadn't been moved and then she took the elevator to his room. The hospital had the same scent of antiseptic cleaners and cafeteria cooking that she always associated with hospitals.

She tapped gently on his door frame when she arrived at his room. He was propped up on his side, reading the *New Haven Register*. No one else was in sight. She was selfishly glad that she wouldn't have to share him.

He broke into a grin when he saw her and she felt it all the way down to her toes. She carefully put the cookies from Nancy on his rolling tray and then reached out to give him a gentle hug.

Sully was having none of it. He pulled her half onto the bed and squeezed her tight. Then he kissed her hard on the mouth as if to reassure himself that she was, in fact, real.

"How are you feeling?" he asked. "Are you all right? No damage?"

"Me?" she asked. "I'm fine. How are you? How's your head? Are you going to get out soon? Is it a concussion?"

"I'm good," he said. "Apparently, my head has the density of concrete, so I was not concussed and the doctors have agreed to release me today."

"Oh, that's wonderful!" she cried. "When? I have Nancy's car. I can take you home."

"Sadly, my doctor is in surgery this morning on a patient

who wasn't so lucky in the head injury department," he said. "I can't leave until he checks me out one last time, which will be early this afternoon."

"Nuts," she said. "Well, I can call out of work and wait for you if you'd like."

Sully reached up and brushed a length of long, blond hair out of her eyes. "Don't worry. My parents are coming in to collect me."

"They must be so relieved," she said.

He nodded. He scooted over and pulled Lindsey up onto the bed beside him.

"I did have an interesting visitor well after hours last night," he said. "Chief Daniels."

"So you know," she said.

"That the man who rented the boat was calling himself *P. Ruby* and that your ex identified him as his landlord, Paul Gavin," Sully said. "Yeah, he caught me up. Why didn't you tell me on the phone last night?"

"Well, unlike Chief Daniels, I didn't want you to be up all night thinking about the situation," she said. The pillows behind her back were soft and she let out a yawn.

"Like you were?" he asked.

"I couldn't help it," she admitted. "It all seems so random and then it's not."

"No, it isn't," he said.

"Did Chief Daniels say what Paul Gavin had to say for himself?" she asked.

"No, in fact, when they went out to his house to pick him up for questioning, he was gone and it didn't look like he planned to be coming back."

"Did you recognize him?" she asked. "Is he really Peter Ruby?"

Sully stretched his neck as he looked at the ceiling. He closed his eyes and Lindsey knew he was trying to decide if the man he saw on the island could have been the man he had known as a child.

"I don't know," he said. He sounded defeated and Lindsey squeezed his forearm in reassurance. "I wish I could say yes, but like I told Chief Daniels, I don't know."

"This must be so hard for you," Lindsey said. "I'm sorry."

"No, I'm sorry," he said. "If anything had happened to you out there, I never would have forgiven myself."

"That's silly talk," Lindsey said. "I'm a grown-up. I knew what I was doing."

"Yeah, but we didn't know someone else had a whole other agenda going."

"True," she said.

They sat quietly for a while. Lindsey turned over the events of the past few weeks in her mind and felt incredibly lucky and grateful that Sully was here with her. When the nurse came in later, Lindsey kissed Sully good-bye with a promise to call and check on him. He said he'd let her know as soon as he was sprung. The gray-haired nurse glanced between them and muttered something about young love, which embarrassed Lindsey to no end but Sully looked delighted.

With a wave, Lindsey left Sully to the nurse's care and made her way back out of the hospital. She glanced at the time on her phone. She wasn't due in until eleven. It was only nine-thirty now. She decided she had time for one quick stop before she went to work. As she wound her way out of the parking garage, she turned onto Chapel Street and headed into the heart of Yale.

Lindsey had loved living in New Haven. It was a small city but it had history on every corner from the neo-Gothic Harkness Tower, whose fifty-four-bell carillon she loved to hear play, to the three old churches that sat watch over the New Haven green like three spinster sisters on a porch.

She followed Chapel Street to College Street until she found a spot on Wall Street to park. She hated to leave Nancy's powder blue rag top Mustang on the street, but it couldn't be helped.

When she had called Patti Fulton, her former boss at Beinecke, a few weeks ago and asked for a referral to a noted cartographer, Patti had given her a hard time about not being in touch. Lindsey knew she could blame it on moving and starting a new job, but the reality was she'd had a hard time keeping in contact because she'd been a bit bitter about being let go. She wanted to make amends now.

She called Patti from her cell while she walked toward the building. As always, Lindsey caught her breath at the sight of the rare book and manuscript library. The building was constructed of squares of white, gray-veined marble, framed by shaped light gray granite. The panels served to filter light so that rare materials could be displayed without damage. The building was a marvel and Lindsey had always felt privileged to work there.

Lindsey pushed through the revolving front door. As always, she was struck by the majesty of the glass tower of books that rose up through the core of the building. She took the stairs that led below to the reading room, classrooms and the offices that circled Isamu Noguchi's sculpture garden.

She tapped twice on Patti's closed door.

"Come in," Patti said. She took in Lindsey with a sharp glance. "You look tired."

Lindsey smiled. If ever she wanted an honest opinion of herself, she knew Patti would offer it up.

"I'm tired but it's fine," she said.

Patti indicated the seat across from her desk and Lindsey sat down.

"How's the job?" Patti asked. She looked at Lindsey over the top edge of her glasses.

"I love it."

"That's nice, but it doesn't utilize your skills," Patti said. Her blunt black hair framed her face in a foreboding manner that Lindsey suspected she used to encourage a certain amount of fear in students who came to use the library's materials.

"No, but I'm learning new ones," Lindsey said.

Patti gave her a sour look. She had been Lindsey's mentor. She was brilliant and could tell you exactly how to preserve an ancient tablet from Mesopotamia or a rare folio from Shakespeare. Lindsey had always aspired to be just like her. Life, however, obviously had other plans for Lindsey.

"Listen, I don't want to keep you from your work," Lindsey said. "I just wanted to pop in and see the old digs."

"You're not interrupting," Patti said. "I always have

time for a fellow archivist." Her voice was uncharacteristically kind and Lindsey smiled.

"Thank you."

"So what happened with the treasure map?" Patti asked. She looked much more comfortable talking about rare materials and not personal feelings. "Was it genuine?"

"I called Dr. Harris, but he's on sabbatical. His assistant Dr. G—"

"You mean Dr. Gavin," Patti said.

"He called himself Dr. G," Lindsey said.

Patti gave an eye roll over the black frames of her glasses. "He's trying to impress the undergrads with his coolness, no doubt. Ridiculous—given that he's in his late fifties. I swear male menopause is so much more embarrassing than the change we go through."

Dr. G. Dr. Gavin. Lindsey stared at her.

"What?" Patti asked.

"What's his full name?" Lindsey asked. She could feel the blood rushing in her ears. Could it be? Was there a connection?

"Dr. Gavin Paul," Patti said. "What's wrong? Your face looks weird. Did you verify the map?"

"That would be hard to, given that it's in police custody," Lindsey said. Her mind was racing. Gavin Paul, not Paul Gavin then. The coincidence was too much to ignore.

"They arrested a map?" Patti asked. A small V appeared in between her eyes as she frowned, not understanding.

"It's being held in an evidentiary capacity," Lindsey said. Her voice sounded far away. Her mind was racing.

Dr. Gavin Paul, the cartographer, and Paul Gavin, the landlord, had to be the same man.

"Lindsey, what's going on?" Patti snapped. Her voice brought Lindsey back to the present.

"This is going to sound crazy, but I need a picture of Dr. G," she said.

"Why?" Patti asked.

"I think he might be a murderer," Lindsey said.

Patti stared at her and Lindsey met her gaze. Whatever Patti saw there must have convinced her because she turned around to her computer and started clicking open files.

"I don't see him around campus much. But I did attend a conference a couple of years ago where he was presenting with Dr. Harris. I think there was a group photo taken of all of us."

It took several minutes but she found a set of pictures from a conference at the Thomas Fisher Rare Book Library at the University of Toronto. She flipped through the photos while Lindsey rose and stood behind her, looking over her shoulder.

"There," Patti said.

A picture loaded onto the screen. It was a group shot at a dinner table. Sitting next to Patti was a man who matched the grainy footage from the boatyard and John's description of a gangly, stoop-shouldered man exactly. Dr. Gavin Paul was John's landlord, Paul Gavin.

Lindsey felt her breath release, making her aware that she'd been holding it the whole time. Now the final question remained. Was Paul Gavin or Dr. Gavin Paul also Peter Ruby?

"Can you print that for me?" Lindsey asked.

Their gazes met and held. Patti understood what Lindsey didn't say. "Sure," Patti said. "I'm sorry."

"Don't be," Lindsey said. "You've just given me another lead. Besides you couldn't have known."

"If he is the killer . . ." Patti's voice trailed off as if it was too scary to contemplate.

Lindsey didn't say anything. Her head was swirling with information.

"Can you get me his curriculum vitae?" she asked.

"I can try," Patti agreed. "It should be on file."

"Excellent," Lindsey said. "Can you e-mail it to me?"

"Sure," Patti agreed.

Lindsey grabbed the picture out of the printer and hurried to the door.

"Lindsey!" Patti called. She turned back and Patti gave her a worried look and said, "Be careful."

"I will."

Lindsey parked Nancy's car in the small lot behind the Briar Creek Public Library and entered the back of the building through the staff entrance.

She put her things in her desk and stepped out of the workroom into the main library. The buzz of the receipt printer from the checkout station and the ping of the computer's check-in chime were welcome sounds as she made her way to the circulation desk.

Ms. Cole was manning her station with her usual erect military bearing. Ann Marie was cracking jokes with Alvin Lawrence, an older gentleman who was doing genealogy research on his family in the neighboring town of Branford.

Beth was sitting at her desk in the children's area. She appeared to be working on a craft that required lots and lots of yarn.

Jessica Gallo was at the reference desk. It was quiet, given the midday hour, and she was thumbing through the latest issue of *Library Journal*, while assisting Eleanor Ziobron, one of their summer visitors, with reader's advisory. Eleanor liked to keep up on the latest bestsellers.

The Internet computers were half full and the cushy

seats by the new magazine rack were full of seniors who were there for their weekly visit from the Seaside Adult Living Community on the edge of town.

Lindsey would have given anything for this to just stay a normal day at the library, but it wasn't normal. Sully was in the hospital. Ruby Island had been torched, and there was a killer among them. Definitely not normal.

Beth glanced up and saw her and waved. Lindsey waved back. Reassured that all was well in the library at least, she turned and headed into her office. She needed to call Chief Daniels and have him look at the picture.

She called the police station. Chief Daniels said he'd be over right away. While she waited, Lindsey fired up her computer and opened her e-mail.

There were several messages from Carrie Rushton, the president of the Friends of the Library, as well as a few from the mayor's office. Mostly, it was about not talking to reporters about Trudi Hargrave or the island.

Lindsey wondered how the mayor's office was handling the press. She wondered if anyone had dug up the fact that Trudi was planning to run for mayor. It would make a nice innuendo-laden piece.

She had just answered and deleted most of her messages when a new message appeared. It was from Patti. Dr. Paul's curriculum vitae was attached. Lindsey scanned it quickly. It wasn't conclusive proof of anything but she noted immediately that there was nothing mentioned before 1983, the year that Peter Ruby disappeared.

A knock on the door interrupted her. She glanced up to see Chief Daniels and Officer Plewicki.

"Hi," she said. "Come on in."

"What have you got?" the chief asked. He had one eyebrow higher than the other and looked a bit disapproving.

"I went in to see Sully this morning. He's fine," she said quickly as Emma had opened her mouth to ask. "When I left, I dropped by the rare book library, where I used to work, to see my old supervisor."

"Uh-huh," Chief Daniels encouraged her.

Lindsey got the distinct feeling he suspected her of meddling, but really this time she was innocent.

"Anyway, Patti Fulton, my boss, was the one who referred me to Dr. Harris, the map specialist. When Riordan asked me to look at his map, I called Dr. Harris but he wasn't in so I spoke with his assistant Dr G, whose full name is Dr. Gavin Paul."

"And?" Emma asked.

"Don't you see?" Lindsey asked. "Dr. Gavin Paul and John's landlord is Paul Gavin. They're the same person."

"Maybe," the chief said. "But with two first names, it could just be coincidence."

Lindsey bent down and opened her desk drawer. She took out the printout and set it on the desk. "I had her show me a picture of him, and once I saw it, I had her print it."

Lindsey spun the printout on her desk toward them.

"It's the same man from the boatyard," she said. "I'm sure of it."

"Whoa, whoa, whoa," Chief Daniels said. He leaned forward and studied the photo. "Are you telling me that your map specialist is the same man who rented a boat just before Ruby Island was blown sky-high?"

"Yes, that's what I'm saying," she said.

They both leaned over the photo.

"It could be him," Emma said. "Neither the video nor the picture are ideal, but there is an uncanny similarity between them."

"I thought so, too," Lindsey said. "I also had his curriculum vitae sent to me. There is virtually no record of Dr. G in existence before 1983—the year Peter Ruby went missing. I think Paul Gavin or Gavin Paul is Peter Ruby."

"No, it's not possible," Chief Daniels said. "I've been thinking about this. If he's been living in Briar Creek all these years, we would have seen him; someone would have recognized him if he was Peter Ruby."

"Agreed," Emma said. "It is the most notorious case in the town's history. He could not have been living among us without someone recognizing him."

"He could have changed his appearance. The only photo of him is an old faded one from the seventies. Maybe Trudi Hargrave put it together and recognized him," Lindsey said. "Maybe that's why he killed her."

Emma was the first to speak. "Okay, bottom line, whether he is Peter Ruby or Dr. Gavin Paul or Paul Gavin how are we going to catch him?"

Lindsey looked at the two of them. She knew it was mental and they probably wouldn't go for it, but she had to offer anyway.

"We need to lure him with something he can't resist." They both looked at her and she said, "The map."

"You don't have to do this, you know," Lindsey said.

"It's the least I can do," John replied. "Besides, it makes sense for me to be taking you since I work at Yale and all."

They were seated in her office. Lindsey glanced across her desk at him and gave him a small smile. She shouldn't have been surprised at his offer of help. John had always been very pragmatic when there had been a crisis to be managed.

Much to Lindsey's surprise, Chief Daniels had been receptive to her idea. The plan was simple. She and John would take the map back to Yale. They were in John's car, which had a tracer on it, and unmarked police cars would be all along the route at designated checkpoints. The theory was that Peter Ruby would be so desperate to get his hands on the map, he would try something while John and Lindsey were en route, thus giving the authorities an opportunity to arrest him.

Very few people knew of the sting operation. Chief Daniels didn't want the information to get out. They had, however, staged a scene at the library the previous evening between Milton, who was in on it, and Lindsey.

Milton demanded that Lindsey turn the map over to the town's historical department and she refused. They had made sure their tiff was in the middle of the library with optimum listeners so that the word would get back to Ruby.

Lindsey still felt Milton had gone a bit far by calling her a snooty academic, but she had gotten a good jab in by calling him a crusty old townie. Milton had looked surprised and then winked at her, letting her know they were okay.

The phone rang and Lindsey could see that it was the number of Emma Plewicki's cell phone.

"Briar Creek Public Library, Lindsey Norris speaking, how may I help you?"

"Nice," Emma said. "I like that you answered business as usual."

"Thanks," Lindsey said. "Is it ready?"

"It's good to go," Emma said. "Are you ready?"

Lindsey fingered the leather satchel on her desk.

"As I'll ever be," she said.

"Excellent," Emma said. "See you on the other side."

Lindsey hung up the receiver and nodded at John. He looked as nervous as she felt. She took a deep breath.

"Nothing may happen," she said. "We may deliver this map to Beinecke without . . . er . . . incident."

"Would it be cowardly of me to admit that I'd be okay with that?" he asked.

Lindsey laughed. It was a loud, tension-busting guffaw that made John laugh in return.

They left her office, appearing much more normal, or at least Lindsey hoped so. Thankfully, Ms. Cole was not in today and so had nothing to say about Lindsey leaving in the middle of the workday. Lindsey had told the rest of the staff that she had an errand to run, and although Beth had given her an odd look when she saw her with John, she said nothing.

Once they were outside, Lindsey leaned close to John and said, "It was Emma who called. The tracking device has been put on your car."

"Good," he said. He stiffened up and then blew out a breath. "I guess I'd better be sure not to speed."

He opened the passenger door for Lindsey and she slid into the seat. She clutched the satchel on her lap. She knew that there were unmarked police cars all along the route. The odds that Peter Ruby or whoever the killer was would actually follow them were not great, so really there was no reason to be nervous—at least, that's what she kept telling herself.

John glanced over at her as he pulled away from the curb. At the stop sign, he reached over and took the end of her braid out of her hand.

"We're going to be fine," he said. At her questioning

look, he said, "You always fidget with the end of your hair when you're nervous."

Lindsey gave him a small smile. She'd forgotten how well he knew her, how entwined all of their silly habits and idiosyncrasies had been.

John turned right onto the road that would lead them out of Briar Creek. Lindsey couldn't help glancing back over her shoulder. Was someone following them?

The road remained empty. She tried to feel calm about that. On the one hand, she wanted to help the police catch the man who had murdered his family and Trudi Hargrave and almost killed Sully, but on the other hand, she felt like a big, blubbering baby who would be fine if they didn't run into a cold-blooded killer.

"Staring at the road won't make anyone appear," John said.

She glanced at him and noticed he was looking in the rearview mirror.

"The watched pot?" she asked.

"Exactly."

They drove in silence for a few miles. No cars appeared. If there were unmarked police cars in the area, they were hiding incredibly effectively. Lindsey felt herself begin to relax. This had been a gamble. With the island and the excavation sight razed, it could be that the killer no longer cared about the map either.

A blue sedan pulled out from a side street and fell in behind them. Lindsey turned toward John as if speaking to him and tried to get a peripheral look at the driver.

"He is really on my tail," John muttered. He was glancing at the rearview mirror and frowning.

They took a sharp turn but the car stayed right on their rear bumper. Lindsey heard the sedan's engine rev as if he were trying to goad John into driving faster.

"I am going to have to speed up," John said. "I'm afraid he's going to hit me."

Lindsey glanced quickly over her shoulder. The driver was wearing a red baseball hat. She couldn't see his face.

John stepped on the gas pedal and his car shot forward. They took three sharp turns and still the blue car behind them shadowed them, never letting them get more than a few feet away from him.

Lindsey glanced at John. His hands were at two and ten on the wheel, his knuckles were white. His jaw was clenched as he sped around the back roads, down a hill and through a deserted stretch of trees with no houses in sight.

Lindsey could feel her palms sweating, her heart was racing and her breath was coming in rapid, shallow gasps.

Bang! The car behind them hit their bumper. Both she and John lurched against their seat belts.

"Oh, my God!" John exclaimed. "He's trying to kill us."

Lindsey scanned the area for another car. Where were the unmarked police cars? Shouldn't one of them have noticed that they were speeding and come out to find out why?

Bang! The car behind them hit them again. This time there was a crash as the taillights on John's car were smashed and a horrible scraping sound overrode the sound of the engine.

"Oh, that tears it," John said. He yanked his steering wheel to the right and pulled over under a train underpass.

"John, what are you doing?" Lindsey cried.

"The bumper is on my tires, Lindsey," he said. "I can't drive any further. My tires are going to pop. We'll have to run for it."

The blue sedan pulled up alongside them and the passenger window rolled down. Lindsey ducked down low and pushed open her door. John crouched low, prepared to follow her.

"Why don't you learn how to drive, old man?" a young voice shouted, and with a squeal of tires and a cloud of blue exhaust, the blue sedan tore off.

Lindsey stopped halfway out the door. She glanced back at John.

"He left," she said.

He peered through the window and then looked at her. "Did you see him? He looked like he was twelve."

Lindsey blinked. "We just got run off the road by a thug in his parents' car?"

"Apparently," John said. Then he let out a slow wheezy laugh. "Looks like we're going to live."

Lindsey slumped back in her seat. The relief was so great it took her out at the knees. She started to giggle. As much as she tried, she couldn't stop it.

She and John looked at each other and they both laughed harder. It was several minutes before they wound down to the occasional snort.

"I don't suppose our trap worked," John said. He wiped the moisture from his eyes. "I think the killer has flown the coop."

"Looks like it," Lindsey said. "Let's start walking. I'll

call Emma. I'm sure the police will pick us up and take us back to town."

They climbed out of the car and surveyed the damage to John's bumper. "I'm going to need to get it towed."

"I'm sorry about your car," Lindsey said.

John shrugged. "Since I thought I was about to lose my life, having a warped bumper really doesn't seem like that big of a tragedy."

"Perspective."

"Indeed."

They walked out from under the train bridge, blinking against daylight as they did. Lindsey could see a car coming their way.

"Oh, here they are now," she said. She dropped her phone and raised her hand to wave as the white sedan stopped in front of them.

Her hand fell to her side when the driver door opened and out stepped the stoop-shouldered man from the boatyard video. The man she had come to think of as Peter Ruby, mass murderer. It appeared their trap had worked after all. Lindsey would have been much happier about this if he wasn't smiling at them over the barrel of his gun.

"Need a lift?" he asked.

Lindsey and John exchanged glances. John nodded back at the car.

"You won't make it back to your car before I shoot you," Peter Ruby said. "And I will shoot you. Now put your hands where I can see them."

Lindsey and John both raised their hands. Ruby approached them swiftly as if he was very much aware that he was short on time. He snatched the messenger bag off Lindsey's shoulder and opened the flap. He checked to see that the map was there and held it up to the light to make sure it was authentic. Then he smiled and put it back in the bag.

He trained the gun on them and said, "Now walk."

"What? Why?" John asked. "You've got what you want. Let us go."

"Nah, I don't think so," he said. "You two are my insurance. Now walk or I shoot."

John and Lindsey started to walk down the road in the opposite direction. Twenty feet past the train bridge, he told them to step off the road and follow a bramble-filled path that cut through the woods.

Lindsey strained her ears, listening for the sounds of police car sirens, search dogs or a helicopter. There was nothing but the sounds of the songbirds in the trees and the swish of leaves and branches of the maple and birch trees as they pushed them out of their way.

They walked swiftly over the uneven ground. Lindsey stepped through a patch of damp ferns that left a trail of dew on her jeans. A mountain laurel thick with pink blossoms blocked her way, and she had to scramble around it to keep going.

Abruptly the woods opened up with a ten-foot drop to a marsh below. Anchored in one of the narrow canals that cut through the phragmites and marsh grass was a small boat.

"Jump," he ordered.

"Surely, you can't believe that we're going to go with you in that?" John asked.

"Oh, did you prefer to die here?" Peter Ruby asked.

Lindsey swallowed hard. He wasn't bluffing. He was as cold and calculating as anyone she'd ever met, and working with the public, she'd met her share of lunatics. She glanced at John. He looked as shaken as she felt.

"Would you like a push?" Ruby asked.

John looked at her and nodded. They jumped together. Lindsey hit the middle of the hill with her feet and half slid on her butt down the jagged dirt slope until the gravel below stopped her.

Ruby followed. He slid down the hill with his feet braced. He looked almost as if he were skiing. He never slipped or faltered, never gave them a chance to overpower him. He gestured for them to head to the boat.

Lindsey stepped into the muddy marsh. It stank of salty dead fish, and the dark brown silty muck pulled at her shoes as if wanting to pull her under.

"You don't need her," John said. "Let her go. Just take me as your hostage."

Lindsey glanced back over her shoulder. John had his back to her. His arms were wide as if imploring Ruby to see reason.

"And who would keep you in line?" he asked. "No, I need both of you."

John looked about to protest, but Ruby cocked his head and said, "Go."

Lindsey felt the cold-fingered clutch of panic grab her spine in its icy grip. She turned back to the marsh and slogged her way to the boat.

She hauled herself over the side. Ruby climbed in and ordered John to push them out through the marsh. He heaved his weight against the boat and it slid back with a groan and a whoosh. John was sweat soaked and muddy by the time they cleared the marsh and he was ordered into the boat.

They were still hidden from the shore by the tall sea grass and phragmites, but it didn't stop Lindsey from scanning the marsh, looking for a sign that someone saw their plight.

"Sadly, I can't steer the boat and keep tabs on the two of you so, Little Miss Librarian, I'm going to need your assistance," Ruby said.

Lindsey glanced up at him and he tossed a roll of silver duct tape to her. She caught it just before it connected with her nose, then she stared at him.

"Yeah, it's the bondage tool of choice for us villains," he said. "Wrap up his legs and ankles and don't make them loose. I'm watching."

Lindsey's fingers were cold and she had a hard time finding the end of the tape and peeling it back from the roll. She kneeled before John and began to wrap his ankles. She glanced up at him and felt tears dampen her eyes.

"I'm so sorry," she said. "I never should have gotten you involved in this."

"Don't," John said. His voice was rough and his hazel eyes so like her own were full of regret. "If anyone is to blame, it's me. If I hadn't cheated on you and driven you away, we wouldn't be here now at the mercy of this madman."

"Madman? Me?" Ruby cackled. He gave them an incredulous look. "I assure you, I am perfectly sane."

Lindsey felt her temper flare. She was done with being frightened. If she was going to die, and it looked like she most likely was, she wasn't going without telling her killer exactly what she thought of him.

"You are not sane!" she snapped. "Does a sane man light an island on fire? Murder an innocent woman? Kill his wife and children? No! That is the work of a stark raving lunatic!"

Anger pushed the cold out of her, leaving her smoldering like a cinder. She wrapped John's wrists, keeping them loose and not caring if Peter Ruby shot her on the spot.

He didn't. Instead he stared at her with a look of wide-eyed wonder and then he laughed. It started as an amused chortle and morphed into a loud guffaw of glee.

"You think *I'm* Peter Ruby?" he asked.

Lindsey rose to her feet and the boat wobbled. She stared at him and then nodded, knowing that by identifying her killer, she was very likely assuring her own demise.

"You dim-witted little book dork," he said. "I thought you would have more brains than to fall for that."

He tucked the gun in his waistband and grabbed Lindsey's wrists in one hand. His grip was punishing but he made quick efficient work of taping her hands together and they were not loose.

He gave her a shove and she fell back onto the seat across from John. The hard side of the boat hit her back like a punch to the kidneys. He grinned at her as if enjoying her pain while he taped her ankles together.

"Fall for what?" she asked.

"I'm not Peter Ruby, but I'm delighted that I got you all to think that I might be. Pure genius renting the boat under the name *P. Ruby* to throw the local sheriff off of my tail if I do say so myself," he said. "But no, I'm not Peter. How could I be, when I'm the one who killed him?"

"There is no record of a Dr. Gavin Paul before Peter Ruby disappeared," Lindsey said. She didn't believe him. He was lying.

"That's because my real name is Paul Gavin," he said. He gave them a silly bow. "I'm not a doctor but I play one in real life."

Lindsey and John exchanged a confused look and Paul Gavin laughed.

"Ironic, isn't it?" he asked. "The only one who knew the murderer's real identity was the visiting professor of criminal law. What are the odds that he would be carrying a torch for the nosy local librarian?"

John stared at Lindsey in alarm. There was no doubt that Paul Gavin was mad, utterly mad.

"I knew that some people believed that Peter Ruby murdered his family and fled the island. I figured if I rented the boat under *P. Ruby*, it would start a manhunt for Peter that would distract anyone from noticing me. Didn't completely work out that way, did it?"

Gavin scowled at Lindsey, letting her know he considered it her fault. He then turned and took the driver's seat of the small craft. They had drifted out far enough for him to drop the motor and turn on the engine. They rocketed out of the small cove they'd been in and out into the open water.

He opened the engine up and they smacked the top of the water as they raced across the waves. Lindsey glanced at John. He seemed to be taking the hammering as well as she was with gritted teeth and a pained expression.

Lindsey leaned over and tried to brace herself with an elbow. It only helped to keep her from falling off the seat. The pounding was relentless. The cold wind tore at her hair and her skin as if it was trying to claw her right off the boat—whether to save her or to kill her, she couldn't tell. They were well past the islands when Paul Gavin finally slowed the boat.

Lindsey took great big gulps of air and pushed off her seat to sit upright. John looked as bruised and battered as she felt.

"Well, now we part company," Paul said. "I have no more use for you two. It looks as if our oh-so-brilliant police department hasn't figured out where we went yet."

"But why?" Lindsey cried. "Why did you kill Peter Ruby and his family? Why did you kill Trudi?"

The boat was rocking and Paul braced himself as he considered her.

"Oh, how clichéd. Is this where I'm supposed to give my predictable confession in a crazed monologue that keeps me talking until help arrives?" he asked. He opened his eyes and looked around in a mocking 360-scan of the surrounding area. "Yeah, no one is coming and I have places to go and things to do."

He hauled John up by the elbow. As if sensing this was their moment to do or die, John laced his fingers together and swung them at Paul's head. It was an awkward move, partly because his wrists were taped together and partly because John was a litigator, not a fighter, and his usual weapon of choice was words.

As Paul easily sidestepped the blow, Lindsey hopped forward on her bound ankles and used her arms to catch Paul on the back. She hit him with a solid blow and knocked him to his knees. The boat pitched wildly in the waves, and without being able to brace her feet, Lindsey fell to the deck. John stumbled as well, catching himself against the seat.

Paul jumped up from the deck. His face had turned an ugly shade of red and the chords in his neck were strained as if it were taking all of their strength to keep his head attached.

"You think you can beat me?" he roared. "I have orchestrated everything. From the day I met Peter Ruby and he told me about his treasure island, until today, when I take the map and that treasure becomes mine."

"You can't get the treasure," Lindsey said. "You've burned the island down and blown up the pit."

"Really?" Paul asked. "Do you think I befriended Peter Ruby thirty-seven years ago because I liked him? Hell no. The bastard inherited the map! Can you believe that—inherited it? Apparently, his family has lived here for generations and that damn map just went right down the line. Is that fair?

"I wanted it, I would have paid him even, but no, he wouldn't do a deal and he was so secretive about it. Finally, I found out that he kept it in a storage shed with all of his other Captain Kidd memorabilia. So I killed his family and him, thinking I could retrieve the map, but no, he outmaneuvered me even in death."

"How?" Lindsey asked. Her heart was pounding and a quick glance at the horizon showed that no one was coming.

"He was on to me and he moved all of his things to a variety of storage facilities all over New England. Do you know what happens to storage units when people die and they don't leave an heir? They get auctioned off. I had no way of knowing where Peter had stored his stuff or who had bought it. I spent years trying to track down the map."

"But Riordan beat you out when he bought it from the Cambridge Auction House in Maine," Lindsey guessed.

"Yeah. I'd heard about the Captain Kidd memorabilia going up for auction, but how could I, an assistant to the map collection, afford the price Riordan could? I wanted to kill him right then, but then I thought, I'd let him do the work for me and have my good friend Trudi steal the map back before he could finish. You see, according to all the legends about Captain Kidd's treasure, it's booby-trapped and the pit is a deadly detour. The only way to get Captain Kidd's treasure is to use a tunnel on the east side of the island during low tide. Peter and I figured it out back when we were working together, but the closer we got, the more suspicious he became. He took the map and hid it. Without it, I couldn't get to the treasure."

He had a maniacal gleam in his eye, but still, Lindsey had to know.

"Why did you kill Trudi? She got your map back for you," she said.

"She wanted a cut of the treasure," he said. "I couldn't have that. I'm not a good sharer, never was. Kidd's treasure is all mine."

Lindsey was stunned by the number of lives he had taken in his pursuit of the treasure. He was a psychopath, and she and John were at his mercy.

Before she realized that he had moved, Paul grabbed John by the shirtfront and gave him a mighty shove. John sent Lindsey a startled look just before he disappeared into the dark gray-blue water with a big splash.

"Oh, no!" she cried and stumbled forward.

Paul Gavin used her momentum to give her one mighty push over the side. Lindsey just had time to gulp a lungful of air before she smacked through the surface of the chilly waves.

Panic made her flail against the tape that held her bound. She jerked her elbows back and the leverage caused the tape against her wrists to snap. Her arms were free. She dolphin-kicked toward the surface.

She broke through the water just as her lungs were beginning to burn. She scanned the waves, paddling to keep herself from sinking. Paul Gavin and his boat were the only things in sight, and he was speeding away as fast as the small outboard could go.

She couldn't see John. A new kind of panic began to beat in her chest. No matter what had happened between them, she did not want to be responsible for his death.

She took a deep breath and dove back down, trying to see if she could find him, trying to figure out where the current might have taken him. He had gone under only seconds before her, but if he hadn't gotten out of his tape, he might be drowning, unable to get to the air above.

Lindsey couldn't see anything but the blackness all around her. It fed the panic that was thumping through her.

Something brushed against her and she was caught between wishing it was John and terrified that it was a horrible unknown.

She reached out, but her hands found nothing except the cold, salty water surrounding her like a fluid shroud. A sob burned in her throat. She had to get air. Her legs were still taped and her sodden clothes weighed her down like an anchor.

Her arms burned from the lack of oxygen as she fought her way up. She was close, but she was tired. She didn't know if she was going to make it. Suddenly, she felt something grab her from behind and haul her up. She broke through the waves to see a boat, Sully's water taxi, bobbing in the water ahead of them. She twisted around to find Sully behind her, propelling her toward the boat.

"John is still down there," she cried. "I can't find him. If anything happens to him—"

"Shh, I'll find him," Sully soothed. "Can you swim?"

"Yes," she said. She didn't mention that her legs were still taped. She didn't want Sully to waste any time helping her when John was still missing.

"He'll be all right," Sully said. "Go to the boat. Charlie is there."

He gave her a shove and Lindsey began to dog-paddle toward it. She tried to dolphin-kick but she was so weak. It was all she could do to keep paddling in the direction of the boat.

When she got within twenty yards, Charlie dove in and swam out to help her. Lindsey was so grateful, she could have wept.

He used a lifeguard's hold on her and side-stroked his way to the boat. The Norrgard brothers were there and they reached down to pull Lindsey aboard. One wrapped her in a blanket while the other ripped the tape off her legs. Lindsey whipped around, looking for Sully.

Her teeth chattered from equal parts terror and cold, and Charlie rubbed her arms through the blanket, trying to get her circulation going.

"What were you thinking trying to swim to the boat with your legs taped?" he asked. "You could have drowned."

"Hey, there he is!" Steig shouted.

Lindsey looked where he pointed and sure enough an arm shot out of the water and waved. Stefan took the boat out of idle and headed in that direction.

Lindsey leaned forward, anxious to see. Yes! It was

Sully and he had John in the same hold Charlie had used on her. Stefan slowed the boat and Steig jumped in to offer Sully a hand. Together they got John to the side, where Charlie and Stefan managed to haul him in.

Once in the boat, Charlie ripped the tape off John's arms and legs and wrapped him in another blanket. Lindsey knelt beside him.

"Are you all right?" she asked. "Good God, if anything had happened to you, I wouldn't have been able to live with myself."

"It's all right," John said. His blond hair was plastered to his skull and his teeth were chattering as well. "Sully got me just in time."

Lindsey turned to thank Sully, but he was taking control of the boat from Stefan. He turned to face them, but he didn't look at Lindsey.

"Everyone, take a seat and hang on," he said. "We're going after him."

John and Lindsey huddled together on one seat. They were both wet and shivering. She noticed none of the others were as cold as they were, and she supposed they were more used to being wet on the open water. All she could think about at the moment was a cup of hot tea and being cocooned in a pile of blankets.

"Look!" Steig cried out as he pointed to the left. "I see him."

The boat pitched to the port side as Sully turned hard. Paul Gavin's boat was smaller and the sea was rougher out here.

As they sped closer, Lindsey jumped to her feet. She staggered toward Sully. He saw her and reached out a hand to steady her.

"Lindsey, you need to sit down," he shouted over the wind, which whipped at his mahogany curls. "It's not safe to be standing."

"I know, but you have to be careful," she said, raising her voice to be heard. She clutched a handrail built into the console. "He's got a gun."

"He's going to be too busy trying to outdrive me to use it," Sully said. He looked at her with a tender smile. "But thanks for the warning."

The boat slammed down onto a wave and Lindsey felt her knees give out. John lurched out of his seat to catch her and he pulled her down next to him. They were drawing up alongside Gavin's boat.

"Charlie, take over!" Sully yelled.

Charlie took the controls while Sully moved to the side.

"Get closer and try to keep us there," Sully yelled.

Charlie did, and before Lindsey could register what was happening, Paul Gavin gave them an evil look but then was blocked from view as Sully made a flying tackle into the other man's boat.

A shriek sounded and it was a heart-stopping moment before Lindsey realized it had come from her. Paul wasn't going down easily. He had his gun and he was wrestling with Sully.

"Get down!" Charlie yelled.

Everyone hit the deck except Lindsey, who was yanked down by Stefan and John.

"He didn't save you so you could get shot," Steig yelled.

"Get closer!" Stefan ordered Charlie, who was trying to drive and duck at the same time.

Charlie cut the wheel to follow the other boat. Paul had left the throttle at full while he and Sully both struggled for the gun. Charlie bumped their boat, knocking them down, and Stefan made an awkward flailing leap into the boat, landing on Paul with a sickening crunch.

Paul let out a scream of pain and then Sully hit him with a hard right in the temple, knocking him out.

Lindsey watched as Sully stood with the gun in his hand. He had blood running down his face from a cut over his eye.

Stefan got off Paul and reached over to pull the throttle back, slowing the boat. Charlie did the same.

Lindsey wanted to jump the gap between the two boats and hug Sully close, but the gap was widening.

"You all right?" Charlie yelled.

Sully wiped the blood off his face with his shirtsleeve and nodded.

"Get back to the pier," he yelled.

Charlie gave him a thumbs-up and opened up the engine again. Lindsey watched as Stefan followed in their wake while Sully stood watch over Paul Gavin, the gun still in his hand.

Halfway back to town, a police boat appeared and gave them an escort in. Officer Plewicki was at the wheel with Chief Daniels riding shotgun, literally. As Charlie navigated their way in, Lindsey saw the sun dip low in the sky. She'd been gone all day. Somehow, she didn't think she'd be going in to finish the evening shift at the library tonight.

A crowd met them at the pier. Standing in front was Preston Riordan. As soon as the boats were docked and they climbed up the gangway to the main pier, he approached them.

"I want my map back," he said. "You had no right to take it."

"It's evidence in a murder investigation," Chief Daniels snapped. Sully handed him the leather satchel from Paul's boat. "I'm guessing it won't be yours for a long time to come."

"You can't do that!" Riordan protested.

"Can't I?" Chief Daniels glared. "Sully, Lindsey and the rest of you, I'll need your statements."

It was a ragtag crew that walked down the pier toward the police station with Chief Daniels and Emma leading Paul, who was in handcuffs, into the crowd. Reporters mobbed them but they refused to comment.

Lindsey was between John and Charlie, and she noted that Sully walked ahead. He was talking to Emma as he towel-dried his hair. Something had shifted between them. She wasn't sure what, but she knew she needed to talk to him before the rift became an uncrossable chasm.

"Here," John said as he threw an arm about her and drew her close, trying to warm her. "Your teeth are chattering so hard they're going to crack."

It was then that Sully turned around. His gaze settled on where John's arm rested on Lindsey's shoulders, his glance met hers for the briefest moment and then he looked away.

Yes, something had definitely changed.

Nancy and Violet showed up with another change of clothes for Lindsey. The evening rolled into night while they all sat on the hard chairs in the station awaiting their turn at being questioned. They nursed tepid cups of coffee and fortified themselves with clam chowder from the Anchor that Mary brought over.

Paul Gavin had been escorted to a room in the back of the station, where he was being treated for his broken arm. He refused to speak other than to curse at the police and the medics. The investigators were frustrated.

Charlie and the Norrgard twins gave their statements to Emma and were free to go. Sully was called to give his statement, leaving John and Lindsey waiting to be questioned while Nancy and Violet fussed over them like mother hens. Beth popped in to check on Lindsey and let her know that everything was okay at the library.

"I can't believe you played a decoy like that," Beth said. Her black hair stood on end and her eyes were round with wonder. "You hate water over your head and you could have been shark bait. You are the real pirate among us."

"Arr," Lindsey said in a faint voice.

"Lindsey, we're ready for you," Emma called to her. She rose to her feet and John rose with her. "No, you wait here. We just want Lindsey."

Lindsey gave him a reassuring nod and made her way to the back of the police station. In the back hall, a stretcher was set up and two EMTs and several state police were escorting it from the building out the back door. Paul Gavin was strapped down and about to be wheeled away, but he saw Lindsey and leaned up against his restraints.

She thought he might scream at her or threaten her; after all she was the one who thought of luring him out with the map. He didn't. Instead he laughed. He laughed loud and long in a creepy, maniacal way that caused the hair to stand up on her arms.

Chief Daniels took Lindsey by the elbow and ushered her into his office. Emma and Sully were there as well as Detective Trimble from the state police.

"Are you all right?" Emma asked.

"Fine," Lindsey lied. She clamped her teeth together to keep them from chattering out loud.

"Can you tell us exactly what happened from the moment you left with the map?" Detective Trimble asked.

"Sure," Lindsey said. Her gaze darted to Sully, but he was standing with his back to the room as he looked out the window over the bay. She took a deep breath and began.

When she reached the part about Paul Gavin admitting that he had killed Peter Ruby, everyone sat up a little straighter. Trimble checked the recorder he had put on as if to make sure they were getting the information.

When she recounted how he had thrown them overboard, her voice cracked and she had to suck in a breath to push the remembered terror back. She ended with Sully saving their lives. She glanced swiftly at him while she told this part, but he never turned around to look at her. Both Emma and Chief Daniels looked at him and then back at her. They shared a significant look but said nothing.

When Lindsey was finished, Trimble shut off the recorder. He made a few notes on a notepad and gave Lindsey a sharp look.

"When it comes time, you'll need to testify," he said.

Lindsey nodded. "I can do that."

"I'll need to get the other witness's statement," Trimble said to Emma. He looked back at Lindsey. "You're free to go. Thank you."

She nodded and rose to leave. Emma walked with her to the door.

Sully turned away from the window and asked, "Are you finished with me?"

Trimble scanned his notes. "Yeah, you can go, but the same goes for you. They'll probably want you to testify."

Sully nodded.

In the waiting room, Emma called for John and he squeezed Lindsey's arm as he passed her to go to the back.

Nancy and Violet rose from their hard chairs and asked, "Are you free to go now?"

"I think so," Lindsey said.

Nancy and Violet exchanged a look. And then Violet folded her arms and gave Sully a hard stare and said, "Well, I'm sure Sully will be happy to take you."

As one, the two women turned on their heels and strode to the door. The waiting room was empty except for Sully and Lindsey.

"Are you okay with this?" she asked. As much as she appreciated Violet and Nancy's intention to throw them together, she feared it was just making the awkwardness between them worse.

"Sure. My truck is right outside," he said.

He strode forward and held open the door for her. Lindsey walked through feeling more and more like something was seriously wrong between them but she couldn't fathom what.

This Sully was standoffish and somber, not the jovial, hug-friendly man she had come to know and lo—she stopped her train of thought right there. She was not going to admit to any feelings for this man, even to herself, until she knew exactly what was going on.

"Are you all right?" she asked.

"Fine," he said.

"How's your back?" she asked.

"Good," he said.

They crossed the yard to the lot. He held open the door to his truck and she climbed in. The windows were down and the cool summer breeze ruffled her hair as he drove through the quiet town to her house.

"So now we know the mystery of Peter Ruby's disappearance," she said.

"Yeah."

Lindsey resisted the urge to kick him, but only because it would be awkward to do so while he was driving. The man was talking in monosyllables, which indicated that he was irked about something but he wasn't talking. How was she supposed to deal with that?

He parked in the driveway and got out to open the door for her. Lindsey was too fast and climbed out of her side without his help. He looked annoyed by this and she was glad to finally prick his icy shell just a little bit.

"You don't need to walk me to the door," she said.

He ignored her and matched his stride to hers. Now he was annoying her just as much as she had irked him. Unlike Sully, however, Lindsey's temper got the best of her. She spun to face him in front of the stairs.

"I said you don't have to walk me to the door!" she snapped.

For an instant, Sully looked furious and then his blue eyes met hers in a look that scorched, and before Lindsey had a chance to suck in a breath, his mouth was on hers and he was kissing her as if he was afraid he might never get the chance again. Lindsey wrapped her arms around his neck and kissed him back with all the fear and longing she had felt since Paul Gavin had taken her and John hostage.

Sully broke the kiss first. He stepped back as if he needed to put space between them. Lindsey felt abruptly bereft.

He reached out a hand but he didn't touch her. "I'm sorry."

"Why?" she asked. "What's going on?"

"When you went missing," he said, "I was a lunatic. I couldn't believe that you'd put yourself in harm's way like that and you didn't even tell me."

"Oh," she sighed. "I didn't think. It happened so fast."

She reached out to him, but he shook his head, obviously not wanting her to come any closer.

"And then I saw how frantic you were when John was missing," he said. He heaved a sigh as if he was forcing himself to accept something that he'd rather not. "You have unfinished business there."

"No, I don't," she protested. "I just couldn't bear the thought of anything happening to him—"

"Exactly," Sully said. This time he did reach out and push back a long, curly strand of her hair. He looked wistful and Lindsey felt her throat get tight.

"No, it's not what you think," she said. "It wasn't because I care about him, I mean I care, but it was more that I didn't want to be the cause—oh, good grief, I'm making a mess of this."

"It's all right," he said. "I'm going to give you some space."

"Space?" she repeated. "Are you breaking up with me?"

"You need to figure out your feelings," he said. "I know how I feel, but you need to do the same."

He leaned forward and kissed her on the forehead, and before she could even process the conversation they'd just had, he was gone. The taillights of his truck winked at her from the end of the drive before they disappeared.

"*Treasure Island* was written after Stevenson had traveled to the United States in 1881," Violet said.

"I didn't know that," Nancy said. "I didn't even know he was Scottish until Sully told me a few weeks ago."

Charlene and Violet opened their eyes wide at her, and Nancy bit her lip and glanced quickly at Lindsey. Lindsey forced a small smile.

"It's okay," she said. "I promise not to break into hysterical weeping if someone mentions his name."

"Good," Mary said. "Because I have a lot to say about my brother and I think you need to listen."

A week had passed since Sully had kissed Lindsey on the forehead and disappeared. She hadn't heard from him and she hadn't known what to say to him, so she hadn't contacted him either. Ridiculous.

Lindsey didn't really want to hear what Mary had to say, so she fussed with the tray of food on the table before her.

It had been Beth's turn to bring the food today, so the spread was healthy veggie wraps and California rolls with coconut water on the side. Beth had been on a health food kick lately, but thankfully, she had also included her lemon-almond cookie truffles. Lindsey had already eaten three and she found they took the edge off her heartbreak just the teeniest bit.

Lindsey noticed that everyone was ignoring their cross-stitch project and watching her. She took another truffle.

"Now here's the thing with my brother," Mary said. "He thinks you still have feelings for your ex so he's giving you some room to figure it out."

"How very generous of him," Lindsey said. "Did you know that Robert Louis Stevenson's *Treasure Island* was originally called *The Sea Cook* when it was serialized in 1881 in *Young Folks' Magazine*?"

"She's irritated," Beth said. "She's getting all scholarly."

"I am not irritated," Lindsey said. "I am royally ticked. What exactly does Sully hope to accomplish by vanishing on me?"

She glared at the group of women. She hadn't allowed herself to dwell much on what had happened. It had taken her a couple of days to get over the near drowning she had suffered and to process that Sully had essentially dumped her.

Now that she was back at work and life was resuming

some normalcy, she found that although she understood he was trying to be kind and give her time, she was severely irritated because she hadn't asked for any time and she felt it was pretty high-handed of him to force it upon her.

Poor Mary was caught in between her friend and her brother, and Lindsey didn't want to put her in that position, but hey, she'd brought it up.

A knock on the door sounded and they all turned as one. John stood there, looking more nervous than Lindsey had ever seen him.

"Excuse me," he said. "I just stopped by to say goodbye."

Lindsey put aside her half eaten cookie truffle and stood.

"I'll walk you out," she said.

She and John were only halfway down the hall when she heard the frenzy of whispers erupt behind them. She had a feeling the crafternooners were not having a deep character analysis of Long John Silver and how, despite being evil, he was an inverted father figure for the young Jim Hawkins.

As they stepped outside into the warm June sunshine, Lindsey saw that John had parked beside the curb. Obviously, he had not been planning a long chat.

"Lindsey, it's been—well, *terrifying* is the first word that leaps to mind," he said.

She laughed. He was so right.

"I'm sorry," she said, trying to gather her composure.

"Don't be," he said. "This is one summer I won't forget too soon."

He laughed, too. His blond hair shone almost white in the sun, and despite the breeze, it still didn't shift out of its precise cut. He wore his usual buttoned-down attire of a polo shirt and madras plaid shorts with a belt and leather loafers.

"What's going to happen with Paul Gavin, Ruby Island and the map?" he asked.

"The map will be evidence for a long time to come," Lindsey said. "Paul Gavin has been arrested for the murder of Trudi Hargrave as well as the murders of the Ruby family. I don't know who his attorney is but I hope he is put away—for life. As for the island, well, the town still owns it, but I don't think anyone is as keen on treasure hunting out there as they once were. Even Riordan has packed up and left town. If Gavin's trial takes as long as they suspect, it will be a long time before the map is released."

"The local girls will certainly miss the Norrgard twins," John said.

"Actually, Steig and Stefan have decided to stay and work for Sully. At least, that's what I heard," she said.

An awkward silence fell between them at the mention of Sully's name. She hoped John didn't press for details of their breakup. She wasn't ready to talk about it yet.

"Lindsey." He reached out and took her hand in his. "I was going to try and be noble and ride off into the midday sun and not say a word, but when I look at you, I just have to ask—is there anything I can say to get you to consider coming home to New Haven with me?"

Lindsey looked down at her brown sandals. The soft

linen of her white dress was being tugged by the breeze, and she could feel her hair being lifted up off her shoulders. As a strand was tossed across her face, she pulled it away and wondered if she should she go home with John.

Patti, her old boss, had called her yesterday and told her that they had a vacancy coming up and they were interested in hiring her back. She didn't know if she could just slide back into her old life—and even if she could, did she want to?

Her gaze went across the bay. She could see the Thumb Islands scattered like stones out in the water's blue-gray depths. Boats moved in and out of the islands in a dance that only they knew the steps to. The smell of the sea air and the cries of the gulls filled her senses. No matter what happened between her and Sully, this town had become her home. She was happy here and she was here to stay.

"I'm sorry, John," she said. "I belong here."

He looked at her as if seeing her for the first time.

"You do," he agreed. "Ah, well, I had to give it one more try."

She hugged him close and he clutched her as if trying to memorize the feel of her as if he knew this was their final good bye.

"Thanks for all of your help," she said.

"I'll always be there for you, Lindsey," he said. "Remember that."

"I will," she promised.

She stepped back as he climbed into his car and waved as he drove away.

When he had disappeared, she turned back to her library. The old stone building sat amid its lush lawn, looking comfortably formidable like a strict father doling out hugs.

As she walked back into the building, she was immediately comforted by the sight of her friends, E. B. White, Stephen King and Barbara Kingsolver to name just a few, waiting patiently on their shelves for when she needed them.

Lindsey walked over to the fiction section. Her glance moved over the fiction shelves to the *M*'s. Mitchell, Margaret, was filed exactly where she was supposed to be. She picked up a well-worn copy of *Gone with the Wind* and read the last line, her favorite last line ever. " 'Tomorrow, I'll think of some way to get him back. After all, tomorrow is another day.' "

If it was good enough for Scarlett O'Hara, it was good enough for Lindsey, and with a smile she returned to her crafternoon friends with a new sense of life's possibilities.

The Briar Creek Library Guide to Crafternoons

When Lindsey finds a great book or wants to revisit an old favorite, the next best thing to reading it herself is sharing it with her crafternoon buddies. Crafternoons are basically a book club that does a craft and enjoys some good food while discussing the book they've read.

Attached are some ideas to kick start your own crafternoon with a readers guide to *The Great Gatsby* by F. Scott Fitzgerald, a cross-stitch pattern for Lindsey's "Books are my homeboys" sampler and a couple of the crafternooners' favorite recipes. Enjoy!

Readers Guide for *The Great Gatsby* by F. Scott Fitzgerald

1. Nick Carraway has led a privileged life. Does this affect his perception of Jay Gatsby? What is Nick's relationship with Gatsby? What is Nick's role in the novel?

2. How does Jay Gatsby define the American Dream? Does the novel find him admirable or despicable? Has the American Dream changed since Fitzgerald wrote *The Great Gatsby* in 1925?

3. What is the difference between East Egg and West Egg? What does geography have to do with the societal class constructs in Gatsby?

4. What is Gatsby's interest in Daisy Buchanan? Is she worthy of his attention? What motivates Daisy to make the choices that she does?

5. *The Great Gatsby* is considered the great American novel. What makes it such a classic that it resonates with readers almost a hundred years after its first publication?

Lindsey's Pattern for Her Cross-Stitch Sampler

Books

are my

homeboys.

Recipes

CHARLENE'S CUCUMBER CUPS STUFFED WITH FETA

3 large cucumbers, peeled and cut into 2 inch slices
6 oz crumbled feta
3 tablespoons plain Greek yogurt
10 pitted Kalamata olives, diced
1 tablespoon chopped dill
2 teaspoons of lemon juice

Use a melon baller to scoop out the seeds of the cucumber slices, leaving enough behind to create the base of the cup.

With a fork, mash together the feta and the yogurt then add the olives, dill and lemon juice. When thoroughly mixed, spoon 1-2 tablespoons of cheese and yogurt mixture into the cucumber cups. Chill in refrigerator until ready to serve.

BETH'S LEMON-ALMOND COOKIE TRUFFLES

1 (8-ounce) package cream cheese, softened
2 tablespoons powdered sugar
½ teaspoon lemon extract
3 cups ground lemon sandwich cookies
The zest of 1 lemon
Almond bark, melted for dipping

Mix the cream cheese, powdered sugar and lemon extract in a large bowl until smooth and fluffy. Then stir in the ground cookies and lemon zest until well mixed. Roll into 1 to 1 ½ inch balls and place on a baking sheet. Refrigerate for about 1 hour. Dip balls in melted almond bark, letting excess drip off. Place in mini cupcake papers and cool in fridge until coating hardens. Because of the cream cheese ingredient, store in refrigerator. Serve either at room temperature or chilled.

Turn the page for a preview of Jenn McKinlay's next Library Lover's Mystery . . .

READ IT AND WEEP

Available from Berkley Prime Crime!

"Of course, you're all going to audition for the play," Violet La Rue said. "It's the kickoff to our community theater season."

Lindsey Norris put down her scissors and glanced across the table at Violet. Violet's warm brown eyes sparkled and her brown skin glowed. She was flushed with excitement for the upcoming production that would be her directorial debut.

Lindsey knew it was going to dampen Violet's enthusiasm to learn that the rest of the crafternooners, with the exception of her daughter, Charlene La Rue, and the children's librarian, Beth Stanley, were not as enamored with being on stage as she was. Violet was a former Broadway actress, and her daughter was a local news anchor. They lived for being in front of an audience. As for Beth, she had been instilling the love of reading in children for ten years with her dynamic story times. She lit up in front of an audience. The rest of the crafternooners, well, it wasn't really their thing.

This theory was confirmed when Lindsey glanced around the table and noted that both Mary Murphy and Nancy Peyton had their heads down, completely engrossed in their card-making project.

The group had decided to get a jump on the holidays by making greeting cards. It was only September but judging by the mess Lindsey was making, she was going to need the next three months just to crank out a few decent cards.

The crafternooners met every Thursday at the Briar Creek Public Library, of which Lindsey was the director, to work on a craft while they discussed the latest book that they had read.

This week they were discussing *A Midsummer Night's Dream* by William Shakespeare. It wasn't their standard fare but since Violet was directing the play in the Briar Creek Community Theater, they had all agreed to read it and give her their input as she was gearing up for auditions in the coming week.

"I think I have a crush on Puck. He's so charming. He carries the whole play," Beth Stanley said. Story time had just gotten out and she entered the room with a monkey puppet on one hand and wearing a banana suit.

It was no surprise that she liked Puck; with her diminutive stature and her black hair styled in a pixie cut, Beth reminded Lindsey of a sprite herself.

"Who in town would make a good Puck?" Nancy Peyton asked. Her blue eyes twinkled when her gaze met Lindsey's. "I'd offer up my nephew, Charlie, but he's too busy with the latest incarnation of his rock band."

Lindsey winced. Nancy wasn't kidding. Lindsey rented the third floor apartment of Nancy's three-story captain's house and her nephew, Charlie, lived on the floor between them. Usually, he only practiced once a week, but with the new band learning his material, practices had been more frequent and both Lindsey and Nancy had taken to wearing earplugs while at home. The only one who didn't seem to mind the noise was Lindsey's dog, Heathcliff. As soon as he heard the bass beat of the drums, he began to wag and howl as if he were the lead singer.

"How about my brother, Sully?" Mary Murphy asked. She'd brought the food for today's crafternoon from her restaurant, the Blue Anchor, so it was a feast of crab salad sandwiches and sweet tea.

Lindsey turned and scowled at her. She knew Mary had been just looking for an opportunity to bring Sully into the conversation. Lindsey had been dating Sully up until a few months ago when he decided to give her some space. Space she had not requested and so they had spent the summer apart.

"Did you know the earliest reference to *A Midsummer Night's Dream* is from 1598?" she asked. "No one knows exactly when it was written."

"Nice segue . . . not," Charlene La Rue said. "Are you telling us you don't even want to picture Sully in tights?"

As soon as she said it, Lindsey's brain flashed on a mental

picture of Sully in tights and tunic with a wreath of flowers on his mahogany curls. It did not help that the man had a sailor's muscular build and tights on him would not be a hardship on the eyes.

"I am so not answering that question," she said, at which the others all laughed. When they quieted down, she couldn't help but ask, "How is he anyway?"

"Pitiful," Mary said. "He worked like a dog all summer, almost as if he was trying to keep his mind off something or someone."

"Humph," Lindsey snorted. "Well, he wouldn't have had to if he hadn't dumped me."

The group all made sympathetic noises and Mary looked as if she wanted to say something, but Lindsey held up her hand.

"No, don't bother," she said. "It's fine. I'm fine. Everything is fine."

"Fine? My experience with the fair sex has proven that when a woman says she's fine, she is anything but," a voice, a male voice with a charming accent, said from the door.

The crafternooners all turned as one. Standing in the doorway was a man with reddish-blond hair, twinkling green eyes, a square jaw and a build that could easily carry off a pair of tights or anything else he wanted to dress it in.

"Robbie!" Violet leapt up from her seat and crossed the room to enfold the man in a warm embrace.

"Violet, my love," he said. "You're more beautiful than ever."

Charlene followed her mother and hugged the man, too; obviously he was a friend of the La Rue family. Beth, who was sitting beside Lindsey, nudged her arm until Lindsey turned toward her.

"Do you know who that is?" she hissed.

"No, no idea."

"It's Robbie Vine," Nancy whispered from across the table. "The famous British actor."

"Oh, my," Mary breathed.

Lindsey glanced at her friends. All three of them looked utterly star struck. She glanced back at the man. He was incredibly handsome and when he smiled his mouth was bracketed by dimples that could have charmed the birds right out of the trees. He looked familiar and then she remembered the movie she had just seen him in. There had been a shirtless scene that had been, for lack of a better word, revealing.

"Let me introduce you to my friends," Violet said and she tucked her hand in Robbie's elbow and brought him to the table. "Ladies, I'd like for you to meet—"

"Hello, Violet!" a voice interrupted her and they all turned to the door. "Robbie."

"Harvey?" Violet asked as if she couldn't believe what she was seeing. "Harvey Wargus?"

She looked down her elegant nose at the stubby, little man who entered the room. His dark brown hair was parted in the middle and flopped down over the sides of his head in a sag that was repeated by the brown mustache over his lips. He had a long body and short legs and a large bottom that added to his overall droopy appearance.

"Well, if I didn't know better, I'd think we were having a reunion," Robbie said. Then he turned and glared at the little man. "But of course I do know better because there is no way in hell you'd ever be invited to any reunion of ours."

"What are you doing here, Harvey?" Violet asked.

Lindsey glanced at the man. Now she remembered him. He had been a theater critic in New York at one time. He'd been on staff at one of the larger entertainment papers when word got out that he was bribable, particularly by up and coming young actresses looking for some positive ink. Unfortunately, a fourteen-year-old actress had been set up with him by her very own mother and the girl's boyfriend had turned them both in.

Harvey pushed up his glasses while fixing a perturbed gaze on Violet and Robbie. "When I heard through the grapevine that Violet La Rue and Robbie Vine were teaming up again, I got myself assigned to review the show. I must say I am really looking forward to it."

"Who on earth would hire a pervert like you?" Violet asked.

"Oh, haven't you heard?" he asked. "I'm working for Sterling Buchanan, you know, the multimedia mogul. I believe *you* know him quite well, Violet."

Violet reared back as if he'd slapped her and Charlene gasped. She took her mother's hand in hers and squeezed it tight.

Beth looked confused and asked, "Who is Sterling Buchanan?"

Violet closed her eyes and Charlene and Robbie exchanged a glance over her head. He glared at Harvey but then gave Charlene a small nod.

"He's my father," Charlene said.

Someone wants to bake a killing.

FROM *NEW YORK TIMES* BESTSELLING AUTHOR

JENN MCKINLAY

RED VELVET REVENGE

A Cupcake Bakery Mystery

It may be summertime, but sales at Fairy Tale Cupcakes are below zero—and owners Melanie Cooper and Angie DeLaura are willing to try anything to heat things up. So when local legend Slim Hazard offers them the chance to sell cupcakes at the annual Juniper Pass Rodeo, they're determined to rope in a pretty payday!

But not everyone at Juniper Pass is as sweet for Fairy Tale Cupcakes as Slim—including star bull-rider Ty Stokes. Mel and Angie try to steer clear of the cowboy's short fuse, but when his dead body is found facedown in the hay, it's a whole different rodeo...

INCLUDES SCRUMPTIOUS RECIPES!

"I gobbled it up."
—Julie Hyzy, bestselling author of the White House Chef Mysteries

facebook.com/TheCrimeSceneBooks
penguin.com

M1146T0712

Answering tricky reference questions is more than enough excitement for library director Lindsey Norris. That is, until another murder is committed in her cozy hometown of Briar Creek, Connecticut, and the question of who did it must be answered before someone else is checked out—for good.

FROM *NEW YORK TIMES* BESTSELLING AUTHOR

JENN MCKINLAY

DUE OR DIE

-A Library Lover's Mystery-

Carrie Rushton, the president of the Friends of the Library, has been accused of murdering her husband. The evidence is stacking up against Carrie, but neither Lindsey nor the Briar Creek crafternoon club is buying it.

When a nor'easter buries the small coastal town, the police are too busy digging out the locals to investigate the murder. With the help of her crafternoon friends and an abandoned puppy they name Heathcliff, Lindsey has to solve the question of who murdered Mr. Rushton before the killer closes the book on Carrie...

facebook.com/TheCrimeSceneBooks
penguin.com

M1148T0712